The Princess Needs a Wife

JM Dragon

Affinity
Rainbow Publications

2026

Also by JM Dragon

Single Stories

The Boars Head Inn
The Black Knight and the Lady
My Dear Vet
Wanted for Christmas
Dreams in a Jar
At Last
The Tempest
Jeager's
Breaking the Silence
The Promise
Do Dreams Come True?
The One
Letting Go
Circus
Falling into Fate
The Fix-it Girl
In Name Only
Death is Only the Beginning
Lonely Angel
Echo's Crusade
A Window in Time
Waterfalls, Rainbows, and Secrets
The Dragon's Halloween Collection
Incantations – A Collaboration
Affinity's Christmas Collection 2010
Christmas Collection 2011
Christmas Collection 2012
Christmas Collection 2014

Series

Define Destiny Series
Define Destiny
Haunting Shadows
In Pursuit of Dreams
Actions and Consequences
All Our Tomorrows
Two Steps Forward One Back
A World of Change

When Hell Meets Heaven Series
When Hell Meets Heaven - 1
Fatal Hesitation - 2

JM Dragon & Erin O'Reilly Collaborations
Racing for Love
Against All Odds
Take Me as I am
Echoes of the Past- WHMH 3
The End Game- WHMH 4
Requiem – WHMH 5
Earthbound
New Beginnings
Atonement

The Princess Needs a Wife

Affinity E-Book Press NZ LTD.
Canterbury, New Zealand

First Edition

ISBN: 978-1-991357-28-1 (paperback)

This is a work of fiction. Names, characters, places, and incidents are the product of the author's imagination or used fictitiously, and any resemblance to actual persons living or dead, businesses, companies, events, or locales is entirely coincidental.

Editor: A Koenig
Proof Editor: Lisa M
Cover Design: Lisa M
Production Design: Affinity Publication Services

ACKNOWLEDGMENTS

When I began writing The Princess Needs a Wife, it was prior to COVID. I had great intentions of completing it within a reasonable timeframe. COVID hit, and my mum died in the first wave. My best friend and co-founder of Affinity was diagnosed with brain cancer and died two years later. Emotionally, I was drained. As everyone was, I wondered what the hell was going to be next. I made a strategic decision to concentrate on keeping Affinity open for women authors who wanted to tell their stories.

My writing took a backseat. Over the last four years, I've written parts and deleted as many. It was like swings and roundabouts, never really getting anywhere. I'm a compulsive writer; I just keep going and going if I like the characters I write.

My friend Ali said it was time to get it out there and gave me a date for completion. I'm good with dates.

Nancy, a great friend over the years, knew how nervous I was about writing another book again. Thank you for your support when I needed it the most.

Angie, a heartfelt thank you for your editing skills. We both know you deserve the accolade with my work.

Lisa, your intensity is to be cherished. I know that you will give all your effort into having an Affinity book be the best it can ever be—thank you.

Dedication

To my brilliant team. I can't do this without you.
Ali, Angie, Lisa, and Nancy.

TABLE OF CONTENTS

PROLOGUE

Of course, it's easy to say in hindsight that you can change things. Quite the opposite, really. I was about to find out big time. I wasn't prepared, god knows who can be prepared when at ten you fall for a princess. It was a story your mom or dad read to you as a fairy tale. Something you grow out of. I wasn't a teenager for goodness' sake, so no excuse there. My dad said I had great taste. My mom said I'd move on. There was no future in that dream. That was twenty-six years ago. Today, I still love my Princess. Does she love me? That's the big question. It's all about protocol and what others dictate. The old fairytales never mentioned so much angst, unless there were wicked witches and dragons. I would prefer fighting dragons over not knowing how she feels about me. Is it possible to love and be loved by a princess? I was about to find out!

Chapter One

"Princess, His Highness requests you assign fifteen minutes from your schedule tomorrow and meet him in the drawing room."

Sophia watched as her father's private secretary, Henry Torvois, a wiry man with a pale complexion, wiped a finger behind a pristine white collar.

"Really, only fifteen. I would have thought my recent escapades warranted at least sixteen, Henry."

Henry blew out his chest. "His Highness was specific. He also mentioned that it must be between nine to ten am."

Sophia frowned. "Of course, nothing must interfere with my dear papa's golf schedule." She shook her head, turning to the window providing a view of the south gardens. Immaculate as always, they probably had always been that way through the centuries. She wondered how many trysts had occurred there when a garden meant something in social circles.

"I will inform His Highness of a time?"

Sophia didn't turn; she could imagine he was weaving his hands together, waiting for her reply. A typical Henry trait when he spoke with her. Anyone would think she made him nervous.

"So be it. You can advise Papa that I will be in the drawing room for an audience at precisely nine-forty-five." Sophia turned and gave Henry a hard gaze. He looked annoyed. "Any problem with that? You did say he only wanted fifteen minutes."

Henry shook his head. "No, Princess." He marched out of the room.

Sophia returned her gaze to the garden, a mass of blooms. Her late mother had had a penchant for flowers. Her father had provided her with an area earmarked for whatever she desired. He even hired a personal gardener for her, rather than the contract hires he used for the rest of the property. Though that was now a thing of the past. There had been an exodus of staff since Sophia had returned home from traveling the world three years ago.

Her phone rang, and she pulled her cell from her pocket and looked at the caller ID. Smiling, she pressed the green answer button. "Claire, I'm surprised to hear from you this early. You were totally drunk at ten last evening." There was a muted laugh on the other end of the phone.

"Says, she who was as drunk as a skunk, ending the evening with her Jag in a ditch. Thank god your father is who he is. No one is going to prosecute you for drink driving." Claire giggled.

"Maybe they should," Sophia mumbled.

"What! Don't go all pious on me, please!"

"Me, pious, hardly. Papa wants an audience with me tomorrow at some god-forsaken time in the morning." Sophia sucked in breath. Her gaze moved to the circular water fountain. Whenever she watched the spouts of water flow from the beak of the stone swan, it made her warm inside.

"Oh, midday. Not too bad."

"Not midday. Before ten."

"Oh, girlfriend, that's cruel. Doesn't he know you have a heavy social life that must be adhered…" A female voice in the background drew Claire's attention from her. "Got to go, Soph. Danny has just arrived to clean the house. She has one beautiful ass; I love watching her work. Tonight, at Dominico's around seven and then Tremont's for supper. I'll book the table, will that work?"

"Yes, I'll see you there."

†

Abigail Ranger gazed at her mother. She looked pensive. Abigail clasped her hands tightly together before venturing toward where her mom was sitting.

"I miss your dad, Abby, especially now." Her mom's countenance became sad.

Abby moved at lightning speed to engulf her in a hug. "I know, me too, Mom. Is there something else?"

She pointed to a box on the table. "It's finally arrived."

"I see." Abby walked over to the box. About a foot long by eight inches wide. Finally, three years later. She caught her mom's expression, grief written all over her face. "How about we put the box away until the time is right."

"I agree. Though your dad waited so long for this to be sent home. I'm sure that was part of why he succumbed to COVID. He stressed so much about your sister."

Abby drew her mom close. "Never! Dad wouldn't have left you for anything."

"Thank you, Abby, for always being practical. Without you, I could never have continued the tenure. That would have broken your dad's heart, more than it was already."

Abby tried not to tense, but her body had other ideas.

"I'm sorry, my darling." Her mother kissed her cheek. "His family have had the tenancy of Osric farm since…"

"1758. Mom, I'm going to work like a person demented to keep up our family tradition." She hugged her mom closely.

"You already do, always have. What life outside of the farm do you have?"

"I catch up with friends when I can. Besides, I love the farm."

"It's the anniversary of the family Tenure. The head of the household meets with the Crown Prince for permission to lease the land for another twenty-five years."

"Well, that's not a problem. Have you made an appointment?"

"Yes. Abby, I need you to do this. You are our future."

"No, Mom. Nope." Abby moved like lightning to the door leading to the laundry room.

"I'm not going, Abby. It's up to you now. The appointment is for eight-thirty."

In her thirty-six years, she had only seen His Highness and the family at tenant yearly gatherings. She had never spoken directly to him, never.

"Please, darling. I heard that there may be financial problems at the castle. They have been reducing staff for months now."

"Mom." Abby shook her head. "COVID hit everywhere in the world, hard." Her mother began to cry. "I'm sorry."

"All I ask is that you meet His Highness and agree on the new Tenure."

"I will. I need to wash up before dinner." Abby frowned as she left the room. *God, what will I say!*

CHAPTER TWO

Crown Prince Claude Maximillian Osric glared at the seventeenth-century mantle clock on the marble fireplace border. It showed nine-fifty-five. *Damn you, Sophia.* With a click of heels, he strode toward the door and threw it open, almost colliding with his daughter. Reclaiming his equilibrium, he said, "What time do you call this?"

Sophia dragged a hand through her mussed-up hair and shrugged. Then she kissed his cheek. "Good morning, Papa."

Claude shook his head. "Good morning, Sophia. Though I suspect you rarely hear that with your social calendar. Why can't you be more like your brother?"

"Whoa, don't go there, Papa. Trust me, two siblings with a head up their backside would be too much for you." He raised his eyebrows. Sophia beamed a smile and entered the room. "You wanted to speak with me; Henry informed me yesterday."

Claude sighed. Her tone was enough to know his favorite child was irked by him sending the message via Henry.

"Yes." He glanced at the clock again; it was two minutes to ten. Frank would be waiting in the limousine to take him to the golf club at Entarie. "See me to my car, we can talk as we walk."

"Of course."

"Look, Sophia, you need to be more careful. Commissioner Foley is naturally upset with your flaunting the rules."

"Then don't let him."

Claude frowned, turning as they opened the front door. "Why do you say that?"

"Maybe, Papa, because…" A large woman interrupted them. She had a ruddy complexion and was dressed in a green overall that had mud patches on the legs.

"I'm so sorry to interrupt Your Highness. There was an appointment scheduled for eight-thirty. I know I'm way late, but there was a problem with the turkeys."

"You are?" Sophia exclaimed.

Claude smiled and placed a hand on his daughter's shoulder. "Abigail Ranger. Her family is as much a fixture here as we are." Claude frowned. "I was expecting your mama."

"Sorry, Your Highness, she sent me in her place."

"Is she ill?"

Abby shook her head. "My mother is well, Your Highness. She asked me to attend the meeting. Unfortunately, there was a drama with…"

Claude nodded. "Turkeys, yes, I understand. I take it you are asking for permission to renew your tenancy."

"Yes, Your Highness."

Claude turned to his daughter. "Perhaps you can arrange to have dinner with me this evening. Henry will know my schedule."

He motioned for his tenant to move closer. "Your Tenure is guaranteed. I shall set up the documents immediately. The paperwork will go through your previous legal representative, I assume." Abigail nodded. "Give your mama my best regards."

He smiled as Abigail Ranger nodded furiously and then sped rather gracefully for her size across the gravel drive toward a walled area, entering it through a wooden door.

Sophia stamped her foot on the gravel. "Oh, of course, you are the sovereign power here. Go, Papa, go. Obviously, she's more important than I am."

He wanted to strangle his daughter. "One day, maybe you will understand." He passed his daughter, hesitating for a moment. "I love you," he whispered and headed toward the car.

†

Sophia glared at the back of her father. True to form, he had let other factors interfere with family. This time it had been related to state affairs, not golf, though that was a close second. *God damn it, I'm just a useless attachment that doesn't even come close to being important. I'm done!* She entered the house and ran up the staircase to her room.

†

Sophia looked at her baggage. *Hmm, too much.* She'd spent two hours condensing her possessions to three suitcases and a vanity case since speaking with her father. The next big question was how she was going to get out of the castle without suspicion. Grinning, she picked up the internal phone.

"Princess, how can I help?" a sexy, melodic voice spoke.

"My car is at the mechanics, and I need to go into town. Can you arrange this?" Sophia heard a sharp intake of breath from the person who listened, not that she knew who they were. The staff were just staff. She hadn't any great contact with any of them, except for Henry Torvois.

"When do you intend to leave?"

"Now. Yes, now would be good."

"Of course, Princess. Someone will be at your stateroom shortly."

"Excellent." Sophia ended the call. She looked around the room that had been hers since…forever! Sadness descended on her heart, yet leaving home was the only obvious thing she could do. It was time to make a life she could be happier with.

†

Abby ended the call with the Princess. "Damn, Frank is with His Highness, and Samuel is with Prince Rupert. Who else do I send?" Frowning, Abby considered several options, but the reality left her. Two meetings with the Princess in the space of a morning were extraordinary to say the least. She called Mr. Torvois; it rang for precisely three rings. If there was one thing you could guarantee about the Crown Prince's aide, though you could call him the head butler and anything else that meant he ran the castle, was that he was predictable.

"Mr. Torvois, this is Abby Ranger. Princess Sophia has requested a driver to take her and several items to a charity establishment. Frank and Samuel are engaged in other royal duties. Who shall I send?" A heavy sigh at the other end of the line was her first reply.

"You take the Princess. Anything else?"

"Well, yes. Who is going to take the calls to the castle when I am gone? I was covering for Anna. Her youngest had to leave school early…"

"They can go to voicemail." He ended the call.

Abby glared at the small box on the desk and flicked the switch to automatic. "I wish I'd never agreed to help today." Then she chastised herself; her childhood friend wasn't responsible. She headed toward the Princess' quarters in the south wing. On the way, she collected the keys to one of the utility vehicles. At least that was a plus; it didn't have to be her farm vehicle. *Darn sure the Socialite Princess wouldn't want the smell of the farmyard all around her.* Abby chuckled.

†

Sophia watched as the broad-shouldered woman hoisted with ease two of the three suitcases she'd packed. It had been an effort to drag each case from her bed. This woman must have the strength of a muscle builder. Staring at the biceps that bulged as the woman worked, Sophia found it a turn on. Mentally, she shook her head. *I can't go there.*

"Want me to help?" The grimace given told a story without words. *Guess not.*

Sophia glanced around her royal apartment. Since her decision to leave, she doubted herself. Was it really time to move out? The simple fact was, she was nothing but a hanger-on. Her brother would inherit the title and the fortune when her father died. The only thing she could expect was an allowance. Her father was generous, but Rupert, when a wife and family came along, might not be so. Though they loved each other, he would have his own family.

"Is this the last one?"

Sophia dragged herself out of her musings and turned. "Yes. Will Frank be driving me?"

"No. I will."

"Exactly, who are you again? You never gave me your name. Though I am sure you are vaguely familiar."

"I help friends out when they need it at the castle. We…"

"I see." Sophia became more deflated than she had been. *I'm not even worth a member of the royal staff assisting me. Darn, this woman looks familiar*. Then the light bulb went off. "Ah, I remember you. Earlier, you interrupted my conversation with my father."

"That was not intentional."

Sophia watched as a red hue inflamed the already ruddy cheeks. "Nevertheless, it happened. Didn't you have an appointment?"

"Yes, but…"

"Ah. I remember you had some excuse."

"Are we leaving? I have other work to attend to." The sharp retort surprised Sophia.

"Yes, of course you do, something to do with turkeys." She motioned toward the door. The woman glared at her and left. Holding the door back, Sophia sucked in a shallow breath as tears welled. "I wish I could say I'd be back. My senses tell me I never will, in quite the same way." She headed for the stairs.

†

Abby regarded her mother watching her favorite afternoon TV show as she knitted vigorously. Her phone rang and she answered. "Hi, it's Abby."

"Abby, how are you doing?"

Abby frowned. "Who is this, please?"

"Sorry, it's Jean. Remember me from Jake's bar."

Abby bit her lip, "Can't quite recall…"

"Hey, no problem. It was a heavy session. Your friend was celebrating a birthday."

"Chantelle?"

"Yep, Chantelle. You kissed me. You said if I wanted to go on a date, to call you. You gave me your number."

I absolutely don't remember this at all. I'm not that forward. Though I did drink a lot that evening, well, more than I normally do. Yeah, right three ciders. What the hell, Mom was only saying I had no life outside of the farm. "That was three months ago."

"COVID had a comeback. I figured I would wait. Want to go on a date?"

Abby had no clue who this woman was, but she needed a change, even if it was with a stranger. *I'm certain I didn't kiss anyone, I'd remember*. "Sure, why not. Where shall we meet? I can pick you up?"

"No, I figured I'd do that. Six pm work?"

"Yes, I guess." The call ended as suddenly as it had started.

Abby was puzzled over the brief conversation. How does she know where I live? I guess cider is more potent than I figured.

†

Henry Torvois eyed the police officer in front of him; he could not be more than mid-twenties. "I'm the Crown Prince's Private Aide; how can I help?" A sexy, chocolate-eyed gaze caught his. Henry drew in a deep breath.

"We had a report that a car driven by Her Highness crashed into a ditch on the Alyse Mountain pass."

Henry sighed. "She broke down. Why is it a police matter?"

The officer cleared his throat, "We have a witness who says…"

"A witness, I see. What is this accusation of wrongdoing? Who is this witness?" Henry calmed himself with a deep but careful breath that would be undetectable to the person before him. He had not paid a fortune for lessons in control for it not to work.

"No, at least not exactly. The witness is adamant that Her Highness was drunk behind the wheel."

Henry shook his head. "Officer…?"

"James, Officer James."

"Officer James. The Princess told the appropriate staff this morning of her mishap. It had nothing to do with alcohol intoxication. Unless the person can prove it conclusively. I would say there is nothing for you to do here."

"May I see the Princess and confirm this myself?"

To the book, okay, applaudable. "I shall ask if the Princess is available. Please wait a few moments." Henry turned away and entered an anteroom off the main vestibule.

God, he's handsome. If I were twenty years younger and not happily married, I'd love to find out if he liked older men. He headed to the communications console and raised his eyebrows when no one responded. Where was that girl? Then it dawned on him. He had sent her to drive the Princess. That was three hours ago! He turned back to the door. I doubt the officer will know if I make a small deception. Adjusting his tie, he re-entered the vestibule.

"The Princess isn't home currently. Shall I ask her to contact you?"

"Yes." Officer James withdrew a card from his pocket. "This is my precinct; please have her contact us as soon as possible." The officer turned to the door.

"Do I need to inform His Highness we have a problem with the Princess?"

"Possibly." The officer left the room.

God, that child has been trouble for years. Why can't she be more like her brother? He took a deep breath and looked at his wristwatch. Three-ten.

CHAPTER THREE

Henry paced around the room, then snorted.

"Is there a problem, sir?"

"Yes. Prince Rupert is late for his meeting with the women's league; they are in the green room." He stared at Charlotte Debussy, the young woman who organized the social calendar of the prince; a relative newbie, she had only been employed for eighteen months.

"He rearranged a meeting this afternoon at three. He assured me that he would be here at the castle for the five-thirty meeting. He's never late." They both looked at their watches.

"Well, that record has been broken. It's six-fifteen. Have you contacted Samuel?"

Charlotte nodded. Glancing at her tablet, she swiped it several times. "He hasn't answered. That isn't unusual."

Henry clicked his heels.

"I'm sure he's on the way, sir."

He watched enviously as Charlotte's fingers zoomed over her electronic device.

"Have you called Prince Rupert's private cell?"

"Yes, he doesn't answer."

Henry narrowed his eyes. "When was this?"

"Prince Rupert asked for total privacy until four." Charlotte's voice wobbled.

"It's well after." He withdrew his phone.

As the muted sounds of sirens approached, Henry looked out of the nearest window to the courtyard. Several police vehicles arrived, including the Commissioner. *Police! Twice in one day, this must be a record for her Highness.*

He sighed heavily. "Perhaps they have the answers." He heard a sharp intake of breath from Charlotte.

†

Claire Demeter slung her shapely legs over the side arm of the cream leather sofa she lounged upon and grinned while her best friend walked over and handed her a glass of champagne. It was always nice to be in the prime suite of the most expensive hotel in the city.

"What are we celebrating?" she asked, accepting the glass and taking a sip.

Sophia sat opposite her on the matching leather recliner and took a drink from her glass. "I've left the castle."

Claire's eyebrows creased. "Why?" She sat upright.

"It is time, Claire. I am thirty years old; I need my own space."

"I would have thought you had plenty of that. You live in the south wing, which has ten rooms, and you are the only living soul in any of them. Unless you invite a guest to stay." Claire grinned, sipping her drink.

"True." Sophia contemplated her glass.

"Okay, what is the real reason? Had another argument with the son and heir. You really do not have to take his crap, you know, he's hardly goody two-shoes from what I hear on the grapevine."

"Not Rupert, I don't care what he says. You must have felt the need to have your own place. You left home three years ago, when we came back from our travels." Sophia placed her glass on the polished wooden coffee table, stood, and walked over to the window.

Claire laughed. "If I had my way, I would still be at the parents' château. They decided it was better I fend for myself in the big, wide world and stop leeching off them. I figured my papa got pissed big time after drinking their cellar dry the first week I was home. His 1996 Dom Perignon Rose Gold, in particular."

Sophia grinned. "Well, he would. I bet he paid at least 60,000 Euros a bottle."

"He forgave me for that. I fixed him up with a little insider stock exchange deal that made him a million Euros overnight."

"And they never let you back home?"

"Well, I made a mistake again," Claire groaned, "though this time I broke Mom's Chinese vase. It was dated 1400s or something. I tell you, Soph, it looked like it was worth less than you paid for those Jimmy Choo's." Claire drank heavily from her glass. "I suppose having my freedom and own place isn't so bad; there isn't anyone judging me." Claire stood and walked over to her friend.

"Precisely!" Sophia turned; they were face to face, their breaths mingling in the still air.

Claire touched the full lips of her friend with a slim finger. "I have said this before and mean it. You have the most delectable lips for kissing." She dropped her head and snatched a chaste kiss and then laughed. "I'm glad we are friends, Soph, and not lovers, or I'd spend eternity in doubt that you loved me."

"Hardly. It would be the other way around. You are such a womaniser, how you ever keep a girlfriend beats me. Ah, of course you do not." They both laughed.

"Drink up, we will go on a bar trip around the harbour area. At least you do not have to drive home tonight."

Sophia nodded. "Sounds like a great plan. Incidentally, you are the only person other than the staff, that know I am here. I know they will not divulge that info."

"Are you saying I will?" Claire pouted.

"No." Sophia shrugged.

"Don't worry, my Princess, you have my total devotion." Claire bowed. "Let's celebrate your newfound independence."

"I like the sound of that." Sophia linked arms with Claire. "I love you, Claire. Thank you for understanding.

"Back at you, Princess."

†

Abby showered and kept a close eye on the time.

The Princess' trip had made her late. She'd arrived back at the farm at two-thirty. Normally, she spent her lunch break preparing the feed for the animals for the next day. Now she'd have to get up even earlier than normal and see to it.

Her phone alarm went off. "Damn, it must be five-forty." Leaving the shower, she wrapped herself in her generous favorite towel. It covered all her body and more.

Ten minutes later, with her hair three-quarters dry, she emerged into the lounge.

"What do you think, Mom?" She gave a twirl.

"You look beautiful as always, darling." Her mom was glued to her favorite soap opera.

Abby drew a deep breath and closed her eyes for a second. Her mother had not even looked at her. "Mom, remember I'm going out for the evening. I'll be home at a reasonable time. Don't wait up." Leaving the house, she hesitated and saw the package that had arrived earlier. *I need this personal time.* She shut the door and left. She took the side garden gate that led to a pathway by the walled vegetable garden, a quicker route to the road via the castle's main gates than the long and winding drive from the farm to their entrance gate. The imposing bricks of the castle she passed had her considering her family's future here long-term. There wasn't anyone else in the family to take over when she died. She shrugged the dark thoughts away. *I'm going on a date; it has been ages*. Minutes later, she arrived at the gate of the castle. She walked a few more yards and found the almost invisible side gate used by employees and tenants. She entered a key code into the side gate and left the castle boundaries. She took a seat on the bench, halfway between the castle gates and the farm entrance. It was regularly used by visitors waiting to glimpse a sight of the royal family.

She looked around and smiled. Although for a time she had wished for a different profession, keeping the family farm alive was a gift. Her father had often warned her of wishing for something better and being disillusioned. She'd laughed at him as a child, and worse as a teenager, even leaving for a couple of years to stay with her mom's brother in America. Once she had reached her early twenties, it dawned on her that he might be onto something, and she returned home. The sound of a vehicle behind the hedge had her stand.

A bright red sports car took the sharp corner at speed and managed it with ease, then came to a dust-enveloping stop in front of the gates.

"My date, perhaps." A small woman climbed out of the car. *If I kissed her, surely, I'd remember. She's a looker.* Abby stood and walked back to the gates.

"Abby. I was not expecting you to be waiting for me. I was hoping for the royal tour."

"Even I need to have permission for that." Abby moved forward, darn sure she'd never seen this woman before.

"Spoil sport. Okay, let's go. I figured dinner at Tremont's and then Club Dominica. Sound good?"

Abby could barely speak, then managed to find her voice. "Are you sure?"

Bright blue eyes turned to her. "Only the best for a date of mine." She turned and headed to her car.

"Okay," Abby whispered. She followed, inwardly groaning at the low vehicle that was going to be hell for her back. She climbed awkwardly into the passenger seat.

†

Claude relaxed, martini in hand, at the exclusive Entarie Golf Club VIP room. As he glanced around, he saw three other members: Phillipe Costas, the mayor; Chey Turner, a guru of something he'd never understood – social media, in the far corner as usual; and Peter Reynolds, who had fingers in more business pies than anyone in the principality and all legitimate according to the police commissioner. Claude looked at the clock on the wall, a wonderful craftsman's piece from the sixteenth century.

"Your Highness, there is a phone call for you."

Claude frowned. “I’m not usually disturbed, Findlay.” He gave the tall, thin man a tight smile.

“It is Mr. Torvois. He said it was urgent. Shall I bring the phone?”

Claude could count on one hand how many times Henry had interrupted him at this time – once. “Yes.” The sharp word resonated in the room.

Chapter Four

"Where is Princess Sophia?" Henry quizzed Charlotte Debussy.

"I have no idea. I'm Prince Rupert's PA. She doesn't tell me anything." Henry snorted.

"I thought you knew where everyone was, isn't that your job?" Charlotte spat out, heading for the door.

"Where do you think you're going?"

"I don't take orders from you, Henry, that much was written in my contract. Now, unless you want me to speak with Prince Rupert about your impertinence, I'm going to have dinner."

Henry moved swiftly and barred the door. He scowled. "Have you any idea what's going on? Or don't you care?"

"The Prince just wants privacy for a few hours. Who would blame him? His every living moment is scheduled, probably to the day he dies." Charlotte glared at Henry.

"How on earth did you get this job? It sounds like you hate the royal lifestyle."

"Oh, I love my job, don't ever think otherwise. I also appreciate that there are times when even a royal needs some time that isn't constantly under the watchful eye. You obviously don't." She reached for the door handle and swung the door open. Henry moved to avoid it hitting him.

As the door closed behind Charlotte, Henry leaned back against it. "Damn that woman." He moved toward his desk and sat at his chair.

†

Abby smiled at every joke her date made, even if she didn't understand some of them, and was as attentive as possible. But when the woman began incessantly questioning her about the royal family, especially the Princess, Abby became evasive, so much so that Jean had called her on it and left for the bathroom. *Thank god. This is torture.* All she'd wanted was a good night out without anything to do with her day-to-day routine and the royal family. That was not happening any time soon, it appeared; everyone had an angle, she should have known that.

"Do you want to order a dessert or coffee?"

Abby mentally cleared her mind as their waitress appeared at the table. "I'm good, thanks. Can you return in a few minutes to check if my friend wants anything more?"

"Sure. She doesn't usually, though. A bit tight, that one, when it comes to an Irish coffee." The waitress left to serve another table.

Abby wasn't sure if she wanted to laugh or be offended by the remark. *How the heck does she keep her job*? Unable to suppress the emotion, she chuckled.

"What makes you happy? I thought you were a sober side?" Jean declared, retaking her seat.

"An innocent remark from the waitress struck a chord. And if you think that, how about we call this evening over? I think neither of us are entirely happy with this date."

"Why do you say that?" The defensive stance had Abby mentally wondering how some people could be so obtuse. Jean must have another agenda, and you could bet your bottom dollar, it had something to do with the royal family.

"Are you?" Abby watched Jean's neutral expression.

"Let's leave this place and go to Dominico's. We can talk about it there."

"Sorry, Jean, not going to happen. I've made my decision about this evening, and frankly, we don't see eye to eye. I'll pay for the dinner. You have a great time partying."

Jean glared at her. "You like her, don't you? That's why you wouldn't talk about her? Oh, don't answer. It's obvious." Jean stood and walked aggressively toward the exit of the restaurant.

Abby watched Jean leave and gave a sigh of relief.

"Guess your friend doesn't want dessert or a nightcap. Told you so."

Abby was startled at first, then grinned at the waitress. She might be over the top and not PC, but hell, that was refreshing, and she would have been a lot better choice for a date. "Guess not. I've changed my mind. I'm going to have a dessert and a nightcap." She grinned.

"Great idea. I'll fetch you a menu."

Chapter Five

Claire discreetly watched Sophia. Something wasn't quite right with her friend. Sure, she'd left home, though how long that would last would be anyone's call. No, something else was bothering her, had been for a while.

"Two Negronis."

Turning to the bartender. "Add it to the bill, Gris." He nodded and moved away.

Claire picked up the drinks, wonderful zesty orange cocktails with a combination of dry gin, Campari, and sweet vermouth. She carried them to their table. "Here you go, one of our favs." She handed one to her friend.

"Wonderful, thanks, Claire." Sophia smiled as she took the drink.

Claire sat opposite her and sipped her drink. "Wow, that Gris knows how to make a fine cocktail." She placed the drink on the table. "I've known you forever, Soph. What's wrong?"

"Nothing, why do you say that?"

The walls were going up again. Typical royal reply, which meant there was something not right with her friend's world.

"Well, leaving home is a big thing."

"Yes. However, at thirty, I'm a late starter. Papa should expect it at some time."

"Sure, he would if you married. Though the person you would want to marry is far from the traditional approval list." Claire grinned and caught a fraction of a smile from her friend.

"Probably. Thank goodness I'm not the heir apparent."

Claire sighed. "Yeah, I wonder what would happen if you were. You could marry me, and I'd be a princess."

Sophia laughed. "We both know that's never going to happen. You must be a virgin, remember?"

"Oh, really, and how can they prove that these days? Besides, no one does that anymore; we live in the enlightened age." Claire rolled her eyes.

"Beats me. Enlightened, really! Conservatives think it a debauched lifestyle most of us live these days. However, I'm highly unlikely to have the opportunity to find out."

"Hi, ladies, mind if I sit here for a few minutes? My friend is on the dance floor with her date, and all the other tables are full."

Claire smiled at the stranger, who was pleasant to look at. *She doesn't know who we are. How refreshing.* The answer to her question had to come from her friend. As a princess, she was outgoing, though careful of her private space.

"No problem." Sophia nodded to the chair opposite her.

"Thanks." The woman took a seat next to Sophia.

"Do you come here often? "The woman looked toward Sophia.

Claire shrugged. Nothing new there, the Princess was always the focus, yet this woman showed no sign she knew who Soph was. "Regulars. What about you?"

"Oh no. I can't afford this place frequently. It's a treat."

Claire smiled, looking toward Sophia. Her expression was tense, her lips pulled into a line. "We are moving on, so you will have the table all to yourself."

Sophia drained the rest of her drink in one gulp. She stood, turning to the woman at her side. "Have a great evening."

"Thanks."

Sophia nodded and walked toward the exit.

Claire grinned at the woman. "Hey, if you want a free entrance, give me your name and I'll add it to our list of VIPs."

"Are you sure, you don't know me?"

Claire winked, "A good deed done is a good deed repaid."

Moments later, a piece of paper was thrust toward her.

Taking the note, Claire checked out the name. "Hi, Jean. Sorry, got to go."

"Do you really have to go?" Claire's hand was taken and gently stroked.

Damn, I haven't been laid in at least a week. This would be easy pickings.

"I…give me a minute." Claire raced after Sophia, finally catching her at the exit. "Soph, I think I've got a date. Why don't we stay a bit longer?"

"Not unusual for you, I guess. With your track record, at least it's someone new. Try to treat her better than you have the previous ones, Claire."

"Oh, you are such a great friend." She hugged her tight.

"Hmm, go or she might find someone else."

"Never going to happen, I'm the best catch in town." She winked. "Present company excepted." Smiling, she headed back to the table.

†

Sophia looked around her as she left the bar. The evening was still young. *What the hell, I might as well have dinner at Tremont's.* She walked alone to the restaurant, which was two streets away. Her papa would have a fit. He had insisted she have some protection, but she refused. In the grand scheme of things, she wasn't the important one; her brother was. *I feel like a normal person doing this. The paparazzi only hound me when I do something wrong.*

When she turned the corner to the restaurant, a line of at least thirty people greeted her. Bending her head, she ignored the line and walked up the steps to the entrance of the restaurant. Several noncomplimentary words were shouted as the door flung open.

"Princess, always a pleasure to welcome you to our humble restaurant."

Sophia nodded. "Thank you, Rafe. Tonight, I'll be eating alone." She was waved inside to the opulent waiting area by the host. His attention to detail for customers was second to none, one of the reasons this place was so successful.

Several people who were sitting, talking, and drinking, waiting for a table to be free, stared at her. She gave them a polite smile, taught to her since she was able to go out in public. *When was that? Ah, yes, around two.*

"This way, Your Highness." Rafe, like a mother hen, ushered her into the main restaurant. As expected, the tables were filled. Again, heads turned at her arrival, and her fake smile appeared as if on cue.

"I have your usual table ready behind the screen."

Sophia looked at the screened area, a great place for privacy. Except tonight, she didn't want that. If she had any chance of having a normal life outside her royal duties, she had to be more open. "Rafe, I would prefer a table in the main restaurant tonight."

Sophia almost laughed out loud at the host's face. Rafe usually had a deadpan expression, accompanied by a tight smile. Right now, he looked like someone had given him a rather invasive surgical procedure.

"I…are you sure, Your Highness?" he nervously looked around the area.

"Yes."

"Please wait here a few moments." Rafe shot off toward the kitchen entrance.

Hmm, that was interesting. Sophia looked closer at the diners. Most of them were strangers, though she noted that several affluent members of the country were visible. *God, I hope Adele Revere doesn't take it upon herself to talk to me. I'll never get out of here until midnight*. Sophia looked toward the inner tables. *Ah, Police Commissioner Foley and his…paramour. Papa would have a heart attack if he knew he was being so open.*

"Princess, please this way, a table is being made available."

Sophia automatically followed her thoughts, still on Foley.

"I'm sorry, madam, but we need this table vacated. You appear to have completed your dinner?"

"No. I'm waiting for my dessert."

"Well, I was informed."

"Abigail?"

"Your Highness." Abby stood.

"No, please. I'm sorry for disturbing your evening, Abigail. Rafe, what's the meaning of this?"

The host visibly shrank from six feet to a miniature you could fit in a bottle.

"I was told…that is…"

"Enough, Rafe." Sophia quietly spoke. "Abigail, do you mind if I join you?"

Sophia watched a frown travel across the woman's features before she nodded.

"Thank you. Rafe. Everything is fine."

"I will bring the menu, Your Highness."

"Thank you." Sophia sat opposite the woman who had helped her move out of the castle. How bizarre that they had met on three occasions on the same day and never before in her lifetime that she recalled. Life was full of surprises, that's for sure.

"So, Abigail, do you often eat here?" Strangely enough, it was the only thing she could think of to say. Her etiquette advisor would be livid with her.

Those massive shoulders shrugged. Sophia had firsthand experience that this woman was strong from earlier in the day. It still sent a shiver down her back.

"No."

"Oh, a woman of few words, I should have known that from earlier." She was given a glare. "Look, I invited myself to your table, and I'm sorry. You don't have to do everything your employer asks."

"You do not employ me, Your Highness. Though technically, your father is responsible for my livelihood and residence." Sophia wasn't sure who was more shocked, she or the woman who said the words.

Raising her hands, she scraped back the chair and stood. "Okay. I'll find another table." As she did, a waitress arrived at their table.

"Is there a problem? I have your menu, Princess." The waitress handed Sophia a velvet-covered folder.

"I need another…"

Abigail stood and faced her. "No problem at all. The Princess is hungry; she, like the rest of us, becomes antsy when famished." The waitress laughed, winking at Abigail.

"Can I get anyone drinks?"

Sophia sat down. Half of her wanted to leave, the other … she had no idea, just like her life, it was a maelstrom of change. "Please, a vodka martini. Abigail?"

"I'll have an Irish coffee." Abby smiled at the waitress, who grinned.

Sophia absurdly didn't like that. She shrugged it off as someone other than herself as the center of attention, and that was a rare occurrence. Sophia retook the seat and opened the menu. She knew it by heart and rarely chose anything different. The braised steak with baby beetroot and asparagus.

"I can recommend the chicken al orange, delicious," Abby softly commented.

Sophia looked up from the menu. Abby wasn't attractive in the usual feminine mode; she had harsher features. *I wonder what Claire would think of her, hmm, maybe too butch looking for Claire, she likes to be in charge.* "I usually have the braised steak."

Abby nodded and turned her profile away. Sophia saw the angular jaw and ever so slightly crooked nose. *I wonder if she's…*

"Here we go, one Irish coffee." The waitress placed the drink before Abigail, who smiled at her. The smile was reciprocated. Sophia almost became the spoilt brat many thought her to be and was about to point out protocol, which meant she should have been served first.

"Your Highness, a vodka martini. Have you decided on a selection from the menu?" The waitress had her pen poised over her notebook.

"I'll have the chicken al orange. I heard it was delicious." Sophia gave the open-mouthed waitress a smile.

"Of course, of course." The woman left immediately.

Sophia chuckled.

"What's the joke?" Abigail asked.

"Nothing really. I usually have braised steak. They probably had it cooking as soon as I entered." She took a sip of her drink.

"It's a nice place."

Sophia held back laughter at the remark. If Rafe had heard that remark, he would have had his underwear in a twist. Tremont was slightly more than a nice place. "Hmm, perhaps a little more than nice. I don't mean to pry, but have you ever been here before?"

"No." Abigail's bushy eyebrows rose.

"Would you come back?" Sophia ran a finger around the stem of her glass.

"Probably not. It's going to cost me a month's salary at least for this evening."

Sophia chuckled. "I hope the reason you came was worth it?" Silence accompanied the question. She watched Abigail's expression turn serious.

"I was on a first date. It didn't work out," she lifted her hands, "as you can see, I'm now on my own."

"Ouch, that must hurt."

"No. To be honest, I was glad she left."

"A bad date. I hope she left before the meal and not after." Sophia emptied her drink, and a waiter arrived at her side as if by telepathy.

"A refill, Your Highness."

"Please."

"And your guest?"

"I'm not…."

"Want another, Abigail, or something else? It's on me." Sophia wanted this woman to stay a while longer, better than being alone.

"I guess I could drink another."

"Irish coffee and vodka martini coming up." The waiter left.

"Thank you," Abigail said. "I can pay my own way."

Sophia nodded. "My treat. Heck, you have had to put up with me muscling on your table and keeping you longer than you expected. It's the least I can do."

Abigail shrugged. Sophia wondered what it must be like to hold onto those solid shoulders. *Crap, I'm fantasizing about the help*.

"Princess." A voice she knew well drew her back to reality.

"Commissioner Foley, nice to see you." She smiled, though her teeth gritted hard. Her orthodontist wouldn't be happy.

"Princess, there is a situation. Your father requests you return to the castle immediately."

"A situation? Can you be more specific?" Damn, someone has told him I'm leaving the castle. Then she glanced at Abigail Ranger. Of course, it's this woman, she's the only one who knew at the castle.

"I'm sorry, Your Highness, he wanted to inform you himself."

Sophia stood. "I don't think so, unless you give me more specifics."

"The Princess will return to the castle, I guarantee it." Abigail quietly said.

Foley turned to the speaker. "Who are you?"

Sophia sighed. "You have no right to say what I will or won't do!"

Abigail nodded. "Perhaps not, but if your father sent the Police Commissioner to ask you to return home. I suspect it's very important."

Sophia curled her fingers into her hands to stop herself from laughing at Foley's strained expression. "Abigail Ranger is a friend; she is entitled to say…something."

Foley and Abigail stared at her.

"Very well, Princess." Foley left and returned to his table. Sophia watched as he departed with a few words to his guests. Several pairs of eyes from his table turned to hers.

"I'm not going to try the chicken after all. I'll add it to my bucket list though."

"You will like it. I think you need to go."

Sophia realized that the woman before her was naive of the baggage she had with the police. Yet she was the only one who knew she had left the castle, or was she?

"Well, Abigail, my new friend, would you like to take me home? After all, it's a friend's duty."

"It would be my pleasure." Abigail frowned. "I don't have my vehicle."

Sophia stood, and Abigail followed. "Leave the transport to me."

Chapter Six

The castle was lit up like a Christmas tree as they arrived. The taxi had to slowly push its way through a line of people to reach the gate access. Camera lights popped like a lightning storm as the car approached.

Sophia frowned. “I…this isn’t about me. I’ve never had this kind of media exposure ever!”

Abby heard the shock in the incredulous words and instinctively clutched the Princess’ hand. “Not everything is about you, Princess.”

Pale blue eyes caught Abby’s. “Then what is it about? I need to find out…”

Abby stopped Sophia in her tracks as she reached for the taxi door handle.

“I think we need to find a less public route to the Castle. Do you trust me?”

Sophia blinked several times, then turned her head to the side window and thrust her hand over her eyes as lights continued to flash. “I…I’m not sure.”

"I would never cause you harm. Why not let your 'new friend' make the next call?"

"Go ahead."

Abby leaned toward the driver and spoke softly. Seconds later, he reversed slowly, and gradually they managed a turn that left the photographers behind. Abby spoke to the cab driver, and a few minutes later, they were at the edge of her farm. "Take the next left. I'll open the gate." Abby hopped out of the car and opened a farm gate. Taking the seat next to the driver, she said, "The road is gravel, sorry."

"No problem. Makes a change from the usual with the Princess. She is usually as drunk as a skunk. Guess, there must be some good news coming from the castle by the looks of those reporters."

"Hopefully." Abby turned to the glass screen that separated her from the Princess. Her heart stopped a beat; she looked so forlorn.

"There's another gate."

Abby nodded. "Last one." The cab stopped. Abby alighted and opened the gate, and as the taxi went through, she wondered what was on the other side for the Princess. She climbed back into the taxi beside the driver.

"She's lucky to have you. That other friend of hers is flaky. She'd have stormed the gate in an alcoholic rage."

Abby frowned. "I don't know about that. Right now, we need to get the Princess home. Something important is going on."

"You don't say. I know you, don't I?"

"They say it's a small world." Abby bit her bottom lip.

"Never forget a face. My wife banks on it." He hummed. "Peter Ranger's kid, right?"

Abby almost choked. "Yes."

"Good man, your dad. Your mom too. I was sorry to hear he died of that god-forsaken disease, COVID."

"Thank you."

The castle appeared.

"I'll have to remember this route. Though I doubt I'll receive help opening the gates. How did you get stuck with babysitting the Party Princess?"

Abby looked at the Princess. "She is hardly a baby."

They drew up outside the castle.

Abby opened the cab door and went to the passenger door and opened it.

"Thank you, Abigail." Sophia climbed out of the vehicle.

Abby smiled. "I hope everything is well, Princess." She turned away, stopping at the next words.

"Thank you for being a true friend, Abigail Ranger. I will not forget it."

"It will always be a pleasure, my Princess."

†

Sophia was ushered by a police officer into the main parlor as she entered the house. Henry swooped on her as she entered the room. He looked unlike his usual self, but she couldn't put a finger on why she thought that.

"His Highness will be glad you are home safe." Henry pointed toward a deep-red leather-buttoned armchair facing away from them.

Sophia walked over and saw her papa huddled there. "Papa, what's going on?" She dropped to her knees next to him.

Her hand was taken and grasped tightly. "Sophia, I'm so glad you are home." Her father's features were ashen.

"Papa, what's going on? What's with the police contingent? Not to mention the howling press at the gates."

"It's your brother, he's gone."

Sophia's stomach reacted like an out-of-control elevator. She clutched her midriff. "I don't understand? Gone. Rupert never does anything out of the ordinary."

"There was a car accident."

"Accident, is Rupert injured?" Tears formed in her father's eyes. She had only seen that once before when she was a teenager, and her mother died. "He's…" she choked off the word, and arms enfolded her.

"He and Samuel are dead. There was a traffic accident." The words floated in the air like fog.

"I don't understand. Samuel is an excellent driver."

Her father stood. "The police found the vehicle in a ravine, below Point Augustus. A tourist saw flames. Rupert was in the driver's seat."

Sophia hugged her father. "Papa, it isn't true. Surely, it's a mistake." She felt her father sag against her. "Papa, sit. Henry, a brandy for my father."

"Yes, Your Highness." Henry walked to the drinks cabinet and began to pour the beverage. "Would Your Highness like a drink too?"

Sophia needed one, that's for sure, but right now, no. She'd consumed enough for this evening. "Thank you, no." Noting Henry's raised eyebrows, she didn't react. *What the hell happened?* Sophia sat opposite her father and threaded her fingers together, her head bowed.

"He will never come back to us, Sophia." The quiet words shrouded them in a dark blanket.

"I know, Papa, I know."

Henry placed a glass in front of her father.

Sophia stood and looked at the man who had organized her life since … probably birth. His ashen features were similar to her own right now. "Henry, please take time to grieve. I'm very sorry for your loss. Samuel was a wonderful person." She stared at the man who must be in tremendous pain, going about his duties as if nothing had happened.

"Your Highness, that is very kind of you. I have a duty to my prince." They looked at the almost nonresponsive man in the room.

"We have a duty to you as well, Henry. Please, he would want you to take some private time. Leave the basics to the rest of the staff." She touched his thin shoulder. "You trained them, Henry; they can do this."

Henry nodded, tears forming. Sophia hoped he wouldn't cry, or she would break down.

"Your Highness. I will take a break. Thank you for your understanding." He bowed and left the room.

Sophia's stomach churned as she walked over to the window that overlooked the main courtyard with its perfectly manicured hedges surrounding the swan waterfall, now lit with multicolored lights. A memory of her fifth birthday filtered through. Rupert had tricked her into looking for his birthday gift for her in the fountain, which had been turned off for cleaning. Not that she knew that then. Stepping into the basin, the water began to spout immediately, and she was soaked to the skin. Someone had picked her up and placed her on the drive. That person left a warm feeling that she remembered rather than who it was. Through tears, she saw her brother laughing, and that started their love-hate relationship. It was one of the many tricks he'd played on her in their early years, but he always apologized. His present later had been a teddy bear that she still had today. Right now, she wanted to wrap her arms around the stuffed animal and pray this was all a dream and Rupert would turn up and say it was a joke.

†

"Is that you, Abby?"

Abby rolled her eyes as she entered the house and stood in the dimly lit hallway. "Certainly hope so, or you are in trouble. Didn't think you would still be up."

"I wouldn't be. Except there has been a lot of activity going toward the castle. Do you know what's happening? I didn't see or hear anything about a party at the castle this evening."

Abby removed her shoes and sighed. "I hate a heel, even a small one."

"What was that, dear?"

"Nothing, just prefer flat shoes or my gumboots. How can people wear those skyscraper heels?" Abby smiled as she recalled watching the Princess enter the restaurant – her heels were at least four inches with a red sole. It didn't seem to bother her. She had a wonderful, sexy swagger. Abby shook away the thoughts, but her smile refused to give in. She entered the sitting room and sank into the well-worn sofa in a sea-green fabric. *It's past its best days but so comfortable*.

"What did you see when you came home?" Her mom asked again.

No escape there. "Photographers." Her mother's face turned pale. "Nothing to worry about, I'm sure."

There was a pause.

"I knew eventually this would happen."

"What?"

"Well, it must be something the Princess has done. She isn't afraid of pushing the boundaries."

Abby frowned. “No, I don’t think so. Probably something unrelated to her.” If it was about the Princess, the police commissioner would have insisted on her leaving big time in the restaurant.

“It must be, darling. Prince Rupert is never a concern. Trouble follows that child.”

“Mom, even if, according to you, the Prince is a saint, he might have a secret life no one knows about.”

“Wash your mouth out. Prince Rupert will head our country one day!” Her mother stood and shook her head. “Goodnight, Abby. I’ll see you at breakfast.” She left the room.

“Goodnight, Mom.” Abby watched her mom leave the room and contemplated her words. *Rupert could do no wrong. Sophia, on the other hand, was the devil’s child.* A part of her now wished she’d been able to find out what was going on. Retrieving the TV remote from the coffee table, she began channel searching for something worthwhile to watch. *Mom didn’t even ask how my date went.*

†

Claire took a sip of the drink Jean had bought her. Either she was way too drunk to define things, or the drink was more water than alcohol. That was something she had never encountered in the bar before. Looking at the woman she had dumped a meal with a princess for, she smiled. “How is your drink?”

“Great, what about you. Vodka sweet, right?”

“Perfect. Jean, tell me what you do in the real world outside of partying?” Claire watched as Jean’s eyebrows rose a fraction, and her lips thinned.

“Mundane office work, what about you?”

Claire laughed. “Mundane office work, too. How about we head for a club and dance the rest of the evening away?”

Jean smiled. “Works for me. Will the princess be there?”

Claire shook her head. “Nope. You will have me all to yourself.” She stood and walked the short distance to her companion and took her arm. “The drinks are so much stronger at Svengalis.”

“I’ve never been there; it’s only for the elite,” Jean replied, her eyes wide.

“Guess you’ve met an elite. I’m a member.” Claire was astonished but happy when Jean kissed her full on the lips. “With a response like that, I’ll have to show you some of the other clubs in the city.”

“Lead the way,” Jean said as she hung on to her arm.

CHAPTER SEVEN

"This is a blast; I wish Soph had stayed, she loves this DJ combination."

Jean twirled her finger around the rim of her scotch glass. "Pictures in the tabloids don't do her justice. Wow, it must be a very privileged life you lead, being the best friend of Her Royal Highness?"

Claire laughed. "Hardly. I was already privileged."

Jean cringed. *What an ego*. "Really, are you a princess, too?"

"Sure I am." Claire grinned. "To my parents anyway." She clutched Jean's hand. "Want to get out of here? My apartment is only a short cab drive away?"

Jean pulled the hand that enclosed hers toward her lips and kissed several knuckles. "I have work early tomorrow. I need to go, it's almost midnight."

"Wow, Cinderella. Where do you work? I might be able to wrangle a little magic and get you a few days off."

Jean pulled away gently. "You are so wonderful. I'd rather not deceive my boss. What about we meet up at the weekend? I'll guarantee it will be worth it." She pulled Claire closer and gave her a deep kiss.

When they came up for air, Claire withdrew her phone. "Absolutely, what's your number?"

"A lady never gives her number on the first date." Jean flashed her eyelashes. "You give me yours and I'll call you."

Claire gave her a sharp look, then grinned. "Ah, you don't think I'm a lady…maybe you are right. Another first for me tonight. Here you go."

Jean noted the number on her phone and pulled Claire in for another deep kiss.

"Goodnight, Claire. I'll be in touch soon. It's been a magical night." Jean extricated herself from Claire's arm encircling her and left the club.

†

Abby threw down the remote and looked toward the castle. Lights hadn't dimmed at all; in fact, there were more, she figured. She looked at the clock on the wall her parents had bought in Bavaria on their honeymoon. It struck two in the morning with a drummer boy heralding the hour. She stood and gazed around the surrounding areas of the castle. Lights were everywhere. Not normal. She clenched her fingers several times and then shook her head. "The Princess said I was her friend, and right now I'm intrigued. As a friend, I should ask if everything is okay." Switching off the TV, Abby entered the hallway and stood for a minute, listening for any movement or noise from her mom. There wasn't any sound other than snoring. Smiling, she put on her shoes as quietly as possible, opened the door, and left the house.

†

Charlotte Debussy walked across the drive and entered the castle by the servant's entrance. She sped along the corridor to the main house entrance and entered.

A police person stood in the main hallway. She walked toward the woman, who was using her phone, and tapped her on the shoulder.

The officer shrieked. "What the hell?"

"I was ordered to be here. Debussy."

The officer with red-flamed cheeks recovered her composure. She pressed the button on her radio and spoke into it. "A woman called Debussy is here." There were several electronic sounds, and the officer turned to her. "The Commissioner needs to speak with you."

"I know, he sent for me. Why else would I get up at this hour for a meeting?" As she spoke, the door to the family parlor opened, and Princess Sophia entered the hall.

"Princess."

"Charlotte, we hope you can help with any information about my…Prince Rupert's last official agenda."

"Princess, I will do my best."

The officer she had embarrassed, spoke. "Ms. Debussy, the Commissioner is ready for you now."

"I guess that's my cue, Princess."

"Charlotte, no matter the outcome, tell them everything you know about my brother. It may help to understand what happened." Princess Sophia turned toward the entrance.

"I will."

The Princess swung her gaze back, "I appreciate that," then opened the door and left the house.

"The Commissioner doesn't like to be kept waiting."

Charlotte stared at the officer. "I'm sure he doesn't." She gave the front door one last look and then entered the parlor.

†

"This is the right thing to do," Abby muttered, knowing the only one who would hear her was Basil the owl, who lived in the barn next to the garden shed.

"What is the right thing to do?"

Abby almost pissed her pants at the voice that was etched forever in her brain and never forgettable.

"Princess?"

"Yes, very perceptive."

"I…it's unexpected…wandering the grounds at this time of night."

"It's in the am."

"Of course, it is." Abby hung her head. *This is stupid.*

"Why are you out at," Sophia looked at her watch, "two-thirty am."

Abby pondered that question, obviously for too long.

"And?"

"I thought I heard a problem in the chicken compound, a fox maybe."

"Really, I thought you had turkeys?"

Abby balled her fingers into her palms. *Lie, Lie.* "We have both. I was worried about you." *There, I've said it.*

The Princess stared at her for what seemed a decade.

"Thank you, Abby. Do you mind if I call you, Abby?" Abby simply nodded. "My description of you as my friend is well warranted."

"At your service."

"What about those chickens and turkeys?"

Abby grinned. "Maybe it was a wily fox. It led me to you."

Sophia gave a short laugh. "I'm not sure being equated to a wily fox is quite how I'd want to come across to our people."

Abby's body flooded with warmth. "How can I help you, Princess?"

"There has been an incident."

"I figured that. The only time that there have been so many lights during the night this long was when your mom died." Abby wished those words away as the Princess' expression became ashen. "I'm sorry. That was insensitive. Is anything wrong with the Crown Prince?"

"No. No! My papa is well." Abby reeled from the emotive explosion that underlined the narrative.

"Prince Rupert?"

"Yes." Sophia lowered her head. "He and Samuel are dead. I…I don't understand, Abby, why did this happen?" She began to cry.

Abby moved closer, instinctively enveloping the Princess into a hug. They stayed like that for a while before Abby gently distanced them. "Life is never a certainty, no matter who you are. Do you know what happened?"

"No. The police are looking into whether there was any foul play. God, I sound like an advert for a mystery novel." Pale blue eyes sparkled with tears.

"My Princess, do you want to sit and have an almost stranger, who by chance is a new friend, hold your hand for a while?"

"Yes." The Princess' grasp felt like a vice.

Abby held on and knew, at that moment, she was going to make sure that her Princess had a happy ending, whatever that might be.

†

Commissioner Foley pulled at his pointed chin. The interview with Charlotte Debussy hadn't given any sign that anything had been amiss when the prince had left the castle. He scratched a psoriasis patch on his left temple.

"Other than this massage establishment that he went to regularly, is there anything else?"

"No, sir. He followed the expected schedule."

"I'm damn sure he did. Yet we didn't know about the massage interlude. What happened to the intelligence about the Prince? He's next in line, or has everyone forgotten that?"

"He was the next in line."

Foley grimaced, then threw the few papers in his hand into the air and watched them fall onto the parquet surface.

There was a general silence around the room.

The door opened, and the Crown Prince entered.

"Sir." Foley bowed slightly as the ashen-featured man walked toward him and then stopped a foot away.

"My son, Commissioner, do you have any news on how this happened?"

Foley wanted to be anywhere but here. He had this man to thank for his position and keeping it through a few tremors in his tenure. Mostly infidelity problems, which, had the Crown Prince's late wife been alive, he'd certainly have lost his position. "Sir, I'm sorry there is no news. We are looking at every avenue in his recent activities, thanks to his PA. To establish a timeline."

"Do you think someone else was involved in the accident?"

"No, but it's best to be sure. Samuel was an expert driver.

"Samuel wasn't the driver though. My son was in the driving seat. I think the pathologist said that in her initial report."

"I will give you the conclusive results as soon as I have them."

"Do I need to take action to safeguard my daughter?"

Foley almost choked on a laugh. "No, sir. The Princess is perfectly safe."

"Now, why do I believe that. Ah, yes, because she, in your eyes, constantly makes errors in judgement, in her lifestyle, and you know where she always is."

Foley dropped his gaze. "Sir, I don't…."

"Don't bother, Commissioner. Tell me when you have the conclusion about the accident." The Crown Prince turned rapidly, opened the door, and then turned back. "My family is not the only one wanting answers. Samuel's next of kin will need the same. I assume you are giving them the same courtesy you are my family." He left the room.

Foley bristled at the veiled insult from the Crown Prince and turned to the people in the room who had heard the engagement.

"I'm going to see the pathologist. Has anyone talked to the other victim's family?"

Silence filled the room.

†

Sophia wiped tears away with a linen handkerchief, which she had retrieved from one of the numerous pockets in her cargo pants. The sound of sirens and several vehicles leaving the property had her fantasizing this was just her brother's first-ever fault from what was expected of him, and he would be waiting for her with his wonderful smile and that wink indicating everything was okay. Leaving her again to be the unnecessary royal in the eyes of her people. She looked at Abby, who stood silently staring at some plant or other. It must be so simple to live a normal life without the trappings of royal expectation. It was time to move forward, maybe pursue a career to help people, instead of the aimless lifestyle she had been born into. After all, the royal title always went to the next male in line.

"Abby."

"Yes, Princess."

"I've decided to become a better person,"

"Princess, you are a good person, at least to me." Abby frowned.

"I may be to you and other loyal supporters. However, not to the public. Can you help me achieve this?" She saw hesitation. Evident in the movement of the strong shoulders and tightness of the full lips. "You can say no; it isn't a royal decree." Sophia gave a tight smile.

"No, no, I'm sure it isn't."

Abby's frown had Sophia moving away a fraction; those bushy eyebrows might consume her any second.

"You agree to be my friend?"

"Yes, my Princess. Whatever you need," Abby spoke slowly, and Sophia wondered if it was lip service to her position.

"Thank you, Abby. I guess I'd better go home and see if there is any news concerning my brother's accident. Papa doesn't need the stress." Sophia held out her hand and saw Abby hesitate before she shook it vigorously.

"My pleasure and honor, my Princess."

Sophia took her leave and headed back to the house.

†

Henry Torvois drew in a deep breath as he contemplated the mirror in front of him. To anyone observing he would look composed and in control. He nodded at the mirror. Then he turned to the empty bedroom he should now be sharing with Samuel. He held back a sob threatening to explode his chest. He slowly walked around the generously proportioned room with a king-sized bed dominating the area. He closed his eyes. *Life was never going to be the same again*. He cried like he hadn't since his mother had passed away.

CHAPTER EIGHT

Claude gazed at the portrait of his late wife on the wall in his study. The painting had been commissioned privately when Adeline had agreed to be his wife. She had, of course, said it was a ridiculous waste of money that could be used elsewhere, helping those less fortunate in the principality. He'd given her his best, sad puppy-dog look, and she agreed. Not without having him pay the same fee due the artist to a local charity. As he stared at the image, he could not imagine her sorrow at their eldest child's death.

"He had your eyes, my love, though not the warmth beneath. Sophia inherited those." He sighed; there was a rap on his door. "Enter."

Henry appeared, and though he looked the same, the shadows in his eyes acutely conveyed his loss.

"Henry, you should be mourning. Please take the time."

"Sir, I could say the same to you."

"Indeed, you could." Claude waved Henry to a leather armchair, and he sat in the opposite one.

"I wanted to make sure you were coping, sir."

Claude stared at the man who was his…not a friend, no. Probably the only person who knew all his secrets and the rest. "I will ask the same of you, Henry?"

There was silence between them that encompassed their loss.

Claude stood. "Henry, in all the years I've known you, I do not know what you drink?" Claude walked to the drinks bar in his study.

"Sir, if you need a drink, I will…." He attempted to stand.

"No! Henry, tonight…today. The people we love have died. We share the same pain. Please allow me to at least dispense something that might numb our pain for a short time. I'm going to have a triple scotch." Claude looked at the man who had been his rock since he employed him decades ago. "You?"

"The same."

"Good man."

When they had their drinks in hand, Claude drew his glass up and Henry did the same. "For the fallen whom we love and always will."

Henry nodded, and they chinked glasses. "May they rest in peace."

An hour later, as the door closed behind Henry, Claude looked at the portrait of his wife and cried like a baby.

†

"Abby, for goodness' sake, wake up." A vigorous shake of the bed had Abby groaning. "It's important, Abby."

"Mom, what's wrong?"

Tears glistened in her mother's eyes, and Abby reached out to hug her close. "Mom, what's happened?"

"It's the young prince. Rupert, he's…he's…" Her mother sobbed.

"Hey, take your time, Mom." Another sob, and her mother looked directly into her eyes. "He's dead?" Her mother cried in her arms.

Women crying in her arms was becoming a habit right now. Should she tell her mom she already knew? No point.

"Will you find out the details?" Her mother wailed.

"I will, Mom." She climbed out of bed and began retrieving her clothes. "I'll go now."

"I'll take care of the chickens and turkeys." Her mother left the room.

Abby, dragging on trousers, staggered one-legged toward the family bathroom, cursing when she knocked her leg on the side of the shower door. Finally getting her other leg inside the trousers, she looked at herself in the mirror and groaned. *No oil painting*. She reached for the mouthwash, swirled it around, and then spit it out in the basin. Locating the T-shirt from the day before, she mussed up her hair.

A few minutes later, she was out of the farmhouse heading to the castle. Halfway to her destination, she regretted not taking a shower and a better choice of clothes.

†

Sophia stared blankly at the picturesque gardens below her bedroom window. Her eyes burned with the tears she'd shed since Rupert's death. Her initial reaction had been disbelief. How could it not be? Yet her father was adamant. It wasn't his words that convinced her but the expression of heartbreaking loss that immersed every facet of his features. She had seen it only once before when her mother died.

She turned to contemplate her room, missing many of her private items, stuck at the hotel apartment she had rented. Right now, something childishly familiar that she could clutch close and know that the pain of the loss would diminish…at least for a short while. There was one item, a small white bear with a black eye. It wasn't the Steiff bear Rupert had bought her, but for some absurd reason, she loved the poor fellow more. She'd had it for as long as she could remember and took it everywhere. Her friends in school, at Uni, and even the rare girlfriend she had allowed into her private sphere had commented it was childish. The only person who hadn't belittled her fascination with the bear had been Claire.

Turning back to the window, she saw a figure moving toward the side entrance. She watched for a few more seconds, then left her room.

†

"Antoine, I hear that Prince Rupert has died, Samuel too. You didn't sound very sympathetic when I opened the door." Abby cornered the royal chef and stared directly into his dull grey gaze. From what she heard as she entered through the back door of the kitchen, he was less than complimentary about the situation. The man wasn't intimidated by her gaze because he outstared her. Withdrawing the direct confrontation, she glanced toward the skillet on the kitchen burner.

"What do you know, farm girl?"

Abby screwed up her eyes. He wasn't the pleasantest man on the planet. "Mom said you told her that Prince Rupert was dead."

"He is, along with that aberration, Samuel."

Abby wanted to punch the lights out of the small, wiry man in front of her.

"Commissioner Foley gave the Crown Prince the news himself. As you know, nothing is secret within these walls, especially to the staff that are close to the family." He sniffed the air.

Abby had never liked this man, and his food was worse. She knew firsthand from the leftovers that circulated, and there were always lots of them. How he became a renowned chef puzzled her. "How can you say that about someone who has just died?"

"Car accident, good riddance."

Abby swallowed hard. She hated the way Antione spoke without emotion. "You are the worst kind of person on the planet; don't you have any sympathy or respect?" Abby rocked back on her heels.

"Rupert was a privileged prick. I heard he was seeing some slut from a massage parlor; he always loved playing with the lower classes. You should know."

Abby snorted back her anger and faced off against Antoine. "You are the prick. If any of the royal family heard what you said to me, you'd be out of a job in an instant."

"Yeah, farm girl, are you going to tell them? They barely know you are alive."

Abby saw the smug smile on his face, and it sent a wave of anger through her. She reached out and pulled him closer. "I'm going to knock the hell out of…"

"Enough!"

†

As Sophia approached the kitchen, she heard raised voices, both familiar to her. Would it be prudent to listen before entering? She waited at the door; tears formed at the conversation. Maybe this was a bad idea. Then she heard the derogatory way the chef talked of her brother and Samuel, and, sucking in a sharp breath, she reached for the door to open it. The next words she heard as she entered had her sighing.

"Enough!" The word sounded strangely authoritative, something she never thought she would ever be.

"Princess."

"Oh god."

Sophia glanced first at the chef. His food sucked big time, but apparently, her father thought his Michelin star status was enough to put up with the pathetic dishes he served. "Antoine, if you believe my brother was a privileged 'prick', exactly what do you make of me? Please don't spare my blushes."

"I…Princess. I'm sure you misheard." He glared at Abby.

"To the best of my knowledge, the royal doctor said my hearing was functioning perfectly. So, is that another person you believe isn't up to scratch?" The chef lost his swagger as he lowered his head.

"My father will want his food on a tray in his room for the rest of the day."

"Of course, Princess. I will personally serve His Highness."

"No."

"No?"

“I will take his meals. Now leave, I’m sure you need to find eggs, or something.” Sophia once again heard that strange commanding tone. *It isn’t unpleasant. I could get used to it.*

“Your Highness, that is beneath your position. We can assign someone to the task.”

“Nothing regarding my father is beneath me, Antoine. As an aside, you disrespected my friend. That is unforgivable.”

“Your Highness, that must be a mistake. I’m sure it must be a misunderstanding.”

Sophia glanced at Abby’s averted head. *Damn, what am I doing?* “Abby is my friend. Antoine, I expect you to give the same respect to her you afford me.

Sophia had seen numerous expressions on people’s faces, but this was a new one. His face turned beet, and she was sure the chef wet his pants at her announcement. Abby, on the other hand, looked like she was choking on something. “I need to speak with Abby. Please leave.”

“Yes.” He rushed out of the kitchen, his apron flapping, much like a frightened chicken.

There was an awkward silence between her and Abby.

“Thank you.” Sophia finally broke the silence. There was no answer, just a puzzled expression. “Thank you for defending my brother’s honor and Samuel’s. They were both good men.”

Abby stared at her with tears in her eyes. “I was hoping it was a dream…last night. I’m truly sorry for your loss.”

Sophia responded to Abby’s pain. It was akin to hers. “Right now, all I know is that…what the hell.” She hugged Abby, and they both burst into tears.

CHAPTER NINE

Claire Demeter groaned as she struggled through the sheets to get out of bed. Glancing at the other side of the bed, she was thankful there wasn't another person there. Slowly walking to the kitchen, she pushed the button on her kettle, and when, seconds later, it beeped empty, she listlessly filled the jug, resetting the timer. Locating her phone, she detached it from the power station. Placing her thumb on the surface, it powered. She was aghast at the number of texts.

"What the hell!"

Ignoring the rest, she concentrated on the only VIP that mattered—Sophia.

Claire, call me now. The time stamp was around midnight.

"Fuck, what have I missed? She never sends me texts, unless…oh crap, she's had another accident."

She swiftly pushed Sophia's number. There was no answer. Leaving it a few minutes, she tried again and still no answer. Then texted her.

"Right, get your head on, Claire." She headed to the bathroom for a shower. Her next move would be to go to the castle and see Sophia in person.

†

"Your Highness, I'm sorry to disturb you."

Claude looked up from his newspaper. "What is it, Henry?"

"The Princess…"

"Is my daughter in trouble?" His heart somersaulted.

"No, no, sir. It's just…"

"Just?

"Sir, she has been a little difficult with the police."

"How?"

"Well, she refuses to stay in the castle. She says that she's perfectly able to go outside the castle grounds and will take her personal aide with her. I did not approve an aide for the Princess."

"Henry, Sophia is headstrong; we are aware of that."

"I know, but the aide, sir, I did not approve…"

"Henry, the only person who can really approve a personal aide is my daughter. Your opinion, even mine, becomes redundant."

Sir, I…it isn't protocol."

"Sophia and protocol have never gone hand in glove. How many times have we had to manage her public profile since she turned eighteen? Sometimes I wish she was still my little girl. She isn't, and her brother," His voice cracked. "Rupert has…had made some interesting decisions we were unaware of it seems."

"Sir, should we have the new aide vetted by the police?"

"Do we know this person?"

"Well, she is a…"

"I can't think about this right now, Henry. Deal with it as you see fit."

"I will call the Commissioner to vet the person."

"Good. If he approves, Sophia can go out in public with this new aide."

"Sir." Henry shuffled out of the room.

†

Paul Foley wasn't a fool. He was aware that his career and reputation were now held in balance. If he stepped out of line in any way that upset the Crown Prince, he was mincemeat. To do his job, he had to speak with the one person who probably had as many secrets as he did, and she wouldn't care if he was fodder for the wolves. Though the opportunity to interview her so-called aide would work equally as well.

There was a knock on the door. "Enter."

The woman that entered was a surprise, though she looked familiar somehow.

"Ms. Ranger, please take a seat; this won't take long."

She took the seat opposite him.

"Ms. Ranger, it seems that you are Princess Sophia's personal aide. Do you mind if I ask when this happened?"

"Not a personal aide. More a new friendship, really."

"You didn't answer the question." He watched a heavy frown appear on her brow. *She needs a facial.*

"Yesterday."

"I see. Can I ask, are you happy to be her aide?"

"As I mentioned…"

"Mr. Torvois wasn't aware of this appointment. He's not happy, and the Crown Prince needs to verify your credibility."

"I, well, like I keep trying to say, it's more a friendship."

"I'll come straight to the point. How trustworthy are you?"

"Very, ask my mom."

"Oh, don't worry, I will. Though I find parents are very protective of their children." His lips twitched into a small smile.

"You can check my passport. What about speaking with my bank manager? I'm not that religious, though, so a priest isn't on my list. I do have another person who may give me a character reference that you would take immediately."

He watched the woman who was at least five inches taller than he was and probably twice his weight. "Really, and that would be?"

"His Highness. Our families have known each other for centuries."

He was puzzled that he was being asked to vet a woman the royal family knew. Henry Torvois must be losing his marbles, though understandable in the circumstances.

"Is that all?"

"At this moment."

He stared at the woman; she was an odd choice for a royal, especially one like the Party-goer Princess. This woman wasn't any kind of party girl. Still, if she was known by the royal family.

"I think you will be good for the Princess. Thank you for your time."

"Thank you, can I go now?"

"Yes, have a good day, Ms. Abigail Ranger."

She nodded and left the room.

He made a call. "If the Princess wants to leave the castle, allow her on the strict instruction that Abigail Ranger is with her 24/7." He ended the call and looked down at his polished black leather loafers. *I need a drink and some good company.*

†

Sophia lounged against the bonnet of her F-type Jaguar, frustrated by the police cordon at the front gate. There was no getting through unless she decided to go on foot. Reaching inside the pocket of her trousers for her phone, she frowned when all she felt was the lining. "Damn, I've left my phone in my room." She kicked the gravel beneath her feet. "Fuck." She looked toward the castle and was surprised to see Abby heading her way. A smile flirted her lips as she watched the woman walk forthrightly toward her.

"Abby, shouldn't you be doing farming stuff?"

Abby nodded. "I had a shipment of fresh goods for the kitchen."

"You work hard, Abby. How do you do it and still smile?"

Abby shrugged. "Practice."

"I need to take lessons from you. Not the smiling, that I learnt when I was a babe in arms. On being industrious."

"Princess, you have work; it is just different from mine." Abby smiled. "I need to go. Unfortunately, the work on a farm is, as you said, never-ending."

"I still feel like a spare wheel." Sophia shook her head.

"Why? Your father needs you, especially now."

Sophia nodded. "I know. I guess since I was a teenager, I've rebelled at anyone who wanted me to conform. I was a spare part of the family, never likely to amount to anything.

Not expected to do anything. Everything was focused on Rupert."

"He is…was heir," Abby softly said.

"How very practical you are, Abby. "

Abby scuffed the gravel at her feet.

Sophia leaned back against the Jaguar. "I should maybe go see how Papa is doing. They won't let me out on my own right now."

"Sounds like a nice way to spend your day. His Highness is a good man."

Sophia raised her eyebrows. "Really, how do you know that?" Abby chuckled, and it calmed Sophia.

"My mom says so, and when are parents ever wrong?"

Sophia nodded. "Abby Ranger, you are good for me. Please, will you join me for dinner this evening?"

"Oh, I can't. I have lots of work to do."

"What if I demanded it?"

"Then I would have to be there."

"So, I demand."

"I would arrive, greet you, and leave."

Sophia threw up her hands and stood next to Abby. "Now I know even more why I like you. Any chance you might meet me in the walled garden after dinner, just to chill? It's halfway between my home and yours?"

Abby grinned. "I can do that. What time?"

"Father eats at seven. Nine work for you?" Sophia noted a slight grimace from Abby.

"Yes. See you at nine." Abby turned to walk away.

"Abby, thank you."

"You are very welcome, Princess." Abby walked away, and Sophia watched until she was out of sight.

"There is something about Abby I'd want to be more like. Though right now, having a drink with Claire would be great." She gave a longing look at the gate guarded by the police and turned back to the castle.

†

Claire arrived at the castle gates and pressed the intercom. "Hi, it's Claire." Fully expecting the gates to open, she was surprised when they didn't.

"Are you expected?" A voice Claire had never heard before replied.

"Not exactly. Princess Sophia will want to see me."

"If you are not expected or do not have an official appointment, you cannot enter."

"Call the Princess, she will be upset if I'm not allowed in," Claire growled.

"If the Princess adds you to the official list of visitors, then you may enter."

Claire clenched her fists, reached for her phone, and tried Sophia's number. Again, no answer. Angrily, she reversed her Porsche Boxster and headed home. "I need a drink."

†

"Papa, how are you feeling? And please don't give me the protocol crap. That everything will work out. It won't, we both know that." Sophia twirled the napkin she held around her fingers.

Sophia watched as her father dropped his gaze for a few moments. Then he looked directly at her, they were in the small dining vestibule for private family meals, fairly normal at only three feet apart.

"I should be asking you that question."

"I asked first." Sophia gave a tight smile.

"My darling, I'm devastated. You should never outlive your children." Tears formed in his pale blue eyes. "Your mama could never get over that she wasn't going to see you grow, but she said at least she would not outlive her children."

Sophia gulped back a sob. "How did this happen, Papa? Rupert was always the one we could rely on to do the right thing. It doesn't make any sense. Samuel was an expert driver. Why wasn't he driving? Rupert could barely hold the wheel in a straight line." Her tears flowed, and seconds later, she was wrapped in a loving hug.

"My darling, cry as much as you need." Sophia looked up at her father, his tears flowing freely. Together they comforted each other.

†

Abby had been successful in avoiding Mr. Torvois for most of her visits to the castle. Then he cornered her as she was leaving the kitchen.

"Ms. Ranger, do you have something to tell me?"

"I don't think so."

He coughed. "The Princess."

"The Princess?"

"There is a rumor that you are her personal aide, ridiculous, of course, because I approve all household employment."

"I think a rumor has been started, and…we are just friends."

Torvois shook his head and waved a hand around but didn't say anything.

"Sometimes a person needs help in a terrible time. I believe in helping if I'm able."

"Very noble," Torvois gruffly replied. He turned and walked toward the door to the main hall.

"Mr. Torvois."

"Yes?"

"I'm here, and so are many of the royal staff if you need us."

"What do you mean?"

"Samuel was a great guy."

The name floated in the air like a specter.

"I don't need pity."

"That wasn't what I or the others will offer. If you do, because you will, we're here. I know from experience. My mom has some great tales about Sam. He spent more time with us in the early days when he arrived. My dad called him the son he never had." Abby walked by the unemotional statue that was Henry Torvois. She gently touched his shoulder and left.

†

Jean Randle pressed the intercom connected to Claire Demeter's apartment for the fifth time. Again, no response. "Fuck, I wonder which bar she is in. I need this story," she muttered, then gave the intercom one last shot at the woman being home. She turned at the roar of a throaty engine as a sports car that cost more than three years' salary sped down the ramp into the underground parking lot. Her thoughts travelled to earlier that day.

Entering the small office that hosted her editor, John, and Ed, the guy who did everything else. She was amazed when they pounced on her.

"Jean, baby, what the hell do you know?"

Jean hated John Sinclair. He was her boss but a womanizer. She'd forgotten how many times he'd hit on her since she worked here. When she had pitched a story on the Party-girl Princess, he began to take her seriously for a scoop. Fate had been kind to her two months ago when she'd been in a bar and there were drunken women on a hens' night talking about a member of their party who lived at the castle. She didn't have a clue who it was; all she could find out was that the name was Abby Ranger. It had to be her way in, so she listened. That had been a disaster. The woman was nice but didn't have any connection that would help her article. Then miraculously, she'd hit gold with Claire Demeter, the Princess' best friend. She was a looker and great in bed. Sometimes you get perks.

"Hey, shouldn't it at least be good morning first?" Jean threw her backpack on her desk and stared at her pudgy, owl-eyed boss.

"You texted you were with Her Highness, what's the news? The police are all over the castle. Never seen that happen in my lifetime." Beads of sweat formed on his forehead.

"I have no fricking idea. Maybe there is going to be a social occasion, and they need security advice. Her royal privilege brat was normal when I saw her, no drama."

"When was that?"

"I don't know, it was at Domenico's. Day before yesterday." A low whistle came from the back of the office, and Ed winked.

"I wasn't paying, right?" John blustered

"Hey, we lesbians keep it in the family. I was well taken care of." Jean wanted to laugh out loud at the beetroot red that John turned.

"What a good reporter would have asked is what time was that. Timeline is everything."

John pulled at his dark brown tie and coughed.

"I don't know. The Princess left to have dinner. I was with…someone who was close to the Princess until about eleven. You had me running around yesterday on that stupid photo shoot about a monkey. What the hell aren't you telling me?"

"Rumors are that Prince Rupert is in trouble. Get to that person who is closer to the Princess and find out what she knows. I have a feeling in my bones that this is a story of the century for this principality.

Jean looked at the sparsely populated street, one of the most prestigious in the principality. She turned back and looked at the keypad of the apartment block. *I really should have given her my number.*

Her steps pounded the pavement as she walked away.

†

Sophia looked at the clock on the onyx mantle in the room her mother had used as her private sanctuary. The time made no imprint on her consciousness. Closing her eyes, she tried to recall the happy memories she'd had here. Then a memory from her early childhood pushed through.

"Big bear, big bear, where are you?"

"Sophia, you know it's not nice to be unkind to your brother."

"Mama, he looks like the bear in the story. I love those stories."

Her mother raised a slim finger to her lips.

She dropped her gaze. Then muttered, "He does though. I love Rupert Bear. Why is that wrong?"

She was engulfed in a bear-like hug. "I love you, too, Soph."

As Rupert released her, she grinned. "Hey, better than Pooh Bear, right?"

"I'm no smelly bear, but I do love honey." He touched his bourgeoning belly.

Laughing, they had a playful fight.

"My children, it is so good to see you both enjoying each other's company. As you grow, things will change. Please always remember this bond. Family support is our lifeblood, in love and protocol, family transcends everything.

"I forgot, Mama. I forgot to support Rupert and Papa. I've ignored my heritage and what it means to our people." Tears caressed her cheeks as she stared at the family portrait on the wall. "I'm not sure I can make it better, Mama, but I will try. I will." Then her phone rang. "Hey."

"Hey, yourself. I've been trying to call you forever! Are you okay? You flooded my phone with messages. I came by and wasn't allowed in. What's that all about? You aren't in trouble, are you?" Claire sounded frantic and probably was.

"There's been an incident. It isn't about me. It's Rupert," Sophia softly replied.

"Thank god. That makes sense then. Son and heir is the reason I couldn't get past some ridiculous security man at the gate earlier today."

"Yes."

"So, want to meet me in town or at your hotel apartment? You can tell me all about it over a drink or few."

Sophia wanted to shake Claire. *God, why is everything about a drink*? "I'm giving up the apartment. My things are being delivered back to the castle tomorrow."

"His Highness didn't like it, right? Soph, I can pick you up in…"

"Why is everything about pleasure with you, Claire? You haven't even asked me what the problem was with Rupert. Goodnight, Claire." Sophia ended the call. She gazed at the clock again. It was nine-forty-five. Something niggled in the back of her mind that she'd forgotten…something. "I guess if it's important, it will come back to me." She left the room.

†

Abby paced the gravel walkways between the rose garden plots. Each had its own variety and was her mom's favorite flower. Even her dad had succumbed to the rose, building a small rose garden behind the farmhouse, though Abby suspected that was because he loved her mom so much. He was more a shrub man.

The lights were brightly burning at the castle. Nothing unusual at nine in the evening, but this was going to be another long night for the family. She brushed back tears as thoughts of Samuel and Prince Rupert surfaced. She sat at the bench situated halfway between the white and red rose varieties.

Had the Prince been a good man? He seemed to be. There weren't news reports like those that followed the Princess. A smile tugged at her lips at the thought of Her Highness. Glancing at her watch, she saw it was almost ten.

She stood, looked around the garden, and left for home. It had been a long day, and she wanted her bed. Four o'clock came around so quickly.

†

Claire entered the bar nearest to her apartment. Normally, she didn't frequent it, too close to home, but tonight, her call to Soph had her on the back foot. Her friend was annoyed big time. *Maybe the son and heir isn't as squeaky clean as everyone thinks.*

She heard her name called, then it amplified. She looked around and, with a smile, headed to the booth and slid opposite the woman. "Hey there, I didn't know you came here?"

"I don't. I was hoping you might. I was right."

"I rarely do. You must have second sight." Claire had to admit this woman gave her the hots, but there was something else that didn't quite gel. "Want a drink?"

"I thought you'd never ask." Slim fingers wound around the almost empty beer glass.

Claire headed for the bar. At least tonight might not be a total loss.

†

Henry Torvois sat in his favorite high-backed chair. His slim fingers traced the multi-colored brocade covering. Tears spilled as he recalled Samuel presenting him with the gift five years ago. Chronic back pain through years of service in the royal household had taken its toll. This magnificent chair had eased the pain significantly. His head bobbed down, and through his mind's eye, he could see Samuel sitting at his feet as they watched some ridiculous reality show about sewing. He closed his eyes, but tears forced them open immediately, and he wept for the man who had taken the chance to love him without reservation. He'd never experienced that before. What was left for him now, a lonely sad life with nothing to look forward to. He brusquely swept away the tears and stood. He had to be strong for the Crown Prince because, without that, he would be crushed underfoot by his emotions. Bright lights, from outside, flooded his room.

"What's going on?" He strode to the window to see that the gatehouse entrance to the castle was a mirror of light. Frowning, he left his room to find out what was going on.

†

There was a tentative knock on the door of Sophia's room, and she sighed.

"Enter." She was surprised to find the salt-and-pepper head of her father peeping around the door.

"My dear, we have visitors, lots of them. I think the news is out about Rupert."

Sophia scrambled off the bed where she'd been looking through photos on her phone. She watched the nervous tick appear above her father's left eye, barely noticeable, but a sure indicator he was stressed. "I'll find out." She walked up to her father and held him close. "Papa, it's going to be okay, I promise."

"The only promise I want, Sophia, is that you stay safe and well. You are all I have left now." The words floated in the air between them, a promise but also an acknowledgement for them both that things would never be the same again.

"I know, and I promise to take great care. I'll be back soon."

They left her room. Sophia descended the stairs as her father watched. She waved as she opened the front door and left the castle. Pulling the collar of her sweater tighter to ward off the cool air, she marched toward the gatehouse. The idea that she had forgotten something earlier burst into her mind like a jack-in-a-box.

"Damn, Abby." Her eyes travelled to the walled garden, where she had last seen Abby leave. She stopped and debated the merit of contacting Abby, first to apologize and then ask for support. Shaking her head, she knew that it would be wrong. Using people, no matter what the paparazzi thought, wasn't part of her makeup. She resumed her pace to the gatehouse.

As she arrived, a police officer stood in front of her ten feet from the gate.

"Your Highness, I'm sorry, but it isn't wise for you to go any farther."

"Why?"

"It's the reporters." The police officer looked like he was just out of graduate school. Fresh-faced and innocent—*oh, how was that going to change over the years*?

"I've been through the gamut with the newshounds before, officer. What do they want?"

"I'm not sure."

Ah, right, not everyone was in the know about my brother's accident. "If you don't mind, I'd like to find out. It's disturbing my papa." Sophia wanted to laugh at the shocked expression on the young man's face.

"I will escort you, Your Highness."

"Very well." They turned toward the gate and the blinding lights. As they got closer, voices began shouting.

"Is it true, Princess?"

"Where is Prince Rupert?"

"Why do you have police at the gates?"

Sophia listened to the barrage of questions, many inaudible. As she neared the gates, some of the faces were old friends. One, she thought she'd seen recently, but not in this context. Placing a dutiful smile on her lips, she threw out her hands. "Please, how ridiculous are your questions."

"We have a good source that says Prince Rupert is dead. Is it true? Come on, why all the police activity if it isn't?"

"A good source, really? Nelly, you've been watching too many Netflix murder series."

"So, you are saying that Prince Rupert is alive?"

The words cut Sophia deep. However, she was an Osric; the mantra was never reveal emotion in public or be forever wounded by it. Words drilled into her from a child. "I prefer to say that it isn't any of your business." She smiled.

"That didn't answer my question, Princess."

"Yeah, answer the question." There were several other murmurings of the same in the crowd.

"I have given you my answer, now please leave, there isn't anything for you here." Sophia turned away.

"Afraid to answer."

Sophia clenched her fists and turned, glaring at the woman who had called her out. "Do I know you?"

A sneer crossed the woman's face. "We shared drinks a couple of nights ago." There was a crackle of laughter from the crowd.

Sophia frowned. Finally realizing this was the woman Claire had been enamored by. *What the hell was her name? Ah yes. Jean.* "If I recall the event correctly, you joined a table that I left almost immediately. I'd hardly call that sharing drinks." Sophia closed her eyes, fully expecting a barrage of questions.

"I'd agree. Their Highnesses will update you on Prince Rupert's situation in the morning. If you want a true statement, then I'd allow Their Highnesses to have some rest."

Sophia's body relaxed. Abby was here.

"Yes, tomorrow at ten am, there will be an announcement."

There was a cavalcade of voices at the gate.

"Let's go." Abby placed a hand on Sophia's arm.

"Your Highness, I will take care of the reporters." The young police officer said, heading for the gate.

"Thank you." Sophia turned to Abby. "How did you know I needed your help?"

"I didn't. Those darn lights were keeping my mother awake. She told me to check it out."

"God, I'm so grateful for your mother. Abby, I'm sorry about this evening." Sophia stopped and stared into Abby's plain features. Right now, they were the most comforting and beautiful thing in her life.

"No problem, my Princess." They walked another ten feet, and Sophia stopped again.

"It is a problem. I should have at least called you to tell you I couldn't make it."

Abby knitted her brows then shrugged. "Do you even have my number?"

Oh god, no, no, I don't. "True. Though I could have asked the staff."

Abby grinned. "Works. Though you may have ended up talking to my mother."

"Look, Abby, I'm…"

"It's all good, my Princess. You need to put His Highness' mind at rest, as I do my mother's.

"Yes, yes of course." The castle entrance loomed.

"Goodnight, Princess." Abby smiled and began to walk toward the walled garden.

"Thank you, Abby."

"You are very welcome, my Princess. Goodnight." Abby opened the door to the walled garden and entered.

Sophia watched the door close behind her, and a big part of her wanted to follow. Something about Abby called to her soul. But right now, she had to give her papa priority.

"Goodnight, Abby," she whispered before entering the castle.

Chapter Ten

Commissioner Foley threw down one of the numerous tabloids he'd read that morning: one way or another, all the headlines read *Prince Rupert suspected dead.* He picked up the phone, punched in a number, and growled down the receiver, then slammed it down.

There was a knock on the door of his office.

"Yes?"

The door opened, and Sawyer, the pathologist, entered. As usual, she was dressed more for a visit to a country hoedown than work. Black Levi's and a blue cotton shirt, buttoned to the top, greeted him.

"Doctor, I hope you have news."

"I wouldn't be here if I didn't." She strolled farther into his domain and settled in the seat opposite him.

"And?"

"He was the driver."

"The driver—he was a terrible driver!"

"Mr. Samuel Anderson had COVID. He was probably feeling pretty crap, the obvious explanation for His Highness to drive. He was crushed like a bug when the car wrapped around a tree. He hit the windscreen and the impact jetsoned him into the tree. The poor man had no chance."

Foley knitted his heavy brows together.

"The prince?"

"He died from a massive head trauma. If that hadn't killed him, his right leg was trapped, and he was bleeding out rapidly. To put it in a nutshell, it was a terrible accident, and neither man had a chance of survival." Sawyer turned away toward the door. "Forensics is going over the vehicle for any trace of 'foul play', and they will have that report for you in…" She glanced at her watch, and the phone rang. "Now I suspect." She left the room.

"I really don't like that woman." Foley answered the phone, "Yes."

"Sir, there is no evidence of any tampering to the vehicle or mechanical fault. It's a preliminary report now but fairly conclusive."

Foley growled. "Have the definitive report on my desk by the end of the day." He ended the call, picked up his briefcase, and left the office.

†

"It's time, Henry." Crown Prince Claude smoothed down his jacket.

"Sir?"

"Time for us to acknowledge our loss and allow the public to mourn as we do."

"Yes, sir."

Claude sighed. "Henry, we do this together. I understand your pain is akin to mine. Together we can do this."

"I don't understand…"

"Henry, I have a daughter who loves women quite as I love women. I have my most trusted royal aide who 'loved' a man. It is not something we talk about; indeed, we don't talk at all about it. I confess that I should have. Love, as my wife once explained to me," Claude sucked in a slow breath, "is never about gender. Simply, that another soul calls to yours and the rest is history."

"Sir, I…I."

"Henry, today, as we face the public and our sad story is told, it will be hard for both of us. More, I believe, for you, since Samuel will be barely spoken of. I want you to know that the family Osric will know and grieve as you do for our combined loss." He reached out and touched Henry's shoulder. "Together we will withstand this, and then be allowed to grieve in peace."

"Thank you, sir."

"Thank you, Henry. I could not do this without you."

They left the room.

†

Sophia, dressed in a Balmain black A-line dress, stood beside her father. She touched his shaking hands, hands clasped behind his back. He turned and gave her a slight nod.

"Sir, is Prince Rupert dead?"

"Was he murdered?"

"How did he die?"

The voices of the paparazzi reverberated around the room.

Sophia watched her father go from nervous to completely composed. He held up a hand and waited for the noise to abate. Within a minute, the room was so quiet that you could hear a pin drop. She had always envied her father's grace in difficult situations. This was another example and a reminder that there was no way she could ever do this.

"My son, His Highness Prince Rupert, has had his life tragically cut short." Her father looked at the reporters, then cleared his throat. "We only know the circumstances of his demise and that of his aide, Samuel." Her father glanced for a mini second toward Henry on his left side. "There was a tragic traffic accident that claimed their lives. The full details are yet to be acknowledged. Commissioner Foley is working toward that solution. Currently, we ask for privacy at this time to grieve." Her father turned away from the reporters.

"Sir, what does this mean for the succession?" Sophia glared at the reporter who had spoken. It was that woman again.

"My…" Her hand was gently clutched. Her father looked deep into her eyes. The message clear: *Do not engage*. She nodded, and they walked away.

"There are times to speak, Sophia, and others to just let be. Today is a let it be day." He gave her a weak smile. "Tomorrow is another day, my love."

"Yes, Papa." Sophia bit down on her lip. Right now, the actual recognition, publicly, that her brother was dead, hurt so much she wanted to scream her rage out loud.

"Commissioner Foley will not be happy with this publicity event."

"That is true, Your Highness."

Sophia had almost forgotten that Henry was still with them. *He must be hurting like hell.*

“Henry, maybe if I say to hell with Foley, you might actually not want to reprimand me?” Sophia gave him a small smile. He looked tighter than a drum about to explode as he turned to her.

“Princess, I agree entirely.”

Sophia was sure her mouth opened like a guppy at his words. “Great minds.” She turned to her father. “Papa, do you mind if I catch up with …”

“Do what you need to do. Tomorrow at ten am, Sophia, meet me in my study.”

“Yes, Papa.” She kissed his cheek. “I’ll see you at lunch and dinner.”

“Not today, Sophia. I need personal time.” He pulled her close. “This is about how I grieve. I love you so much. I need to spend my time with your mama.” He released her.

Sophia watched him walk toward the castle with Henry following. Tears had filled his eyes as he’d spoken.

Her chest hurt and she thought it was caving in.

†

“Mom, what’s wrong?” Abby took the few steps to her mother, who was crying as she stood next to the TV.

“I just can’t believe Prince Rupert is dead.”

She wrapped her mom in a hug. “I really don’t know what to say, Mom.”

“I thought you and the Princess were close now that you are friends. Shouldn’t you be there supporting her?”

Abby withdrew a little and stared into her mom’s eyes. “I think it’s a convenience, the friend thing. I haven’t a clue where she is or what’s going on.”

“She was on TV, supporting her father. You should have been with her. I saw how fragile they were.”

"Mom, the Princess is hardly fragile. She can handle anything that they throw at her. I've seen it firsthand." Abby sighed. "Mom, we are commoners, and they are royalty. They don't care what we think."

Her mom's eyebrows rose. Then there was a knock on the door.

"I'll get it." Abby headed to the door. An arm stopped her.

"I can answer my front door." Her mother walked the few paces and opened the door.

Abby's heart sank at the next words.

"Princess, I'm so sorry for your loss. How can I help you?"

Abby watched as her mom walked over to the Princess. Then her jaw dropped as the Princess threw herself into her mom's arms and sobbed.

"I'll make tea," Abby mumbled.

†

Abby held her mom's hand as the Crown Prince announced officially to the household his only son's death in a tragic accident. She felt the tremors through her mom's body at the news. There were cries of anguish, some genuine, others not so much as Abby scanned the household staff. She and her mom, along with other tenants on the Prince's land, were invited as a matter of protocol.

"We need you all to pull together. Every one of you is part of the Osric family and will face the inevitable barrage of questions from the press." A silence engulfed the room.

Abby watched the Crown Prince intently. He looked less than well. In the circumstances, understandable, but his pallor was grey, and he appeared short of breath.

Why wasn't his backup, Henry, taking better care of him? Then she mentally smacked herself. Of course Henry would be grieving his loss too.

Abby released her mom's hand and stepped forward a few feet to stand opposite the Crown Prince.

"Sir, are you okay?" she whispered, as eyes she was becoming familiar with looked in her direction. Abby saw a slight smile hover over his lips.

"As well as one can be, in these circumstances. Thank you for your concern, Abby." He turned back to the staff. "Please take time to grieve. Thank you all for your service."

There were a few moments of silence as the Crown Prince left the room. Then the voices began. Hushed at first, then louder.

Abby looked at her mom. "Shall we go home?"

Her mother gave her a teary smile. "Do you mind if I have tea here with Mrs. Castle and the other girls?"

Abby glanced over at the portly housekeeper and the four women who made up most of the staff. Hardly girls, but hey. "Sure."

"Do you want to join us?"

"Davy takes on my tasks at the farm if Anna needs my help for a break. I'm sure right now she does. It would be testing his generosity if I just sat around and had tea. Besides, I'd rather work; it will help."

"Oh, my darling, what a wonderful person you are. Always so concerned about others." She smiled and left Abby standing alone in the middle of the room.

She was still reeling from the Princess' visit earlier that morning. The tea had been awkward, and the Princess had left soon after. *I wonder why she came to us, of all people. What about her best friend?* Questions she probably would never know the answer to, at least today. Leaving the room, she headed for the switch room, once a broom cupboard. If she thought about it, Harry Potter's bedroom at his Muggle home was larger. She chuckled and opened the door.

"Hey, Anna, do you need a break?"

Anna Winter turned and gave her a heartfelt nod. "Abs, you are a godsend. Has the Crown Prince spoken to the staff?"

"Yes, just finished. I expect you know what he said."

"Well, I have been briefed by Charlotte, such a tragedy."

"I guess it was just their time," Abby said before she realized that might sound harsh.

Anna walked up to her and laid a hand on her arm. "I know what you mean, Abby. Is it okay if I leave now? I need to see my kids and break the news when they get home from school. Though they will probably know by now." Abby nodded. Anna picked up her coat and handbag from the small coat rack on the wall and slipped the jacket on. "You do know what this means."

Abby frowned, "What?"

"Will the Crown Prince change tradition and announce the Princess as the heiress to the crown on his passing, or will he stick with tradition and go with some idiot male relative?" Anna shrugged. "Love you, Abby, and thank you. I hope one day I can help you as much as you do me."

"You do; Davy is very understanding. Love you, too, Anna."

Anna grinned. "He should, or he won't be getting his dinner when he arrives home." She gave Abby a hug and left the room.

Abby sat at the desk and pulled her phone from her jeans. Seconds later, the call connected. "Davy, sorry, earlier than I expected. Anna needed to go home and break the news to the kids. Can you hold the fort a little longer?"

"I told you I would. Hell, Abby, you've helped us out so many times in the past and now once again. My kids will thank you for it, and we love you for it."

Abby smiled. "Thank you, Davy. I'll catch up with you tomorrow." The call ended.

Davy Winter was a cousin twice removed on her father's side. He had been a bit of a rolling stone until he met and married Anna ten years ago. Her father had employed Davy as a casual farm hand to help them out. She had employed him full-time when her father died. Now he knew everything about the farm and probably could run it better than she could, and it seemed these days he did.

She glanced down at the switchboard, groaned, and changed the covers on the earpieces to clean ones. Immediately, the ten external lines buzzed for attention. *God, this is going to be one long session.*

†

Sophia called Claire for the fifth time and got no answer. *Where the hell was she?* Glancing at her Cartier watch, her mother's, she saw it was six pm. She closed her eyes, knowing exactly where Claire was, or at least probably, a bar. Then the familiar voice answered.

"Soph, god, I'm so sorry for your loss. I…shall I come over?"

"No, no." There was a moment of silence.

"You said that last time we spoke. Have I done something wrong? I'm here for you, always have been, you know that, right?" Claire quietly replied.

Sophia could see in her mind's eye her friend's frown. She loved Claire but knew her so well. It was affection for a sibling rather than what she knew Claire hoped might happen one day—it wouldn't. "It's not about you."

"I know. Look, Soph, you need me right now. You must be in pieces. I can't even imagine what your father is going through."

"He's coping rather well in the circumstances. I've called you several times, but you haven't answered."

Claire cleared her throat. "Sorry. I forgot to put my phone on charge last night, and it died on me at lunchtime. I had a meeting this afternoon and just retrieved it. I'm so sorry, Soph. Look, I'll come over and we can talk or not. I'll just be there for you. I want to be there for you."

There seemed to be desperation in Claire's plea.

It would be good to see Claire and accept her friend's comfort. "Okay, I'll let the jailers at the gate know you are coming. See you in half an hour."

"Wonderful. Get the drinks on ice." She ended the call.

Sophia simply stared at the item in the palm of her hand.

That was Claire's solution to any problem—drink.

†

Abby stretched aching muscles and stood, removing her earpieces. She couldn't remember how many calls she'd taken and had to divert, probably twenty to one that she had put through to others in the castle. Most had been news media of various kinds. One had been aggressive. She was sure she had heard the voice before, but then, after all those calls, it could just be someone trying incessantly to get through to a member of the royal family.

The door opened, and Henry Torvois entered.

Abby waited for him to speak, but he just stood silent. "Mr. Torvois, can I help you?"

No verbal interaction. *Okay, now I'm puzzled.* She gazed at his pale features. He was never that flush, but right now he looked like a ghost. "Are you okay?"

"It is ten pm, Abby."

"Oh, really, time flies." Abby smiled.

"Thank you."

"You are welcome."

"You only needed to help for Anna's shift, and that ended hours ago."

Abby knitted her eyebrows. "Math was almost my worst subject. I lost track of time."

Henry nodded. "We both know different, Abby. You have been here for ten hours that I know of."

"Really? That long."

"Why?"

Abby didn't dislike Mr. Torvois; he was just a cold man in her eyes. He must have had some redeeming qualities if Sam had loved him. "The family needed it. Anna needed to talk with her kids about the situation. Then no one else turned up."

Henry frowned. "Sybil didn't appear for her shift?"

"No, I figured she needed time to grieve as His Highness mentioned."

Abby would never have expected, in her weirdest dreams, what would happen next. He hugged her hard and whispered, "Thank you." Then kissed her cheek.

†

Claire lounged on Sophia's chaise, a glass of vodka in hand. "Soph, I heard on the grapevine you have a new friend. I said it was ridiculous. You have me."

Sophia took a sip from her watered-down vodka. God knows drinking herself to oblivion would be wonderful. Not tonight. There was a pull on her heart that didn't make sense, but prevented her from drinking as she usually did with Claire.

"Ridiculous, of course. I have you," Sophia cagily replied.

"Want another?" Claire raised her glass.

Sophia lifted her half-full glass. "Still okay."

Claire stood and moved toward the drinks at the small bar. "Hm, running out of ice. I'll get some more from the kitchen." She picked up the ice bucket.

Sophia took it from her. "I'll get it. I know exactly where in the kitchen it is."

"Wow, I'm being waited on by a princess. I love it." Claire chuckled.

"Be right back." Sophia left her room and heaved a sigh of relief.

The first hour was, as expected, full of condolences. The second was reflective. Now it was… I just want to go to bed and cry. Why doesn't she just go? If she loves me so much, she should understand.

Sophia made her way swiftly down the staircase and turned toward the corridor that led to the hall, then she heard voices. Glancing at her watch, she saw it was ten pm. Frowning, she switched direction, opened the door to the small office, and stepped inside. Her eyes flared, and she was sure her eyebrows hit the ceiling at what she saw. "Pardon my interruption." Sophia croaked and was halfway out of the room.

"Your Royal Highness, please, this isn't what it seems." Henry moved swiftly to hold the door open.

"I…" Her eyes moved from his to Abby. She had turned her back. And was taking a call.

"Princess, do you need anything?"

"Yes." She held her head high. "I've run out of ice in my room."

"I will attend to that, Your Highness." Henry smiled.

Sophia looked again toward Abby, who was involved in a conversation. "Good. Don't take forever." She walked briskly away back to the staircase.

Right now, getting blind drunk is a good call.

†

Abby finished the call and navigated around Henry to pick up her belongings. "Goodnight, Mr. Torvois."

"Goodnight, Abby."

She was less than two inches from the door closing when he spoke again.

"Do you know where the ice is?" Abby suppressed a laugh.

"Probably the walk-in freezer." The puzzled look that crossed his face had her shaking her head. "I'll get the ice."

Henry's phone rang. His face became professional, much as she saw every day from him. "Yes, Your Highness?" he nodded several times. "Yes, Your Highness, I will be there immediately." He turned to her as he replaced his phone in his pocket.

"It's okay. See to the Crown Prince, and I will take the ice to the Princess."

Henry nodded and left the room.

What the hell was Henry doing, giving me a kiss on the cheek? He must be losing it.

†

Claire was still in the same place she had been when Sophia left.

“What, no ice?”

“It’s on the way. “Sophia picked up her drink and downed it in one.

“There was me, thinking you knew where something as mediocre as ice was kept. Come on, let’s drink to something?”

Sophia loved her friend, she really did, but right now, Claire was an itch that needed eradication.

“Hey, what’s the point in having staff if you don’t use them?” As the words were out of her mouth, she hated them. “Get me a drink, I want a large one.”

Claire grinned. “About time.”

Ten minutes after she arrived back in her room, there was a knock on the door. Sophia didn’t know why she had such vicious feelings for Abby or even Henry. Yet she wanted to smack them both.

“I’ll get it.” Claire lithely slipped from her chair and opened the door. “Great, can’t have a decent drink without ice, just leave it on the table over there.” Claire waved to the coffee table.

Sophia opened her mouth to thank Henry and became mute when Abby stood in the room.

“I brought two bags. Do you want to put them in your fridge and take them as needed? The castle is a bit short-staffed.”

Claire shrugged. “Whatever.” Reaching for one of the containers, she fumbled desperately with the bag and threw it down. “Open it.”

Sophia's heart accelerated. "I'll do it, Abby. Thank you."

"Soph, it's the hired hand. She can do it."

Sophia dropped her gaze and stared at the beautiful wool-blended carpet that had been bought internationally. Her mom had loved her honeymoon in New Zealand, so much so, she'd commissioned a special wool carpet for the main family bedrooms.

"Yes, she can." Sophia sucked in breath. "Abby, thank you. I'll take it from here."

Sophia wasn't sure why she was so magnanimous when minutes earlier she had wanted to smack the woman.

"Thanks, it's been a long day. Good night, Princess." Abby left the room.

"Let her off lightly, Soph. Now we have ice. Want a Claire special vodka concoction, made from my very own recipe?" Claire moved toward the drinks area and picked up the vodka bottle.

"You know my brother is dead...right, and you ask me what we are drinking to?" Sophia shook her head. "I think it's best you go, Claire. Right now, I need to be alone." She walked to her bedroom and slammed the door behind her.

Chapter Eleven

Crown Prince Claude twirled the ring on his wedding finger for the thousandth time, or that's what it seemed. He was seated at his normal position in the dining room. Sophia was unlikely to attend breakfast unless it was under duress. He stroked a hand over his two-day stubble. Closing his eyes, he wondered what Adeline would have thought of the situation. Devasted, of course. His thoughts traveled to Sophia. "Ah, Sophia, who has had all the bad publicity, but in actuality, she is showing how remarkable a person she has become."

The door opened, and Henry entered with a large silver tray. He placed it on the long table on the wall opposite the dining table.

"What's this, Henry? I have never seen you serve breakfast in all the years I have known you."

"You did give permission for the staff to take time if they needed it. Many have, Your Highness." Henry headed for the door.

"I'm sorry, Henry, you should, of all the household staff, be the one taking time away."

"Nothing to be sorry for, sir. I'll be back with the final tray and then prepare the accompaniments." He left the room.

Claude sighed. "Damn."

The door opened again.

"I'm sorry, Henry, I should insist." A faint tinkle of laughter lifted Claude's heavy heart.

"I'm sorry, Papa, have the last few days taken that kind of toll on me?"

"My darling, of course not, you are as beautiful as you always are. You rarely attend breakfast, why today?" Claude stood and engulfed his daughter in a tight hug.

"Probably the same reason you have given me a hug; you haven't done that since I was a teenager, and I'm sure you did it to annoy me." She smiled. "Papa, you need to release me if I'm to cat."

Claude released his daughter and simply stared at her.

"Papa, you are staring."

"Sorry, I'm just…"

Sophia kissed him on the cheek. "Happy to see me?"

Claude nodded. "There will never be any doubt of that."

They sat opposite each other, the distance a chasm. Claude stood and moved so that they sat next to each other.

"Henry will not be happy you moved, though not I." Sophia took his hand and squeezed it gently.

"I really don't care. Right now, being close to my daughter is the only thing that matters."

"Papa, what happens next?"

"My darling, we must wait for the coroner's final report. Commissioner…"

Sophia shook her head. “Papa, I meant the preparations for the funeral.”

“Ah, yes, of course.” He clasped her hand. “I have a meeting with the family undertakers this afternoon to discuss the situation.” He dropped his gaze to the slim fingers threaded through his. *This should not be happening*.

“Papa, I would like to attend the meeting.”

“No. No, my darling, it will be too hard on you. I will take care of the arrangements.”

“Then who will take care of you?” The solemn question floated in the air between them.

He dropped his head, and tears filled his eyes. He couldn’t show his child his weakness. He waved a hand over his eyes. “Henry will be by my side. I trust him. He has been and will be indispensable to me during this time. He suffers the same.”

The door opened, and Henry appeared with another silver platter.

“Henry, where is Jacob?” Sophia asked.

As he carefully placed the platter next to the one already on the table, he turned to them. “He’s taken time off.”

“Time off?”

Henry threw back his thin shoulders. “Yes, Princess.” He opened the platter, and steam vented into the room. “I will make the toast and whatever else you wish. Please let me know.” He turned on the small burners.

Claude thanked Henry, then turned to his daughter, who was frowning. He smiled. “Sophia, Henry has been very diligent for breakfast this morning. I think it only right we eat.”

Sophia stood and whispered in his ear. “He wasn’t the cook, too?”

Claude shook his head. "I think not." He moved to the table and selected a porcelain plate. "Henry, I would like two rounds of rye toast.

"Me too, Henry," Sophia said.

"Oh, and Henry, please join us. It is a request. Not a demand." He smiled at the flustered man. "Henry, we all need to eat to get through this." He looked at Sophia, who appeared surprised. "Is that not right, Sophia?"

"Yes."

"What say you, Henry?"

"Thank you, Your Highness. I do need to eat."

Claude nodded and looked at Sophia. She rolled her eyes and then gave him that smile. It was the one that she gave him when he'd done something she totally agreed with but couldn't hug him in public to acknowledge the action.

"Let's eat breakfast before we face the day. I believe it is going to be a rather long one."

†

Abby woke and looked at the alarm clock on the bedside table, then groaned. Five-thirty was hardly a sleep-in after the hours she worked yesterday. Her nose twitched. The smell of bacon and eggs never got old. Ten minutes later, she was dragging out a chair at the kitchen table. "I guess you couldn't sleep either, Mom?"

"Sleep, sleep. Who can with this tragedy enveloping us? I was awake all night."

Abby pursed her lips to prevent a smile. Her mom had been snoring loudly when she finally arrived home at eleven and passed her bedroom on the way to hers. "True. Everyone knows the Prince is dead. I was thinking about the funeral and the family. All the traditional protocol." Abby forked up a pile of eggs on a hash brown.

"He isn't the Crown Prince. There will not be a time of state mourning. The family will be talking to advisors about the arrangements. If it's like Princess Adeline's funeral, then in two weeks we will bury the young Prince." Her mom shook her head. "He will at least now be reunited with his mother. She loved her babies so much."

"Mom, is the Princess next in line?" Abby held her breath waiting for the answer.

"Traditionally, the principality has always passed to a male heir. Prince Alfonso, her distant cousin, is the likely heir on her father's demise. He will likely be here more often. The Princess will be financially secure, of course. She may marry into a wealthy family." Abby frowned. "There are a lot of wealthy families with lesbian children, darling."

Abby groaned. "Why can't she be the next heir? It seems so unfair." Abby plunged her fork at the bacon on her plate.

There were a few moments of silence, and then Abby felt her mom's arm go around her shoulder.

"Old traditions, my love. More so in these small royal houses. The Princess knows her role. From birth, she has been indoctrinated in the tradition that the male line rules."

Abby looked up. "I don't think it's fair."

"I know, my darling, because you were brought up to be on equal par to anyone regardless of gender or status." She kissed her head.

"I love you, Mom."

Her mother returned to her seat at the table. "I love you. Now let's eat, instead of butchering that poor pork sausage again."

†

Claire woke up with a hangover. Nothing new, but today it pounded louder than the cathedral bells at a coronation. She twitched her wrist, and even the colored dials of her watch hurt her eyes. “Crap, it’s eleven-thirty.” She scrambled out of bed, and the room began to spin. Groaning with a hand to her head, she slipped back into her bed and pulled the pillow over her face. “Tomorrow, I’ll go to work, tomorrow.”

†

Sophia found herself in the walled garden. She didn’t really know why. If she thought about it, in her lifetime, she’d been behind these walls perhaps five times. Two of them recently. For some absurd reason, it drew her in, relaxing her. Taking a seat beside the roses her mother loved, she wasn’t surprised her father continued to nurture the area. She closed her eyes. Her mind began to traverse the myriad situations Rupert’s death had created. Not least her own future. *God, what the hell will I do when Papa dies?*

“Princess?”

Sophia’s body warmed, a smile tugging her lips. She looked at the tall and generous stature of the woman who had spoken. “Abby.”

“I’m sorry, Princess, am I intruding? I was just…”

“No, not intruding. I think, Abby, of all my acquaintances, you are the least likely one to intrude.” She saw Abby’s strong shoulders relax. “You were just?”

Abby smiled. “It’s Anna’s day off, and the replacement has called in sick.”

Sophia nodded. More likely, Abby was the only one available that fell for a sob story from Henry, especially after his admission of staff problems at breakfast. "Then, I shouldn't keep you."

Abby walked past, then stopped. "Do you need anything, Princess?"

They both gazed at each other. Sophia shook her head. "No. Thank you for asking." She watched as Abby moved to the exit. "Abby."

Abby turned." Yes, Princess?"

"I need to take a few days away from the castle and process what life will be without my brother. Would you be interested in coming with me?"

Abby frowned. "Me?"

"Yes, you. After all, you are my friend." Sophia watched the heavy eyebrows furrow. A rabbit would no doubt have enjoyed frolicking inside them. "Tomorrow, is that too short notice?" Abby gave her a long stare. Sophia wasn't sure she'd been inspected so closely since her last medical exam.

"I…Princess, I must work. The farm and helping at the castle. I'm sorry, it's not a good time for someone like me to just take a few days away." Abby shook her head; those eyebrows furrowed even more.

Sophia didn't understand that a simple request like taking a few days away was so difficult.

Abby glanced at her watch. "I need to go, Princess."

"When you are free of your work, will you call me, and we can discuss the situation?"

Abby nodded and left.

Sophia didn't know why she'd said that. Her papa needed her, and she was blithely thinking of walking away. *I'm so selfish.*

†

Sophia looked at the clock on the marble fireplace in the room her mom called her normal family room. As much a place where the family could be normal as you could be as a royal. Her mom hadn't been brought up royal, but she wrapped the role around her like a consummate actress because she loved her prince.

She clenched her fists and walked over to the picture window that overlooked the side garden. It was difficult to see anything at this time of the evening.

"Papa doesn't need me or doesn't want me to help. No one does." The pathetic words echoed in the room. She had never been stupid enough to think she was special except for the title.

The internal phone rang. Who knew she was here? Striding to the phone, she picked it up. "Yes?"

"Hi, it's me. Oops, sorry, Princess. Abby calling."

Sophia smothered laughter at the statement. "Hello, Abby calling."

"I'm sorry it's taken so long to get back to you."

"I figured you were busy. Not working now, I hope." There was a moment of silence.

"Yes, the main switchboard is open until eight."

"Well, that means only another forty-five minutes."

"I wish."

"What do you mean?"

"No one to cover the house system. That is covered until midnight. When it's a party at the castle, it can be a twenty-four-hour situation."

Sophia frowned. "Why?"

"The family and guests may need something."

Sophia swallowed hard. Hadn't she been a culprit of that practice, even recently? "Do you want company?" There was a drawn breath at the end of the line. "Sorry, I know it's …"

"No, no, I'd love company. But, Princess, you must surely have more important things to do."

"My father is at a meeting in town and staying overnight, regarding Rupert's funeral arrangements. He didn't want me there." Sophia knew her tone was harsh and regretted it.

"Your father is probably shielding you from more hurt. It's what parents do."

"Perhaps."

"How about you have dinner and keep me company afterwards."

Sophia smiled. This woman was selfless. "Want me to bring you a snack?"

Abby laughed. "My mom will have supper for me when I get home."

"Okay, that's a no. See you soon."

"Yes, thank you, Princess." The phone went dead, but Sophia still held the receiver to her ear. In the short space of time she'd conversed with Abby, her mood had risen a thousand-fold.

†

Abby was glad there was no one in the room with her as she fumbled with the equipment on the desk. How had she been so forward as to say what she did when calling the Princess? Okay, she appeared cool about it, but... *God, if Mom knew, she would be appalled.*

A call came through. "Hello, how can I help?"

"Put me through to Princess Sophia." The slurred words told their own story, but she also knew the owner of them.

"I'm sorry, I can't do that."

"Sure, you can, you are the help."

Abby hesitated. “May I have your name and the reason for the call?”

“I’m not giving my name to you. You know my voice. I’ve called a million times. It isn’t your business why I want to speak to her. For fuck’s sake, put me through.”

“No.” Abby sucked in a breath. Then she heard another voice in the background, though she couldn’t work out the words.

“I’ll have your job when I speak with the Princess.” The call ended.

Well, that was interesting. If she is such a good friend, why didn’t she call her on her cell? Abby sighed. The Princess needs to find new friends.

An incoming call pulled her back to the task in hand.

†

Henry watched as the Crown Prince discussed the formal preparations for the funeral of his son as if it were just another task in his daily routine. He knew, of course, that wasn’t the case. He’d been with the Crown Prince through his parents’ deaths and his adored wife. He had thought the Crown Prince might never recover from that trauma. He’d been so angry when Adeline had died. If it hadn’t been for the children, he doubted the Crown Prince would be with them today.

“Henry.” He turned to face the Crown Prince.

“How can I help, sir?”

“The car, please.”

“Yes, sir.”

†

Sophia grinned as she knocked softly on the door to the coms room that had less space than her shoe collection. There was no answer, so she opened the door and stepped inside. About to announce her entrance, she stopped.

"Hello, how can I help?"

Sophia smiled and simply listened as Abby took several calls.

"Oh, yes, it is tragic. I will pass on your condolences to their Highnesses. I'm not exactly sure what you are inferring." Sophia saw Abby's expression turn pale. "The royal family is not a subject for speculation."

Sophia's heart warmed at Abby's handling of awkward questions the public asked. The call ended.

"Hi."

Abby turned, and her cheeks colored a delightful pink.

"I'm sorry, Princess, I didn't hear you enter the room." Abby attempted to stand, but Sophia waved for her to remain seated.

"Looks like you are having a busy night."

"That's an understatement." Abby smiled. "Unfortunately, not unusual in the circumstances."

Sophia took a standing position against the wall and then remembered something as she delved into the pocket of her trousers. She withdrew a small package. "I brought you something. It's only a smoked salmon sandwich, but I figured you might be hungry."

Abby grinned and took the sandwich. "I'm starving. I was hoping that Mr. Torvois would find a replacement, but everyone is taking His Highness' option to take time off. I guess it's a free day or two. Gosh, I hope it isn't forever. I need to get back to the farm." Abby unwrapped the wax paper around the food and bit into the sandwich.

“You’ve been working since I saw you this morning without a break?’ Sophia frowned.

Abby shrugged and continued to eat, though the switchboard lit up like a candelabra as she did.

“Please let me help. I’ll answer those as you eat. If you press the right buttons.”

“Princess, that’s not possible.”

“Why? Don’t you think I can do some work for a change?” Sophia prised herself from the wall and stood over Abby, not easy to do, but she managed it. The warmth of the woman was intoxicating.

Abby slipped off the headset and reached for the clean ear covers.

“Don’t bother.” Sophia took the headset.

Abby pressed the first line and placed it on speaker mode.

“Good evening, how can I help?” The first two calls were relatively easy to take care of; the third was another matter altogether.

“Good evening, how can I help?”

“Well, I hope you are more helpful than the last fucking idiot I talked to.”

Sophia sucked in a breath. She didn’t need to know the caller’s name, but that voice she’d know anywhere. “I’m sorry, can you please speak civilly, or I’ll have to end the call.” There were at least another five expletives in the background, so she turned to Abby to end the call.

“I want to speak to the Princess now!”

Sophia’s nostrils flared, clenching her fists. Abby stood and held out her hand for the headset. Sophia shook her head. “I’m afraid she’s busy. Who can I say is calling?”

"Claire Demeter. Please don't give me that shit. She's never too busy for me. I'm her best friend. Put me through, or I'll have your job."

"Really, well, I'm sorry, but you aren't qualified enough."

"You impertinent fuck. You are worse than the other one."

Sophia clenched her jaw, hearing another voice in background. "Go on, don't take no for an answer."

"Put me through to her now! I demand it. You are just a servant."

"Actually, I'm not a servant. The people who regularly work on this switchboard are not servants. I believe, Claire, you have totally overstepped the mark this time in our friendship." Sophia heard a choking sound at the other end of the line, but didn't care. "I think you can say you are now my ex-best friend. Don't ever call me again unless you can be civil." This time, she did end the call. Her hands were shaking when Abby gently took off the headset and replaced it on her head.

"Please sit, Princess."

She did, only because shock was overriding any other emotion. Why hadn't Claire called her on her cell?

Sophia looked at Abby, her gentle giant. Yes, Abby certainly fit that bill. Her body began to relax. "I'm sorry you have to take calls like that."

"All part of the job. Besides, I don't normally. My friend Anna does. I have to say it has been an education of late. I'm going to stick to farming." Abby smiled.

Sophia placed her hand on Abby's. "Then Anna needs a pay raise. Thank you. Thank you for many things that I probably don't even know about." Sophia drew her eyebrows together. "I probably better go."

Abby nodded. "Probably. Thank you, Princess, and I'm sorry you had to listen to…"

"Please don't apologize, Abby. It was all Claire's problem. In a way, I'm glad this has happened. For a while now, I've been trying to figure out where I stand in the world other than as a waste of space."

"You will never be that," Abby fervently replied.

"Thank you, Abby. However, right now that's exactly what I feel." Sophia headed for the door.

"Perhaps you just haven't found your place in the world. It will come. I never wanted to be a farmer, but here I am, and I love it."

Sophia's spirits rose so much that she wanted to hug Abby and never let go. Instead, she nodded. "Thank you, Abby, goodnight."

"Goodnight, Princess."

Sophia left the room and entered the main hallway. She looked around her and realized, for probably the first time in her life, that there were things she could fight for. Even if it was as simple as respect for another human being in her own home.

As she ascended the stairs to her room, tears welled. Claire had been her bestie forever. It hurt like hell to say the words she had. *If I hadn't, what would that say about me?* She reflected on her life at this moment. *I asked for punishment for my excesses, and right now I think it's raining repercussions.*

†

Abby switched off the console at midnight exactly. She looked around the room and then saw the wax paper that wrapped the sandwich the Princess had given her. *It was a great sandwich. Better not tell Mom.* She grinned as she checked the area once more and left the room. Sleep right now was a priority.

†

The Crown Prince paced the Panama Hotel room, permanently at his disposal if he chose to stay in the capital city.

"Sir, is there anything I can do for you?"

Claude gave his PA a sharp look. "Can you bring my boy back?" Henry hung his head; it told the story. *No one could, and it was wrong of him to ask this man. He wanted the same thing for his own partner.* His thoughts travelled to the conversation he'd had with Paul Foley before his meeting about his son's funeral arrangements.

"Your Highness, I'm so sorry to bother you at this time, but I have news." Foley looked uncomfortable; his loose-fitting suit, probably two sizes bigger than he was, looked ridiculous.

"Paul?"

"We now know the Prince was driving. "

Claude sighed. This was old news. "And?"

Foley shuffled. "The coroner was satisfied that it was a tragic accident. The investigative team who worked on the vehicle agree."

He turned to Henry. "Bring the car around to the front; we will be late." Then he returned his gaze to the commissioner of police. "Remove your people from my home by the morning. We need to mourn, as do our people."

Foley nodded and left the room.

"Henry."

"Yes, sir."

"From now on, the Princess is the most important person in the royal household."

"Sir, what about you?"

Claude gave a weak laugh. "Me, I'm the old guard, Henry. My daughter is the future."

Henry frowned, "Yes, sir."

"You doubt this?"

"Sir, if anything happens to you, the principality traditionally goes to the next male edition."

Claude laughed. "Edition. It makes us sound like a publication." Henry frowned. "Don't worry, we are all editions of someone."

"Yes, sir."

"My daughter is special. She will find her way, and when she does, everyone around will benefit."

Henry frowned again. Claude placed a hand on his shoulder. "She is her mother's daughter. How can she be anything but the best?"

"Princess Adeline was special."

"Yes, she was. Right now, you and I are going to go over the details of today's meeting. Then we will have dinner and toast those we have loved and lost."

"Yes, sir."

"Have you ever been drunk, Henry?"

†

"I think I've fucked up big time." Claire turned to the woman who had shared her bed numerous times since she'd met her a few days ago.

"She'll forgive you, she always does, right?"

Claire shook her head. "Not this time. God, I must have had too much to drink. I didn't even recognize her voice."

"Hey, it will all blow over. Don't forget she's under stress right now."

Claire shook her head and climbed out of bed. The room swam before her, but she managed to make it to the ensuite, where she grabbed the toilet bowl and retched until she didn't have the strength to vomit anymore. Noticeably, her companion hadn't bothered to see how she was doing. Nope, all she was interested in was Sophia. *I've been played—big time.*

"I've got to go, Claire. How about coffee at Casper's around ten?"

Claire mumbled a reply; not even sure it was a coherent yes or no. A few minutes later, the bedroom door opened and then closed. Shortly afterwards, the front door went through the same motions.

"Jean, you can go fuck yourself." Claire bit out vehemently and then threw up again.

CHAPTER TWELVE

"Wasn't expecting you up this early, darling."

"Couldn't sleep, that new darn rooster we've added to the chicken compound is loud. Doesn't have any time boundaries." Abby grinned.

Her mum chuckled, then stifled a yawn as she padded over to the kettle. "You were late last night. You are a farmer, Abby. Not staff at the royal household. You can't burn the candle at both ends. I didn't even hear you come home last night."

"It's special circumstances, Mom." Abby bit the bottom of her lip.

"Well, Henry is an idiot to use you like this." Her mother put a teabag in her mug next to the kettle.

Abby sucked in a breath. "He didn't ask me to take the morning shift."

"Good, now what do you want for breakfast? You must be starving. Those few beef sandwiches I left wouldn't fill the gap, I'm sure."

Abby smiled. "No, it didn't." She glanced at the clock on the wall; it was six-thirty-three. "How about a full English-style breakfast, like Dad loved."

Her mother narrowed her eyes. "You must be hungry."

"Can you make extra?"

Her mother laughed. "You want a takeout, too?" She headed for the refrigerator.

"Maybe another guest." Abby grinned and kissed her mother's cheek. "I'll be back in ten."

She was gone before her mother could ask any questions.

†

Sophia sat on the edge of her bed. *The idea of running away had been a bad idea. Abby had, in a few words, made her see sense.* She stood and walked to the window. She dropped her gaze to the coverlet and all the trappings that were her life. *I need to step up and not be the privileged person a lot see me as*. Standing, she looked at the clock: it was six-thirty-five. *God, I can't remember when I've ever been up at this time and been sober*. As she left her room, it was clear there was nothing that meant more than family, however complicated that might be.

Descending the stairs, she was surprised when Abby flew out of the side staff door into the main hall.

"Hey, anything wrong, Abby?"

"No, no. Mom woke early, and she is cooking breakfast. I thought you might like to join us…I know it's presumptuous."

"Not presumptuous at all. I will happily accept the invitation to join you and your mother for breakfast. Besides, I need to talk to you."

"Perfect, I was going to say the same thing."

Sophia smiled. "Nothing bad, I hope?"

"No, no." Abby smiled. "Come on, or the black pudding will be burnt to a crisp."

Laughing, Sophia asked, "I've never had black pudding, what is it?"

Abby grinned as they left by the staff door to the kitchen. "Perhaps it's better you ate it first and dissect what it is later."

"Oh, now I am intrigued."

†

Jenny Ranger watched as her daughter and the Princess ate with gusto from the breakfast plates in front of them. It was unexpected, the arrival of the Princess. In fact, it quite threw her to the point that she almost disintegrated the black pudding. Thankfully not, a little charred but edible.

"Mom, that was great. Dad would be proud." Abby announced, polishing off the final slice of toast on the plate.

"Are you sure? The black pudding wasn't quite…"

"Oh, Mrs. Ranger, the black pudding is to die for." The Princess frowned. "Sorry, but you know what I'm saying."

"I do indeed, Princess. Thank you."

"We need to talk, Princess." Abby sighed.

"Yes, we do."

Jenny felt tension forming in the room. "Why don't you go into the lounge and talk. I'll take care of the dishes."

Abby was about to protest; she knew that about her daughter. "It's okay, darling." Jenny kissed Abby's cheek and moved toward the kitchen bench.

"Thank you for a wonderful breakfast, Mrs. Ranger. If I'm honest, it's the best I've had in years. Maybe I would have gotten up earlier each day if this were in the offing."

Jenny felt her cheeks grow warm. "Thank you, Your Highness. However, I'm sure the years of this kind of breakfast would not be good for the figure."

"I'd take my chance."

Jenny laughed and shooed them into the other room.

†

"I need to say I'm…."

"I can't go with you on your break…."

They both looked at each other and then burst out laughing.

"I guess we both agree. We are staying here and helping Papa?"

"It's in my DNA, helping the Osric family."

"It's in mine, too. Though I have you to thank for bringing it to my attention. Abby, I trust you. Will you help me through the next few weeks?"

"Of course, Princess. You only ever need to ask."

Sophia sighed. "I feel like I can contribute when I'm with you. Why is that, I wonder?"

"I don't know, Princess. All you need to know is that I will be here if you need me."

"Any time? Anywhere? For anything?"

Abby frowned.

"I'm sorry, it's the spoilt child in me coming out again."

"I was going to say yes."

"So, what do you want in return?"

"Nothing. Why would I?"

"Because everyone wants something from someone, even if they say they don't?"

Abby took a moment to answer. “Then perhaps you are relying on the wrong people. Friends, family, and lovers don’t.”

Sophia raised her eyebrows. “Perhaps it is you who are living in a fantasy land. Everyone wants something. Trust me, I know from experience.”

Abby’s phone rang; she looked at the caller’s number. “Sorry, it’s Mr. Torvois.” She answered and listened for a few moments. “Yes. I can’t do as many hours…” There were a few more moments of conversation, then Abby placed her phone in her pocket. “I have to go.”

“Abby, if you don’t want to do this, say no.”

Abby gave Sophia a shrug. “We both know that’s impossible right now. When you need me, you know where to find me. Have a good day, Princess.”

Abby left the room.

†

Jenny saw her daughter leave the house hurriedly. *That isn’t a good sign.* She wiped her hands on a kitchen cloth, opened the door of the kitchen, and saw the Princess standing in the hall. She looked so forlorn. *That must have been some conversation.*

“Is there anything I can do?” Jenny wasn’t sure she was going to receive an answer when she received a softly spoken reply.

“No.”

“I have some leftovers if you are still hungry?” What else can I say? The no said yes in a bizarre way.

“Not sure I could eat anything at the moment.” The Princess turned to her. “You have a very special daughter.”

Jenny smiled. "I do. Though I don't think she feels that way. Which is a good thing."

"A good thing?" Princess Sophia moved toward her.

"Of course. It means she understands the importance of respect for people. Her father was the same. I'm unfortunately one of those who say how it is and don't care about the fallout."

A frown appeared on the Princess' face. "I've been that way for so long. Abby makes me want to be…something so much better. I wish my mother was still alive."

Jenny moved closer to the Princess. "Come here, darling." She held out her arms, and the Princess rushed into them. "Abby will take care of you if you are in trouble. But never lie to her. She can't tolerate lies."

"I haven't. We seem to be on the same wavelength."

"My one piece of wisdom regarding my daughter is keep it that way." Jenny moved to have the Princess at arm's length.

"I will, why wouldn't I? She is so very nice to everyone, even some she shouldn't."

Jenny laughed. "That's my Abby. Come on, let's have tea or coffee, your preference. If you want, we can gossip about Antoine."

The Princess laughed. "Well, in that case, yes, I'd love a tea and one of those black pudding creations."

†

Abby sat at the console and reflected on the conversation she'd had with the Princess. Especially when she said, *Perhaps you are living in a fantasy land. Everyone wants something. Trust me, I know from experience.*

The more that question revolved in her subconscious, the harder it was to deny that she didn't. The bigger question was what did she want from the Princess?

The board in front of her lit up, and she happily began answering the calls. Then it dawned on her what she wanted—to be seen as her equal.

"Hello, Osric Castle, how can I help?"

CHAPTER THIRTEEN

Jean Randle contemplated her current circumstances in light of the fact that Prince Rupert was dead. The news was still sketchy. The worst thing was that she should have been the one with the scoop for her paper, not some nerdy reporter who had camped outside the morgue for any tidbit of information. Nope, she had been bedding the Princess' bestie in the hope of getting a juicy story. All she'd gotten was drunk off her head. Along with being laid more times in the last few days than she had in a year. *Crap*!

She switched off the TV and looked at her phone. Her boss had called her pretty much every five minutes since the story had broken. Damn, he was going to crash her service with his messages. She didn't need to hear them; they would only go two ways: why had she missed the story, or you're fired.

Her heart hardened. She wanted these pretentious, privileged people, who thought nothing could touch them, to feel some retribution for their frivolous acts.

She listened to the last message from her boss.

"Missed that one, Randle. The young Prince is dead, so other than the funeral, it isn't newsworthy. I think you made a great call in associating with the inner circle of the royal family. The best is yet to come. Talk to me."

"Fuck."

†

Henry looked through the picture window of the hotel room where he'd spent the night. "It isn't easy, Samuel." He touched the cold glass. "You were my savior. Loving me for who I am, not what you thought I could be."

The sunrise finally peeked through and heralded the morning.

"Another morning without you, Samuel. It hurts so much, and it's not fair. I can't explain to anyone how it feels. His Highness and even the Princess are very supportive. I hadn't expected that." He dropped his head, and tears struck his cheeks.

His watch broke the silence in the room, reminding him that he had reached a fitness goal. "Damn you, Samuel, you always wanted me to keep fit for my health, so we could see our senior years together." Tears obscured the information.

His phone rang, returning him to the reality of the moment. "Sir?"

†

Crown Prince Claude stared at the wonderful early morning sky. He loved this time of the day. Not that he saw much of it these days. He recalled times when he'd returned from illicit, if you could call them that, dates with Adeline. When he began courting her.

"You were beautiful, my love." He smiled; his heart swelled at the memories. Adeline loved this time of the approaching new day. A time to start again. Forget yesterday and be better today.

"I'm going to do that now, darling." His eyes went skywards. "I'm glad that you never had to go through losing our firstborn. I'm going to accept our daughter is as strong as you were, my love. It's time for a shift in protocols that work for today." He smiled.

There was a knock on the door. He walked over and opened it. Henry stood there, a small valise in hand. "The car is waiting, sir."

"Thank you, Henry. Today is going to be the start of a new era. When we arrive, will you arrange for my daughter to have lunch with me?"

"Yes, sir." Henry walked into the room. "I'll have your bags collected immediately."

"Thank you." Claude nodded as he looked out of the window one more time. "Forget what I said. I'll speak with Sophia about lunch, Henry." He left the room.

†

Claire gazed at a photo of herself and Sophia vacationing at St. Moritz, where, as experienced skiers, they'd had a ball. Now that could all be over, and where did that leave her…alone.

Her video intercom buzzed; she saw the visitor. "What do you want, Jean?"

"Look, I'm sorry about earlier. Can we have lunch and talk?"

†

Sophia had been pleasantly surprised that her father, on his return home, had sought her out, asking her personally if she'd have lunch with him. A part of her tried to rebel as it always had, but another part, one that was growing exponentially within, readily accepted.

Now she sat on his left as they ate. Surreptitiously watching her father, she saw something had changed. He had smiled and kissed her cheek when she arrived. When she'd taken her usual seat in the middle of the table, he'd immediately boycotted that, motioning her to sit beside him to his left. The only person who had ever sat there when it was a family meal was her mother. Hesitantly, she'd taken the seat.

"Papa, I know you don't want me to get involved. I insist. How did the arrangements go?" She fully expected him to wave a hand and dismiss her question.

"As well as you'd expect in the circumstances. Lots of condolences and then the traditional preparation for the funeral. We agreed on a date. Two weeks from today." He gave her a weak smile. "Are you free?"

Sophia sucked in breath. Her father had never been one to joke or alleviate a somber situation with humor. He'd done it all. When it was in the worst possible taste.

"Yes, of course, that's a given."

She dropped her gaze to her plate; the food was like eating sawdust, almost inedible. *God, I'd rather be having lunch at Abby's.*

"Of course, it wasn't a question. There would be no way you wouldn't be there. You loved your brother. My darling,

I'm sorry, I've never asked how all this is affecting you." He placed a hand on hers.

"Papa, I suspect it's affecting me exactly how it is for you. In truth, Rupert was a pain in the derriere, but he was my brother, and I loved him. He was the better part of us as a family."

Her father chuckled. Again unexpected.

"I guess the food is getting to you." A stupid retort, but her papa was acting oddly, and the food was …God, even Abby probably wouldn't eat it. The thought of Abby again started a glow inside that made her happy.

"Food is food. It sustains us."

"Papa, are you telling me that you really don't care what you eat?"

Her father laughed. "I lost my taste bud sensations when I was a teenager. Not sure how, an allergy, I think they said.

Sophia raised her hands. "Papa, I never knew that."

"Why would you? I can eat anything and give a smile of enjoyment. Isn't that what we royals do?"

"Are you telling me that Rupert, god bless him, and I have had to put up with terrible food since Mama died?"

"Antoine was well recommended when Maxwell retired. Your mother loved Maxwell; he had a Michelin star. I thought replacing the same with the same, how could I go wrong?"

"Papa, it must be a fake star. He's a terrible chef. Hasn't anyone mentioned it when you've had formal dinners?"

Her father rubbed his chin and frowned. "Not to me. Henry, perhaps."

"Of course, Henry. He would never tell you such mundane things."

Her father stared at her. "You didn't either. Why not?"

Sophia bit her bottom lip. "To be honest, it wasn't my place."

"I'm sorry, Sophia. I didn't know. Should I ask Henry to terminate his employment?"

"I'd say yes. Better check with Henry. He'll know the right rules regarding employment." As she spoke, she wondered if he was too long in the tooth and didn't understand today's employment rules. His treatment of Abby was almost slave like.

"Yes, of course he will." Her father played with the meal in front of him. "You really don't like this?

"Papa, I really don't." Sophia grinned. "I could ask Mrs. Baker if she'll rustle something up for us discreetly."

"I concur."

†

Abby finished a twelve-hour shift and was exhausted. There wasn't anyone to take over for her to have a meal break. Even her toilet breaks had been out of desperation. The switchboard had been on fire, and she'd done her best.

Switching the board to automatic, she glanced at the small room where she'd pretty much been a prisoner. *Thank goodness I spend most of my time outside*. Shaking her head, she left the room and walked to the side entrance that the staff used from the main house.

"Miss Ranger, why have you left your post?"

The nasal tone told its own story. "Mr. Torvois, hi." She smiled.

"I asked a question. It's only seven-fifteen."

"I've been here without anyone to give me a break for over twelve hours. I need a break."

"But you haven't asked permission?"

Abby softly snorted, wanting to give Henry a punch in the nose. It wasn't usually something she thought of doing to someone, but right now, he was being a pain in her ass.

"Is it okay with you if I leave?"

Henry frowned. "No, not until you find a replacement to cover the next three hours."

Abby sucked in an indiscernible breath. Smiling. "Remember, I don't work here, I'm just trying to help. I guess you are it then." She opened the door to the staff area and left. As the door closed behind her, she was sure she had heard choking.

†

Sophia looked at her phone, and it had been bombarded with messages from Claire. Her best friend had been cruel and stupid on so many levels in the past few days, maybe years, and she'd never realized. Now she had to. Rupert was dead, and for a time, anyway, she needed to help her father overcome his grief, especially as her father was acting positively weird. Sitting on the sofa opposite a portrait of her mother when she turned twenty-one was one of her favorite places to contemplate problems. Claire was a big problem. You couldn't suddenly give up on someone after being such close friends for so many years. She loved Claire like family. As with all families, members do odd things that you really hate, but at the end of the day, they are important to you.

"What would you do, Mama, I wonder?" She shifted on the sofa so her legs could rest on the brocade fabric of the footstool in front of her. Even now, she dared not put her feet on the sofa—not after being scolded by her father when she was six that this sofa had been in the family for hundreds of years and it wasn't to be disrespectfully treated.

Her mother had given her a wink, and two weeks later, a footstool had been placed next to the sofa. A quarter of a century later, it looked well-worn but respectable.

The internal phone rang, and she picked up the handset on the coffee table next to her. “Yes?”

There were a few moments of silence, and then Henry’s panicked voice replied, “Princess, your father informed me that you would like to change the current chef?”

Raising an eyebrow, she was surprised that Henry hadn’t simply come to her in person to ask; it was more his forte. “Yes, is that a problem?”

“No. I will need to discuss why? When I talk to Chef Antoine.”

“Of course, I’m free now.”

She heard his throat clear.

“I’m sorry, Princess, I’m not free until ten this evening, and then I can meet if that is still convenient?”

Sophia considered his reply. “What is so important that allows you to disturb me with the question at this time, but you are unable to actually attend a meeting?”

“I’m covering the switchboard until ten this evening, Your Highness. I was let down rather badly by Ms. Ranger. I need to go, the board is on fire with calls.”

“Of course. Henry, tomorrow at eight in my office.” She ended the call.

There were two things on her mind. Did she have an office in the castle, and better yet, what had Abby done to have Henry be the switchboard operator? Chuckling, she looked at the portrait of her mother. “You would love Abby, Mama, she is just a good all-around person who cares.” As she said the words, an idea occurred. Removing her feet from the footstool, she stood.

"Abby, of course. She will know what to do about Claire." A glance at the clock told her it was seven-forty-five. She left the room on a mission.

†

Abby sank into the bubble bath her mother had drawn as she ate her evening meal. Her smile grew larger as she settled into the hot water and wriggled her toes while her body relaxed. "Ah, now this is luxury." She closed her eyes and simply let the world as she knew it wash away.

Abby wasn't sure how long she'd been immersed in the water when she heard her mother talking. Unable to hear anything but muffled sounds, she relaxed back against the porcelain tub and closed her eyes again. A soft knock on the door had her open them.

"Is something wrong, Mom?"

The door opened, and her mother popped her salt-and-pepper-haired head around the door. "The Princess is here to see you. I did say you were taking a bath, but she said she'd wait. What do you want me to tell her?"

Abby sighed. *When am I going to get some time for myself*? "Give me five minutes." The door closed, and with a regretful look at the foaming bubbles, she stood and grabbed a towel from the rail and toweled herself down.

True to her word, five minutes later she padded in her slippers and fleecy nightgown toward the lounge. Opening the door, she was surprised when no one was there. Frowning, she headed for the kitchen and, sure enough, the Princess and her mom were talking over a cup of tea and scones.

"Have you left any for me?" Abby walked inside and sat opposite the Princess.

"Of course we have, darling. Want a cuppa to go with it?"

"Thanks, Mom." Abby looked at the Princess. *I hope this is urgent because I was really enjoying having some relaxing time.* Of course, that's what she wanted to say. "Princess, a pleasure as always to see you. How can I help?"

"Abby, I hope I didn't disturb your bathing." Abby shrugged. "I need your advice on something important."

Her mother placed a cup of tea in front of her and a plate with two scones. "I'll leave you two. It's time for me to watch my favorite soap." Before either of them could answer, her mother left the room.

The Princess looked puzzled. "She has a favorite soap; she's going for a bath?"

"A TV show she watches."

"Ah, of course."

"This advice you need?"

"It's about Claire."

After the day she'd had, Abby wanted to leave the room and say, *Go to hell.* Instead, she curled her fingers into a fist under the table.

"Okay."

"I know she's done a lot of things wrong. I miss her. We have known each other most of our lives."

"And you need my advice for?"

"Well, do you think it's a good idea to reconnect?"

"I think that if that's what you want to do, then you should. I barely know the woman other than the odd conversation. It isn't my place to say either way."

The Princess toyed with the crumbs on her plate. "I guess I was just hoping that you might have an opinion as a friend or whatever." Sophia waved her hand in the air.

"I don't think it's my position to advise you on this. It's a personal matter. Don't you have other friends you could ask?" Abby bit into the scone, *delicious*.

"Perhaps. Thank you for your time. I'm sorry I disturbed your bathing session." The Princess stood, and Abby remained seated.

"Not a problem." Abby took another scone and bit into it, and almost choked at the next words from the Princess.

"You look cute in that bathrobe."

Abby, scone in hand, was stunned as the Princess left the room.

†

Sophia walked slowly back to the castle. As a child, she had always been awed by the lights that shone from the building. Even today, she felt that sense of wonder. The building was like a beacon of hope that beckoned her to a safe place. How had she forgotten the pull of her home and what it meant to her? Why had it taken Rupert's death to show her that her life was here, at least until her father died? She shuddered and drew her jacket closer around her body. Then she cheered up, recalling her conversation with her father about Chef Antoine. At least, the meals will be better soon.

Her phone rang and she looked at the caller ID—Claire! *Abby is right, I have to make the call, no one else can do it for me.* She answered. "Yes?"

"Oh, thank god. Look, Soph, I'm so sorry about everything. What can I do to make it right?"

Sophia considered the words carefully before replying. "I'm not sure you can. Tomorrow."

"Tomorrow?"

"Yes, at nine, St Agnes' coffee shop." Sophia heard a deep release of breath.

"Don't you want to go to a bar?"

Closing her eyes, she sucked in a silent breath. "Nine am, Claire. If that's not convenient, then this conversation is over."

Silence seemed to last for minutes rather than the actual few seconds.

"I can do nine am. I'll be there, Soph, and thank you for giving me a second chance."

As she ended the call, Sophia shook her head; a part of her was sure this was a bad idea. It could only go two ways. Claire wouldn't change. Claire could change, just as she was going to do, if she found the right reason.

Sauntering toward the house, she smiled, recollecting Abby in the nightgown. She most definitely looked cute, and those breasts. *I love a woman with breasts that I can suckle. Argh, I need sleep. I'm drooling over the help.*

†

Sophia's meeting with Henry had gone surprisingly well and quickly, mainly because he wanted to check that the switchboard was manned. A slight smile twitched her lips when he'd mentioned that. *Way to go, Abby*. The thought of the woman, softened any hostility she felt toward Henry.

"Your Highness, if you need anything, please don't hesitate to let me know. The royal staff are now at your disposal." He opened the door.

Sophia frowned. "First, Henry, you must get them back to work. Though what does that mean exactly—now at your disposal?"

"Your father's request. The household affords you the same privileges that your late brother had." He glanced at his watch. "Pardon me, Your Highness, but I must go." He left the room.

Really? Sophia blankly stared at the closed door. Then she sank back in her chair. "Papa, what's going on?" She peered at her watch; it was eight-thirty. "Damn, Claire." Groaning, she picked up her purse and car keys and left the room.

†

St. Agnes' coffee shop was, by anyone's definition, basic, and in one of the poorest parts of the city. Had Soph gone all philanthropic since her brother's death? That was the only possible explanation.

Claire arrived at eight-fifty. There was absolutely no way she was going to be late, hangover or not. Opening the door, she slid inside and almost ran back out. Plastic tables and chairs that had seen better days, or maybe years, dotted the small room. There was a small counter to the left as she entered, and a chubby woman in black clothing stood there. She was probably about fifty with a ready smile.

"Hello, are you lost?" The woman's voice was melodic and friendly.

"Actually, no. I'm meeting someone. Do I order here?"

"Why not take a seat, and I'll send someone for your order. Do you want to see our breakfast menu?"

Claire gulped back bile at the mention of food. "Thanks."

"Excellent, I'll be back when your friend arrives?"

Claire walked gingerly over to a table that was almost hidden from the world. What was Soph thinking about meeting in this godforsaken place? She glanced at the chair and cringed as she sat down.

I hope this isn't a prank, Soph.

Claire took out her phone and smiled as she saw a text message from Jean. Last night had been something else. She wasn't sure what hurt most, her head or between her legs. The woman had been insatiable.

She replied to the text, and all else faded as she began conversing with her lover.

"Hi, Claire."

Claire didn't immediately reply as she finished her text. She looked up and groaned. "Sorry, Soph." She stood and was about to embrace the Princess, who sat before she could.

"Have you ordered? I know the breakfast menu is good here."

Claire blinked rapidly. "I…no. I was waiting for you. Do you want to eat?" Her stomach rolled at the thought.

"Yes."

Claire fumbled with the menu on the table.

"Hello, Your Highness, do you want your usual?" Claire stared at the woman who had been behind the counter earlier. *How did Soph know about this place? Better yet, why don't I, if Soph came here and they know what she likes to eat?*

"Of course, Sister Ann. You know I love Sister May's hash browns. Coffee, dash of milk, no sugar. Claire?"

Claire really didn't know what to do. "Same, thank you."

"Have you been here long?" Sophia asked.

"No, not long." She smiled. "I'm so glad you agreed to talk. I miss you."

Sophia looked around the deserted room. "Claire, we can't go back to what we had."

"Why!"

"Because Rupert's death has changed everything. I need to support my father."

"Doesn't mean we can't be friends, right?"

"No, it doesn't mean that. It does mean I need to step up my game. Drinking into oblivion and partying most nights can't be in my wheelhouse right now." Soph took her hand and squeezed it. "It never will be again, Claire. I want you in my life, but it can't be like it was. I have responsibilities."

"Oh, come on, Soph, you've always had responsibilities. That didn't stop you in the past."

"It should have. I understand that now, and it does. Claire, you have been my best friend forever. I miss you, but it needs to change."

"You mean I need to change?" Claire snorted.

"We both do."

They looked at each other.

"What do you need from me?" Claire frowned.

"I want you to be there for me. A friend I can rely on."

"I can do that. I've always been that. Soph, nothing has changed."

"I've changed, Claire."

Sister Ann arrived with a laden tray.

"Thank you, Sister Ann."

"My pleasure, Princess. Enjoy."

Claire's stomach double flipped as she saw the food in front of her. Grabbing the coffee, she gulped it down.

"Soph, how do you know this place?"

Sophia grinned. "Remember five years ago and that terrible bistro we went to after partying at Franc's twenty-fifth party."

"Fuck, Soph, I can't remember yesterday most days. Tell me." She reached for her fork and hoped it was a good decision.

†

Abby made a decision as she brushed her teeth. *I'm thirty-six years old and live with my mother. I have no life outside of working.* One more vicious brush later, which was hard with an electronic brush, the darn thing was upset and stopped several times. *I need to find my own way in life.* She replaced the toothbrush on the charger and wiped her mouth on the towel. *How do I do that though?* She walked out of the bathroom and smelled the aroma of bacon. *God, Mom, you do know how to make me forget leaving. I'm such a wuss.* She opened the kitchen door and, just for a moment, hoped the Princess might be sitting at the table. *Damn, she turned up at some unusual times.* She was a princess, for goodness' sake, she could do anything.

Her smile dipped ever so slightly as she saw her mom at the stove and no one else in the room.

"Good morning, Mom." Abby regenerated a ready smile and walked over to give her mom a kiss on the cheek.

"Breakfast will be ready in a few minutes, love. Want to put some bread in the toaster."

"For you, anything." Abby placed four slices in the toaster. "Mom."

"Yes,"

"Mom, I'm in my mid-thirties, and I've been thinking."

"I know how old you are. I gave birth to you. Let me tell you it was difficult."

"Mom, I've heard the story for years. I think I need a change, not forever but now." A plate of bacon and eggs was placed in front of her. "Thank you."

Her mom sat opposite her and stared at her. "Darling, your father and I knew at some time, you would decide what was best for you, and it seems now is the time."

"I don't understand?"

"Abby, because your father and I love the farm, doesn't mean you will want to spend the rest of your life here. In fact, I was surprised when you took on farm management. Your dad worried you did it for tradition."

Abby frowned. "Really?" Her mom nodded. She filled her fork with a mouthful of scrambled egg and ate quickly. "I thought you and Dad expected me to follow the family tradition; I was the eldest."

Her mom swallowed her food and then looked directly at her. "You never said you wanted to do anything else."

"Oh." Abby scratched the side of her neck and chewed on a piece of fried bread.

"Darling, what do you want to do, other than what you said as a child?" Her mom picked up her mug of tea and drank it.

Abby's head moved upwards so fast she was sure the outcome would be a broken neck. "What do you mean what I said as a child?"

Her mom chuckled. "You said you wanted to have enough money to marry a princess."

Abby's jaw dropped.

"Please, darling, catching flies wasn't part of it."

"Why would I say that?"

Her mom smiled, "You were ten, and we were in the walled garden. Princess Adeline arrived with Princess Sophia. I think you were so mesmerized by her you hid behind us. I doubt she even saw you."

Abby felt lost at the information.

"Princess Sophia likes you."

"She's a princess. I'm sure she likes all kinds of people. Princesses do, right?"

"The big question is…"

"What, what is the big question?" Abby's heartbeat was so fast she thought her mom would hear it.

"Do you still want to marry a princess, especially your Princess?"

Abby frowned, "She doesn't think of me that way." Moving her fork around her plate.

"That's my answer right there." Her mom stood, walked around the bench, and hugged her. "Darling, find your dreams, wherever it takes you. Maybe they might not be too far away."

Chapter Fourteen

Sophia slowly approached the castle that was her home. Not the prison she had always thought. Rupert's death had galvanized her senses to what was important, for her anyway. It was time to serve her country and not be the entitled brat she had grown into over the years. Now she had focus. Though it might be only for a short number of years, since her papa's health wasn't exactly robust. It was time for her to pull her weight. Her father needed her, and who knows, maybe her fellow countrymen.

Stopping outside the garage area, she glanced at the walled garden. A smile creased her lips. Behind those walls and beyond was a normality that, until recently, she hadn't understood the meaning of. She climbed out of the vehicle, and her pumps crunched the white gravel, heading toward the castle side entrance.

"Hi."

Sophia turned and grinned. "Hi back at you. Don't tell me Henry persuaded you to take control of the switchboard again?"

"No."

Sophia smiled. "Excellent."

Abby shuffled for a few moments. "I have decided to concentrate wholly on the farm. I'm about to tell Mr. Torvois that, as far as helping on the switchboard, I will no longer be available. It means that I'll stay on my side of the walled garden."

Sophia felt her insides rock. Her eyes pierced the narrator's.

"I know it isn't a good time at the castle right now. It will get better, Abby."

"There will always be a bad and good time, Princess. I do need to have some private time. I'm sure you understand that."

Sophia gathered her scattered wits. "Yes, I understand." She sucked in a silent breath. "You are just over the walled garden, right, if I need you?"

"Yes. Though it is our busy time. I'll not do anything more than work and sleep." Abby smiled. "Though if ever you need me, I will always be…"

"Just over the walled garden?" Sophia nodded. When emotionally unsure and all else failed, as her etiquette teacher had drummed into her from an early age, remain stoic. "Take care of your farm. Abby, please take care of yourself and your family."

"Thank you, Princess."

Sophia walked as fast as she could to the door, allowing her to enter the castle. Once inside, she placed her hands over her face and cried.

"Princess, are you alright?"

Sophia threw her head back, drew in a deep breath, and turned to the speaker. "Yes, something in my eye. Is there anything else, Henry?"

"No, no, Princess."

"Good. Abby will be advising you she can't work at the castle anymore. I want it to be without rancor."

"What will we do? She's the only one who is reliable."

Sophia wanted to strangle the man; he was such an idiot. "You mean the only one who was respectful to our family's needs. She didn't take advantage of my father's option to allow people to mourn my brother. She worked when everyone else left their post."

"I did, also."

"Yes," she replied softly. "Yes, you did. You, of all people, Henry, deserve to take the break and mourn a dual loss." She saw tears forming. "Where is my father?"

Henry took a few moments to settle himself. "His Highness went for a walk. Said something about seeing Mrs. Ranger."

Sophia raised an eyebrow. "Thank you."

Sophia debated her next step. The staircase to her room or a trip to Abby's family farm.

†

Claude sat next to Jenny Ranger on a bench overlooking the fields. "Your daughter, Abby. She is good for mine. I'm hoping her influence will continue."

"Abby barely takes any social time. She works like a trojan on the farm and recently helped out a friend at the castle on the switchboard."

"Pity. Sophia has been different somehow, and I believe it is your daughter I must thank for that."

"Maybe the Princess will visit from time to time, we both enjoy her company. Since Paul died and of course…" Jenny's voice cracked.

Claude placed his hand on Jenny's. "I'm sorry, Jenny, bereavement is a terrible thing, especially when it is the ones we love most dearly." He shook his head.

"I lost my child the day she boarded that flight to the USA. As you know, she never came back. It is only Paul's death that might have brought us closure. She was his favorite, and he never stopped searching for her when we lost touch during the COVID-19 outbreak. I did have one ridiculous expectation that might bring her back to us earlier."

"That was?"

"She fell in love here as a teenager and remained single. It gave us hope she might return one day.

"I'm sorry to hear that. The young man or woman obviously didn't reciprocate her feelings."

"Well, it was a first love. To be honest, it would have turned out to be a fairytale ending if it had."

Claude nodded. "I'm sorry to hear this. Alas, the boundaries of love are a minefield to go through. I thank God that Adeline never doubted my love for her." He stood, gave Jenny a slight bow, and turned toward the castle in the near distance.

"Would you accept a commoner into your family?"

Claude chuckled as he turned to face Jenny. "Honestly, Jenny, at this moment I'd welcome any good news. Commoner, robot, any fleeting slice of future happiness." He sighed. "I hope Abby does occasionally have some free time, and she spends it with my daughter. Otherwise, I do believe that my darling girl will be losing a great opportunity." He strode away.

†

Abby had been surprised when Henry had accepted her announcement without any aggravation. She'd expected him to blow his stack. Sighing, she rested her arm on the desk and her head in her hand.

Her mom's revelation about the Princess still had her reeling. I don't think that at all now. I'm sure she got it wrong. Besides, I was twelve, she was only six, for goodness's sake. That's baby snatching. Abby groaned. I think I'm doing the right thing, concentrating exclusively on the farm.

A ringing in her ears drew her back to reality, her last shift at the castle. "Hi, you've reached Osric Castle. How can I help?"

CHAPTER FIFTEEN

Three weeks later.

Life should never be so cruel. I've buried a wife and now a son. How much more do you want from me? Claude looked up at the heavens, but they did not comfort him. *I will not outlive my darling Sophia.* His conversation with Jenny weeks before had him thinking. *Could Sophia and Abigail become more than friends?* He stroked his chin. Perhaps it might be the way to bring the country back into the light for a good reason. The more he considered it, the more it made sense.

He picked up his phone, and seconds later, his call was answered. "Sophia, are you free?"

"Now? I'm scheduled to meet with my new PA."

"You think that is more important?"

"No!"

"Good. I will see you in an hour." He looked at the time. "Lunch."

"I was going to have..."

"Again, do I need to ask who is more important?"

"I will be there."

†

Abby sighed heavily. Her friend had cancelled afternoon coffee because she had a stinking cold and didn't want to pass on any germs. She looked around in her bedroom. It was home, and yet there was something missing. Going to the US was the right decision. They had to know in person the details behind her sister's death and the rather cryptic reference to a problem she had left behind. Her mom wouldn't rest until they knew the truth.

Her phone pinged again. Smiling, she answered. "Are we still good for lunch?"

"Sorry, look, what about dinner tomorrow? We can go where we first met. I promise not to break the date."

"I'm busy. Remember, I leave the day after tomorrow."

There were a few seconds of hesitation at the other end. "I will see you before, though, right?"

Abby hesitated. "Sure."

Wow. I've been dumped twice in less than a minute, must be a record. Abby scrunched her hands together. Maybe going to the US wasn't such a bad thing; it would give her time to reflect on what was happening in her life right now. She threw her phone on the bed and left the room.

†

Sophia sat two feet away from her father at the small family dining table in the parlor. She had always liked this room, probably because it brought back good memories, especially of her mother. When there had been banquets in the main dining room, her mother had always allowed her and Rupert to stay up that bit longer and enjoy some of the magnificent feast that was to treat their guests.

"Papa, you said it was important. Yet we've eaten lunch and not a word has passed your lips except for polite conversation." Sophia eyed her father. He looked tired, and who would blame him? Rupert's death had taken a heavy toll. Four weeks since his passing, and it was still hard to believe he wasn't going to come sauntering into the room and beam them both a smile, and perhaps the odd raised eyebrow in her direction.

"Having lunch with your father is not important?"

"I didn't mean that." She placed her napkin on the side plate and reached for a glass of sparkling water.

"What do you know about Jenny Ranger's daughter?" Her father pierced her with a friendly look.

"Hmm, Abby?"

He nodded.

"Well, she's loyal, capable, and frankly, she is missed around here as the person to go to when no one else is available. She's now concentrating on the family farm, leaving her no time to associate with the royal household." Sophia almost choked on the water as she sucked in a deep breath. "She's going to the United States of America on Sunday."

"Really, do you know why?" He took a sip of the dark beer, his signature drink at lunchtime.

Sophia frowned. "Why are you interested?" Her father nodded slowly, too slowly, usually meaning he was about to hit her with a bombshell. "I don't know any details. She is not my confidante, Papa."

"Does that matter to you?"

"Matter, Papa?"

"Well, you thought she was good enough to be your new friend when all hell let loose after Rupert's death. From the stories I've heard, she ensured your safety and backed you to the hilt."

Sophia frowned. "Why is it such a big deal now? What or who has been saying things about her?"

Her father gave her a raised eyebrow. "Commissioner Foley has always enlightened me on the car accidents and hundreds of other misdemeanors, Sophia. Was Abby complicit in some of those and became your new best friend at a very difficult and personal time?"

"Abby? For god's sake, Papa! Abby would have turned me in when I jumped my first red light if she'd been there." Sophia sighed. "No. Absolutely not! Abby has never been complicit in any of my stupid actions." Sophia stood up. Her fingers moved at such a rate, it looked like she was counting money.

"Finally, you've come to some sense. I believe Abigail Ranger a far better friend than Claire." Sophia gasped. "Are you ready to accept responsibility at last?" Her father stood, then moved within inches of her personal space.

Sophia drew in a deep breath, stilling her fingers. "I will not comment on my friendship with Claire; that is my business. On the question of responsibility. Yes, of course. I realized that after Rupert died, and maybe sometime before. What do you need from me, Papa?"

He hugged her for a few moments and whispered in her ear, before releasing her, "Simple, really, I need you to marry."

Sophia opened her mouth; a guppy would have been proud. She watched her father walk toward the door. "I…I don't understand?"

"Find a suitable wife. I'll expect to hear engagement news soon. We need some feel-good in this country right now. You are it, my darling Sophia." He opened the door. "Oh, and it needs to be a commoner. I think the entitled are over-rated this season." He left the room.

What the Hell! Sophia's body froze. Then her brain engaged. Oh, no, surely, he doesn't want me to marry a man; he couldn't be that cruel?

†

"Hi." Abby listened, then shook her head. "I can be at the castle in about an hour." Her eyebrows furrowed. "When I leave, I will call you." She ended the call and bit her bottom lip.

"At least this way I will have the chance to say goodbye before I leave," she mumbled as she made her way to the forklift and the pile of hay bales waiting to be stacked. *God, I hope it isn't another how do I deal with my best friend again, blah blah from the Princess.*

†

Sophia almost wore the tread from the Persian silk rug in her office as she watched the clock hand slowly pass. It was now ten minutes past the hour that Abby had said she would be here. Then her cell pinged. She smiled as she answered. "I'm in my office, see you shortly."

Sophia calmed herself with a deep breath and then walked over to her chair and rested her elbows on the oak desk. Two minutes later, there was a knock on the door.

"Enter."

Abby stepped inside the office and looked around.

"Like what you see?" Sophia threw her hand around the air.

"Yes, it suits you."

Sophia's heart beat a little faster as she listened to Abby speak. "Papa wanted me to have Rupert's old office suite, but this room suits me well enough. Please, Abby, take a seat."

"Thanks."

She watched as Abby chose the horsehair-filled leather half sofa.

"Good choice. My mother loved that sofa. She said it was her peaceful-thinking seat."

Abby smiled. "I can understand that." Her large hand stroked the armchair.

"I'll get straight to the point, Abby; I need your help."

"Okay, how can I help?"

"My father has asked…no," she sucked in a breath, "told me to marry and marry soon. Do you think he means a man?"

"I have no idea, I wasn't there. Didn't you ask him?"

"I was too shocked."

"What exactly did he say?"

"Well, marry and soon, oh, and…" Sophia paced the room.

"And? I'm not a mind reader," Abby gently said.

"Sorry, it has to be a commoner, not one of the privileged." Sophia walked around the room.

"Oh."

"Do you think that dismisses Claire?"

A heavy silence engulfed the room.

"Only you can decide that. Ask her to marry you and find out?" Abby stood.

"How about I ask you to marry me?" Sophia trapped a giggle at Abby's face. Abby's expression turned from boredom to outright shock.

Abby squared her shoulders. "Are you mocking me?"

"No. Abigail Ranger, will you marry me?" Sophia made up the distance between them. "I'm serious, Abby, will you marry me?"

"Why?"

"I like you. I don't know anyone else in my life that…just fits me. You bring out the best in me. God knows I need that."

"It's impossible!" Abby headed for the door.

"It isn't, really. We can have separate lives. You do your farm thing, and I do my royal thing. You will be marrying into royalty; it has its advantages. We just ensure the public sees us together from time to time." Sophia smiled.

"I'm sorry, the answer is no. I'm sure your friend can help you out."

Abby left the room so swiftly that Sophia barely had time to take in her answer.

No. Who says no to an offer of marriage to a princess? Abby Ranger, that's who. Sophia smiled.

†

"Mom, tonight I'm taking you into the city for a decadent meal. I've booked a great place, what do you say?"

Her mom looked at her. "I'd rather just stay home with you."

Abby frowned. "Mom. Let me take you somewhere special. Dad would have wanted you to have a great birthday treat." Her mom dropped her gaze, and she saw tears falling. "Mom, I'm sorry." She moved the distance between them and hugged her.

"I know. He always took me out to dinner on my birthday. It's just so hard, darling."

Abby released her mom and gazed at her. "Let's celebrate big time. It's going to be months before we can take time away from the farm when I get back from the US trip. We can, for the night, be like our neighbors."

"I hardly think we can afford to do that, darling."

"Well, we will do the ordinary people affording the big time. Just say yes?"

A beautiful smile from her mom was answer enough.

"Get your glad rags on, Mom. We leave in…" she glanced at her watch, "an hour."

"I'll be ready, though I don't think I have anything…"

"Whatever you wear, Mom, will be perfect."

Her mom left the room, and Abby contemplated where, at short notice, she could get a reservation in a swanky restaurant. The restaurant where she had dessert with the Princess was her first call.

†

Sophia gazed at the wall of her room. Her life was upside down.

Her father had indicated in no uncertain terms that she had to marry for the "people." She rolled her eyes. *The people, right. Abby was people, and she said no*.

She sank onto the sofa and grimaced. It wasn't comfortable. Rummaging around, she pulled a shot glass out of the corner of the seats. "Claire. Of course, it's always Claire."

She stood up and dropped the glass in the trash. She retrieved her phone from the charger and left the room.

†

Henry sat hunched over his desk. A pile of mail awaited his attention. Normally, he would have drilled through the stack with precision earlier in the day. Instead, it stood in front of him like a gigantic wall he was unable to demolish. The phone rang and he automatically answered.

"Princess, what can I do for you?"

"Henry, I need your help."

He frowned. The Princess asking for his help was surely a joke. "I will try."

"Are you aware of my father's plans for this evening?"

"Of course, Princess. He's due to eat at Tremont's with Commissioner Foley at seven."

"And he's where now?"

"He had a private errand to take care of. He is available after six pm." He glanced at the simple but expensive watch Samuel had bought him on their fifth anniversary. It was five pm. He gulped down the emotions that threatened to overwhelm him. "I'm sure he will take your call, Princess."

"No, no, it's okay. Thank you, Henry, good evening."

The call ended, and Henry allowed the memories of his lover to wash over him. It had cost Samuel almost a year's salary to buy the watch Henry now wore on his wrist. Tears spilled, and he simply allowed them to flow.

†

Jean closed her eyes to shut out the maelstrom that crashed around her. Never in her wildest dreams would she have thought she would ever fall in love with a decadent waster like Claire, but she had. Her boss wanted the goods on the Princess and anyone else close to her. That was her goal. She had always wanted equality for everyone. *Why do people with money get a free pass when they do things wrong, and the rest of us get a warning or worse? Total crap.*

"Jean, I just received a text from Sophia. She wants to meet at Tremont's in an hour. Want to join?"

"Will that be okay? She asked you, not me?"

Claire placed an arm around her shoulders and hugged her, then kissed her lips. "It's okay with me. Soph will be cool."

Jean contemplated the answer for less than ten seconds. "Sure. I guess we need to shower and get dressed."

"Hmm, that shower sounds wonderful. Want to share."

Jean smiled and shrugged her principles aside. "I wouldn't want it any other way."

†

Abby waited in the hallway for her mom. Then gasped as she saw her descend the stairs.

"You look like a princess, Mom." Abby grinned.

"Oh, don't be so dramatic." Her mom chuckled. "I do clean up good, though, your dad always used to say."

Abby grinned. "I'm honored." She held out her hand. Her mother smiled and took the proffered arm.

"Let's go and have a decadent meal. Your dad always wanted to take me to Tremont's. We had that on our bucket list." Abby wanted to cry at the words. She sucked in a deep breath.

"Well, let's go celebrate, and Dad can have the spare chair."

"That's my caring girl."

They left the house.

CHAPTER SIXTEEN

Tremont's had lights blazing, a welcome sight in the cool autumn evening. There was a line of customers waiting to be allowed in. Most would be disappointed. The only guarantee of entrance was a reservation, and you usually had to book in advance or, in her case, the royalty card worked every time.

Sophia slid out of her car and locked it, then made her way to the entrance. Several people in the line smiled at her, and others gave her a harsh glance. Whatever they thought or didn't about her, she smiled politely as she headed to the concierge.

"Princess, a pleasure. Are you dining with His Highness?"

"No, not this evening. I wonder if you have a spare table. I have a friend arriving shortly." Sophia beamed a smile, and the man bowed.

"Why of course, Princess." He waved her inside.

She heard several people groan and heard the odd "that isn't fair" grumble as she walked inside. *Of course, in the perfect world, it isn't fair, but when was this a perfect world?*

"Your guest's name?"

"Claire Demeter, she's been here with me before. You will remember her, I'm sure."

"Yes, yes, of course." He gave a small cough. "I'm sorry for your loss, Princess." Sophia nodded as he turned to a woman standing at the front of the restaurant. "Justine, please show the Princess to table sixteen."

A tall woman, whom Sophia vaguely recalled, gave a tight smile and asked her to follow. Gazing around, she saw Tremont's was relatively quiet, busy but not packed. By nine, there wouldn't be an empty seat. Steepling her fingers, she contemplated what to say to Claire.

†

Abby closed her eyes as she saw the line of people outside of the restaurant. When she called for a reservation, she'd been advised that it wasn't possible at short notice. However, if she wanted to wait, perhaps there might be a table free. After her mom said it was on her bucket list, she decided to take a chance. After all, how busy could a place be in the early evening?

"We have a reservation, don't we, Abby?"

Abby bit her bottom lip. "I tried. They did say if we waited…" She trailed off as the line added two more people before they took their place.

"Darling, we will be eating each other by the time they let us in with this line." Her mom chuckled.

Abby laughed. "Stay here, I'll check what the prospects are." She headed for the front of the line and was hissed at a couple of times. When she made it to the front, she remembered the man at the front of the entrance.

"Hi."

He gave her a haughty glance. "Yes?"

"I called earlier to book a table and was told we'd have to wait, but this looks like excessive waiting."

"I'm sorry, madam, it's a busy night. Perhaps if you book ahead next time, you will have a table."

Abby frowned. "It's important. I was here a few months ago with Princess Sophia and…" The whole demeanor of the man changed.

"I'm so sorry. Please, follow me."

Abby was astounded. "I need to get my mom. I'll be right back." Whatever changed the man's mind, she didn't care. Maybe dropping the Princess' name just this once wouldn't hurt. She quickly traversed her route and, without much of an explanation, she took her mom's arm and led her to the front.

The door was opened immediately, and they entered.

"Franco, table sixteen."

Abby grinned at her mom, who smiled back and gave a cute giggle.

"I can't believe I'm actually here."

"You are, and you can have anything on the menu, so don't look at the prices."

"Thank you, darling, I love you."

"Love you, too." They followed Franco.

As they came to the table, Abby's back straightened. "Princess?"

"Abby?"

†

Claire grinned as she held Jean's hand. They had decided to walk to Tremont's, after all, it was only ten minutes away. She laughed as she saw the line. "Thank god Soph has preferential treatment here or we'd be waiting until next week for a table." She looked at Jean. "See, there are perks to knowing the royal clan."

"Ah, but would you get a table if she hadn't invited you?"

"Of course. I have money, too."

"Not royal social status, right?"

Claire pouted. "Oh, that's a bit cruel." Jean squeezed her hand. "True though."

They headed for the front of the line. Several people hissed and booed them.

Claire lifted a finger. Then spoke to the woman at the entrance. "I'm a guest of Princess Sophia."

The woman looked at her and shook her head.

"I'm sorry, may I have your name?"

"Claire Demeter." She scowled.

The woman looked at her tablet. "I'm sorry, but we have no listing. Are you sure about the invite?"

"Yes," Claire snapped. "Find the Princess and ask her. She invited me."

"I'm sorry, but I can't leave my station. Perhaps if you call her."

"Great idea." Claire sneered, moved away, and took out her phone. She walked up and down as the call went to voicemail. After the third attempt, she sighed. "Jean, come on, we are out of here."

Jean shrugged. "Are you sure?"

"Soph isn't answering, and these idiots are incompetent. Let's have a drink at Dominico's—at least there we get service." She took Jean's hand, and they headed away.

†

"Sorry, Justine, I had to take that call. Anything I need to know about?"

"No, just some hanger-on who tried to get in front of the line. I'll get back to my desk. I think it's going to be another great night, especially with the Royals here."

†

Jenny watched the body actions of the two young women. It was like a standoff at the OK Corral, but why? *I thought they were friends.*

"Lovely to see you, Princess. I think there was a mistake. Abby was taking me out for a special dinner for my birthday. Tremont's was on my and my late husband's bucket list."

"Mom, this isn't the time. I'm sorry, Your Highness, for…"

"No, no, please sit. I'd love to know more about your bucket list, Jenny, if you want to share?"

Jenny grinned and took the seat Franco held out for her. "I love to talk about the old times. Your father and I do that when he comes to visit. I think it helps us both cope with our loss." She sighed. "Well, me anyway."

"I know he enjoys the time he spends with you." Sophia gazed at Abby.

"Darling, sit or we will be the talk of the town." Sophia laughed. Abby took the seat opposite the Princess.

"Papa is dining with the police commissioner here this evening. He should be here soon."

"Look, Princess, we came here to eat a special meal. You are obviously not eating alone, so…"

"How do you know that, Abby?"

"I don't, of course. Your friend Claire is usually around."

"Well, clearly she isn't."

Jenny didn't like this animosity between them. Her daughter had always been nice, or at least civil, to the Princess. Why was she so belligerent?

"Abby, I'm sure there is another wonderful restaurant where we can have a special meal."

"Don't go." Sophia stood. Several heads turned in their direction.

"Princess, you weren't dining alone?"

"No. I…no."

"Then Abby is right, we need to leave." Jenny stood.

Abby turned to her. "I'm sorry I couldn't make this a bucket list tick."

"Darling, spending time with you is all I need." Jenny took Abby's hand and squeezed it. "Tremont's is wonderful. I will keep it on my bucket list, and next time we are going to make a reservation that works. Have a lovely evening, Princess."

They turned to leave.

"Jenny, please don't leave. I welcome you as my guest for the evening. You have been so good to me during these difficult months in my life."

Jenny frowned. "Are you sure, your friends?"

Sophia shrugged. "Let me worry about that." She reached inside her pocket and pressed the silent mode on her phone.

"What about Abby?"

"That's a given." The Princess gave her daughter a shrug.

Abby retook her seat. "Thank you. However, I do have a caveat?"

"It is?"

"I pay for dinner."

Jenny watched a turn in the tide. Sophia nodded, and Abby smiled.

†

Sophia enjoyed listening to Jenny regale her with the bucket list she had and why the items were so special. Abby, on the other hand, was silent, except for ordering. Then, when the server arrived, she was quite vocal. Justine, the server, had Abby animated, and that's when she recalled the woman. It had been here, the evening she and Abby dined together.

After Justine left, Sophia turned to Abby. "I think she likes you, Abby."

Abby blushed and looked down at the table.

"Oh, darling, is this the mystery woman you were dating?" Jenny asked.

"No, no, she isn't. Justine is a friend. We have met for a coffee a couple of times recently."

Sophia felt her stomach lurch at the admission. Is this Justine woman the reason Abby isn't interested in me and the reason she refused my marriage proposal? Numerous thoughts washed over her.

"I know she's my daughter, and every parent says this. My Abby is a lovely woman and great company."

"Mom!" Abby narrowed her eyes.

Jenny laughed, as did Sophia.

"I agree. Abby is excellent company. I, too, shall miss her presence. In the past few difficult months, she has been a rock." Sophia stared at Abby, who wouldn't meet her gaze.

Their first course came, and Jenny's mouth opened. "Oh, this is so beautiful. Just like the TV chef's dishes."

"Yes, if I could have poached Chef Daniel from Tremont's, he would be cooking for us. He has two Michelin stars."

"Antoine was terrible. I'm glad you finally let him go," Abby stated. Sophia and Jenny stared at her.

"That's a bit harsh, darling. I'm sure he wasn't that bad."

Sophia chuckled. "Unfortunately, he was Jenny. Our new chef is working out so well as his replacement. Daniel did, however, help me choose Antoine's replacement."

There was a hush in the room, and then most diners stood and clapped. Sophia didn't need to look up to know it was her father's arrival. She was surprised that Abby and Jenny copied the others in the room. Somehow, she considered them family and exempt from the traditional protocol.

"Will you excuse me for a few moments?" Sophia stood, and as her father sat at his table, she walked over to their table.

"Papa." Sophia bent and kissed his cheek.

"Sophia, well, this is a pleasant surprise." Her father stood and hugged her for a few short moments. "What brings you here tonight?" he whispered in her ear.

She whispered back, "I wanted to talk to you about what you said this morning."

"Ah. A discussion for home. I need to discuss some business with the Commissioner; we are only here for appetizers. Then we can leave and talk."

"Well, I'm currently just beginning dinner. Can we talk at breakfast?"

"Oh, anyone I know?" He looked around and then stopped. "Mrs. Ranger and her daughter?"

"Well, they couldn't get a table…" He lifted his hand.

"Sophia, don't be so defensive. You are probably dining with the best people here." He nodded to his guest. "Present company excepted." The Commissioner nodded.

"I'll see you later, father." She gave a short bow and returned to her table.

"My goodness, it must be the highlight of the year for Tremont's to have both royals attending on the same night," Jenny gushed as she loaded a fork. "This smoked salmon pate is delicious."

Sophia took her seat and gazed at her meal. A prawn salad drizzled in Italian herb salsa. "Pate isn't one of my favorite items. I think Antoine's idea of pate and edible were on different flights. Abby, how is your—" She looked at the plate opposite her.

"I like garlic bread. These toasted brioche fingers are good. I could eat another plateful."

Sophia laughed, and her body relaxed. How did this woman do that to her? "Why not ask, after all, you are paying." She checked herself, sucking in a deep breath as Abby's soulful light brown eyes caught her gaze.

"I might just do that."

"Abby, don't forget you ordered the flintstone steak."

"Don't worry, Mom, I'm making sure that I take advantage of this dining experience. Who knows what I'll eat in the airports? Probably fast food."

Sophia began to eat her meal and listened as Jenny spoke about how she had met and married her husband.

†

"Sir, you didn't bring me here to have a social drink. How can I help?" Paul Foley had been surprised at the Crown Prince's invitation this morning. He'd been pondering why all day. Now, when they were here, it had been small talk.

"Since Rupert's death, things have gone back to normal or as normal as one can in the circumstances…."

"Yes, I'm sure it is still very difficult for you and the Princess." He looked over to the table where the Princess sat. Of all the people to have dinner with in such a prestigious restaurant, she chose the help. *Typical, no respect for her position.*

"Difficult, yes. Not insurmountable. My son will be mourned forever in my heart as I mourn my wife."

"Sir, is this about my position and how I managed Prince Rupert's death and perhaps other situations?" He ran a finger around his collar.

"No…well, yes." The prince took a sip of his wine.

"I can explain my actions, sir."

"Oh, I'm sure you can. I want to know that all the findings on my son's case are now complete, and we can go forward without anything coming out of the woodwork?"

Paul took a moment to consider the question. "Yes. The case is closed."

"Good. My daughter will be taking over more of my responsibilities in the future.

"Sir, are you not well?" Genuinely concerned. The Crown Prince was an affable man, and he wasn't afraid to get his hands dirty.

"I'm as good as any man is at my age. Eighty is a fine age these days."

"Indeed, it is, sir. May I ask?" The prince nodded. "The Princess' record so far has been less than exemplary with the principality."

"Then it is time she understands responsibility. Paul, she has her mother's looks and my incorrigible personality. I think, with the right person at her side, she will be a great leader of our people."

Paul's left eyebrow lifted; he hated that it did that whenever he was confused. "Is the Princess about to marry?" He'd heard nothing on the grapevine or the trashy tabloids.

Paul watched as the Crown Prince looked over at his daughter's table. *You've got to be kidding me.*

"Sir, she's marrying a commoner?"

He closed his eyes as the server arrived just as he spoke the words. There was no doubt about the expression on the server's face that he had heard.

"Perhaps."

"How wonderful. We all thought it was strange that you would both attend on the same night," the server gushed, and without asking them a question, headed off toward the kitchen.

"Oh."

"Sir, I'm so sorry. I didn't mean…."

"Forget it, Paul. Are we good?"

"Do I still have a job?"

"Yes."

"Goodnight, Paul."

Paul stood and left. Pleased he still had a job, but he was concerned that the Crown Prince had lost his mind regarding his daughter.

†

Abby tucked into her steak. Flintstone was a bit of a stretch. It didn't look much more substantial than her mom's Friday steak night. She chewed on the steak and attacked a duck fat potato. Wonderful on the taste buds, but the waistline took the hit.

"Want to share?" Sophia asked.

Abby blinked. "Share? You want my steak?"

"No, silly. You look like you are enjoying something that makes you smile. I figured it might be a joke you want to share?"

Abby frowned. "I…no."

"Oh, Abby, don't be mean. What made you smile?"

Abby rolled her eyes. "Okay. Duck fat potatoes." The Princess' face became confused. There was the tell of her smile that lifted automatically, but her expression appeared puzzled.

"I'm not sure duck fat potatoes can do that."

Abby grinned and looked at the meagre chicken salad the Princess had chosen. "Want to try one?" Abby loaded her fork with a roasted potato.

Sophia shook her head. "Doesn't go with my meal."

"Everything goes with these. Dare you to try something new?"

Sophia frowned.

"What's the worst thing that can happen? You like them?"

"Darling, the princess doesn't want to…"

"No, I'll try." Sophia faced off against Abby.

"Look, it was a joke."

"No. Please, now I'm fascinated." The princess moved closer and opened her mouth.

Abby nearly had heart failure.

"Okay." Her reply cracked. She placed a potato in the Princess' mouth, then held her breath.

Sophia chewed on the food, and when she'd finished, her lips curved into a smile. "I stand corrected. I now see why you would smile; it is very tasty."

Abby's breath caught at the back of her throat.

"Want to try a wilted courgette with truffle sauce?" Sophia lifted her fork.

"No, gross." She pulled a face. Courgette? What the hell is a courgette?

"Abby, fair's fair.

"I need the restroom. Please excuse me," Jenny said, pulling out her chair.

Abby watched as her mom left the table.

"It's tasty, I promise." The fork came closer.

I can do this, I know I can do this. She swallowed hard. "Of course, how bad can it be?"

She took the small mouthful and almost puked at the table. She ate it so fast, she wished she was in the restroom.

"What do you think?"

"Okay." Abby picked up her water and drank the contents.

"Hmm, not a vegetable person then?"

Abby wiped her mouth with the napkin. "Some."

Sophia grinned. "You hated it. I love it."

Abby noticed that several of the staff had surrounded their table.

"Is there a problem?"

"No, Princess. We just wanted to be the first to congratulate you both."

"Both?" Abby asked.

"Your nuptials, of course. We are so thankful you chose here to make the announcement."

"Nuptials?" Abby stood and wildly scanned the room. Everyone was looking." Excuse me." This time, she headed for the restroom. *What the hell was going on*?

†

Sophia watched Abby's meltdown. Not surprising. She was remarkably calm in the circumstances. Certainly, she would make a great royalty; her poise was wonderful.

"Princess, is it true you are going to marry a commoner?"

"Are you inferring that my chosen marriage partner is beneath me?" Sophia glared at the concierge.

"No, never, Princess. We just thought it was wonderful."

Sophia watched the man sidle behind the woman who had served them. She didn't look impressed.

"Well, thank you. You are wrong. When I'm ready to release details of my betrothal. I will surely let you all know." Sophia flipped her head, and the crowd slowly dispersed.

She closed her eyes. *God, this is tacky for me. What must it be for Abby*? She didn't dare even think about what the news hounds might report tomorrow.

A seat next to her was withdrawn, and she looked at the intruder. "Papa."

"I'm sorry, my darling. I think someone listened to a conversation they shouldn't have and exaggerated it.

"The damage is done, it appears." She looked toward the restroom.

"Does it matter?"

Sophia glared at her father. "Of course it does."

He took her hand and looked into her eyes. "Why?"

"Well, it's not the truth for starters. Abby and her mother do not deserve this kind of speculation."

"A simple misunderstanding by the staff. A mere note in a cheap tabloid."

Sophia considered a sharp retort. "They, she, deserves more respect."

"Why?"

The question seemed to revolve like a globe.

"Ah, Jenny, how wonderful." Her father stood.

"Your Highness." Sophia watched a red stain appear on the almost flawless skin.

"Would you care to have dessert at my table. I think our daughters need to talk."

"Of course, it would be my pleasure."

"My dear, you have an opportunity, do not squander it." Her father bent to whisper in her ear.

Sophia watched them both leave. "Fuck," she whispered.

†

Abby stared at the bathroom mirror. All the stalls were occupied. Not that she really needed to use them. More a bolt hole away from a ridiculous situation. Had the Princess planned this? She closed her eyes. *No, no, stupid, she didn't even know we were going to be there*. Abby tried to calm her nerves by taking in a deep breath. The Princess had been waiting for someone, yet didn't mind that they were sitting at the table. So, who was the unknown guest? Whoever it was hadn't turned up. Exhaling, she clutched the side of the basin. The flush of a cistern indicated that someone was about to leave and give her the option to hide.

A small woman with a nose shaped like a beak and piercing blue eyes gave her the once-over and then moved to the basin next to her. "It's free."

"Thanks." Abby didn't move.

"Ah. Are you on a date that isn't going well?" the woman asked as she soaped her hands.

The woman's voice was delicate and unintrusive.

"Not a date. Just dinner with my mom. It isn't working out how I planned."

"Family situation then, sucks right?"

Abby shifted her gaze from the mirror to the woman beside her. "Well, not exactly."

The door to the restroom opened, a young woman bustled in, and headed to the free stall.

"Missed your opportunity."

Another stall became free. Abby shrugged. "I'd better go back."

She left the room as the stranger remarked, "Good luck."

Entering the main restaurant, she cautiously glanced around, and everything seemed okay. Her gaze travelled to the table where the Princess sat. She was alone and didn't look upset. Taking a deep breath, she headed in the table's direction. Before she arrived there, she was accosted by Justine.

"Hey. Is it true or fiction?"

"Fiction." Abby gave a tight smile. "I'm not exactly royal material."

"Don't put yourself down, you are the best catch. She wouldn't do any better." Justine smiled. "Call me for a coffee when you get back."

Abby nodded. "I will."

Justine winked. "Got to say I really would love to have the opportunity you have, a Princess asking me to marry her." She moved closer and kissed Abby's cheek, then raced to a table and withdrew her notepad.

Abby stood there a few seconds more before walking over to the table. "Where is Mom?'

A glacial stare caught her. "My father invited her to have dessert at his table."

Abby noted the crisp retort but took her seat.

"What did that woman want?"

"What woman?"

"The help?"

Abby sat back in her chair. "The help?"

The princess smashed her fork into her dessert. "Yes, the woman…the help."

"Hey, Justine is my friend. I wasn't aware that you had the divine right to ask such a personal question. I'm not your wife!" The last word was out before she could stop it.

They both glared at each other.

†

Sophia used all her social etiquette training to understand what was happening in this restaurant. It made no sense to her. The only thing she could do was stare at Abby.

Eventually, she found her voice. "I'm sorry. You are right, that was unforgivable of me."

"Privilege seems to have no boundaries." Abby moved her fork around her dessert.

"I accept your criticism."

"Good, after this evening, it really won't matter. You go your way, and I go mine."

Sophia heard the words, understood them, yet there was an element to them that resonated as a maelstrom in her mind that she wanted to refute.

"I asked you to marry me?"

Abby laughed. "You needed someone expendable who would put up with affairs and simply anything you did."

"I didn't mean…"

Abby raised her hand. "The person I marry will be for love—on both sides. Not some sham. Good luck, Princess, in your search. I'm damn sure you will not have a problem finding a prospective wife." They both stood. Abby walked around the table. Facing each other, she simply kissed her Princess.

Chapter Seventeen

Abby woke to the sound of Sally, the songbird, nesting in the old oak tree outside her bedroom. After Sally had her first brood five years ago, she never left. She'd had yearly broods, but this year things didn't work out. Abby wondered how long songbirds lived. She'd have to look it up.

Climbing out of bed, she walked over to the window and looked down at the verdant view. She could see the parapet of the castle, and her mind wandered to what the princess was doing. She sighed. *Asleep, probably with a hangover.* She glanced at her bedside clock. It was four in the morning.

"Get yourself together. The livestock don't care that I'm in emotional turmoil." Abby shook her head. She glanced again at the castle and headed down the stairs. Pulling on her gumboots in the hallway, she guessed her Princess probably had never owned gumboots or been awake at four in the morning unless it was an extension of her partying. "She is my Princess, and I'm just a farm girl. It would never work."

Tears slowly travelled down her cheeks. She wiped them away and left the house.

†

Henry sat at the kitchen table and contemplated his day.

"Your usual, mate?"

"Yes, thank you." He shuffled the morning papers.

"Not a bonza day for you today, I suspect."

"What do you mean?"

"Read the headlines. Love it myself. Got spunk, I like that."

Henry flicked through the first tabloid. "What!"

"Not the only one highlighting this new royal drama, mate. Great picture, that kiss was cool." Darrel, the new Australian chef, replied. "Is the headline true?"

Henry glanced at the headlines in a few more papers and stood. "Forget breakfast, I have things to attend to." He headed for the door, then turned. "I'm not your mate. I know you are from the Southern Hemisphere, and that description might be okay there. It isn't here."

"My ex-partner was English. He said the staff who worked for royalty thought they were better than anyone else who worked for a living. Never believed them, we all shit the same way. Enjoy your day…mate." Darrel returned to his stove top.

Henry frowned and sucked in a deep breath. I w*ant to…want to do what?* He wrenched the kitchen door open and exited the room.

†

Claude smiled as he saw the newspapers. "It was a rather interesting end to the evening, I have to admit." He chuckled.

There was a knock on the door, and Claude looked at the time. He smiled. "Henry, you are early, enter."

The door opened. "Sophia?"

"Papa, I need your advice." She entered the room and moved swiftly into his arms.

†

Abby walked into the kitchen and hoped that her mom had slept well.

"Darling, I've your favorite breakfast almost ready."

Abby could smell the aroma of bacon, eggs, and her favorite black pudding grilling nicely on the hotplate. Her mom was stupendous. "Thank you, Mom." She went over to the stove where her mom was flipping the eggs. "I love you and I'm sorry about last night." She kissed her mom on the cheek.

"Love you, too, darling. Forget last night. I was well taken care of. Certainly, it was far different from what I expected of my bucket list expectations. In a great way."

Abby frowned. "Mom, I know you need an explanation."

"Abby, you are an adult. Though I have to say the kiss was unexpected."

"Ah…I'm sorry I embarrassed you. And the Princess." Abby slumped in her usual chair.

"I wasn't embarrassed. I thought it was rather wonderful."

Abby dropped her head and stared absently at the wooden pattern of the table. Recalling the aftermath of *That kiss!*

Abby had never felt so many emotions running through her as she broke the kiss with the Princess. Her body overloaded. It was Christmas and her birthday rolled into one on steroids. Her heartbeat pounded in her chest. She figured everyone in the restaurant would hear it. Her eyes were closed. Dare she open them and see the horror of her action on the Princess' face?

Then she felt a gentle touch on her shoulder. "Abby, it's okay." She knew the speaker. It was etched in her DNA. She would for the rest of her life cherish that voice.

Opening her eyes. "I'm so sorry." Then she bolted out of the restaurant into the main street and lost herself in the darkness. As she calmed down on her walk around the town, she realized she'd left the Princess and her mom to clear up the mess she'd made. "They will hate me."

Twenty minutes later, she headed back to the restaurant. Her mom needed a lift home. As she turned the corner facing the restaurant, she saw her mom with the Crown Prince and the Princess. Moments later, amid flashing lights, they left in the Crown Prince's limousine. Abby dipped back into the darkness and headed for her vehicle.

"Hey, darling, are you with me?"

Abby shook away the memories of the last evening. "Sorry. I can't believe I left you behind. I'm such an emotional coward."

"Oh, don't worry about that, His Highness took great care of me. Princess Sophia, too. Your dad would be proud." She smiled and placed the breakfast plate in front of her. "You do need to speak with Her Highness. She is the one who is going to have to go through the cavalcade of paparazzi who want to know all about her and you when you leave for the USA."

Abby stared at the plate in front of her with all the wonderful things she loved for breakfast. Her mom's words had turned her meal to ashes.

"I'll go now and apologize. "Abby stood from the table. "Sorry about breakfast, Mom." She bolted out of the room.

†

Henry muttered under his breath as he paced the floor of his office. Every damn tabloid had the story of *A Kiss*. What was she thinking, riling up the media? Hadn't they had enough media exposure?

A knock on the door distracted him. "Enter."

Charlotte Debussy entered.

"Yes?"

"Sir, what a marvelous opportunity for the family to be more upbeat and move forward for the future. Have you read the papers this morning?"

"Of course, I have!"

The woman sat in his favorite chair and pulled out her tablet. "It's going viral. You couldn't pay for this kind of publicity. Is it true?"

Henry had never really understood this woman; she always had her attention to the small screen in front of her. That wasn't real life. "Is what true?"

Charlotte showed him her tablet. "A kiss like that publicly, involving a royal and a commoner. The headline speaks for itself—do we have a royal wedding on the horizon?"

"It was a chaste kiss."

"Not a chance. That wasn't a friendly kiss from anyone's point of view."

Henry snorted.

"Okay, I get it, you think she's not good enough for our Princess. Henry, it doesn't matter. You can pay colossal amounts of money for this kind of publicity. This was freely given. It's good news, too; we need that. The royal family needs it after Prince Rupert's death. How are we going to respond?"

"I thought this was your last week here?"

"It is. Doesn't mean I can't do what I'm good at. It wasn't my choice to leave."

"What are you good at exactly? I was never sure."

Charlotte snorted. "Sam, god bless him, loved you. He also knew that you would never embrace the world as it is today on social media."

Henry clenched his fingers into his hands. "Sam didn't think I could keep up to date?"

"Are you?"

"I read the newspapers every morning. I know what is going on."

"What about social media?"

Henry hesitated. "Sam was my compass."

There was a silence that stretched longer. "Henry, I loved Sam, too, obviously not the way you did. He was such a caring person. I'd have left after two months if he hadn't encouraged me to stay."

"Why?"

Charlotte shrugged. "He said the royal family needed to know what was being said beyond the local media. He thought I was the person to keep track of that."

Henry felt a pain in his chest that hurt close to the bone.

"At first, Prince Rupert was hard work since he never wanted to be on social media. Sam helped him see that it was the future as much as we might not want it. Our privacy is in the toilet these days, unless we take charge of what the media are informed about."

Henry took a deep breath. "You think this new situation with the Princess is a good thing?"

Charlotte grinned. "Do you mind if I show you?"

He nodded and sat opposite her.

"This is the elixir of life for royalty. A total spin on what is expected of them."

"The Princess is a lesbian, isn't that enough of a spin as you call it?"

Charlotte laughed. "Oh, not these days, unless you live in a country that doesn't respect choices." Henry frowned, nodding for her to continue. "Surprisingly, there are many, and some you would never think of."

"Name one?"

"Indonesia is harsh. Africa, too. Beginning to wonder about the USA."

Henry shook his head.

"Sometimes it depends on the government at the time. Hey, sorry. I'm a woman. I come from a long line of actionist women who want better for women, and others in the same position."

Henry considered her comments. For the first time, he saw raw passion in the woman's demeanor. "How do we exploit this situation without it being obvious?"

"Now you are speaking my language."

†

Claire opened her eyes and blinked them shut. The light was excruciating.

"Ah, sleeping beauty is awake."

Claire groaned. "Why are you so cheerful in the morning?"

Jean dropped a kiss on her lips. "Better than being grouchy.

"Hmm, what time is it?" Claire opened her eyes again and faced a more beautiful sight. *I could get up to see you every day.*

"Seven-forty-five."

"I hope you mean pm, not am." Claire moved out of the duvet cover and stretched her body before she stood.

"Sorry, am." Claire groaned.

"You do have a job, right? You never seem to go to work when I'm with you?"

"Yes, but the hours are at my discretion."

Jean walked over to the window. "Family money?"

"Yes, well, kind of." Claire ran her tongue inside her mouth and hated the texture she found there. "I need the bathroom."

"Want me to make breakfast or shall we eat on the run?' Jean asked.

"Eat on the run, I guess. My larder is bare."

"I'll go get eggs and stuff, so next time we can at least have breakfast. Go have a long shower." Jean left the room.

Claire watched her go and smiled. Maybe getting up early wasn't such a bad thing with the right person beside you. She headed for the shower.

Claire felt better after her shower. Jean hadn't returned yet with breakfast provisions, so she reached for her phone and sat on the sofa. Then she told Alexa to switch on the TV. She settled back in the leather surroundings and then jolted up as she heard the breaking news report.

"Princess Sophia is being tight-lipped about her lip-smacking kiss in public with a woman who can only be described as a mystery person. What do you think of this news, Sara?"

Claire glared at the screen. As a picture of the kiss appeared on screen. *What the fuck have you done now, Soph? She's the help for god's sake.*

"Well, Peter, as an observer at the time, believe me, it was a surprise. I met the young woman in the restroom."

"Oh, goody, do we have a scoop?"

"Scoop. No, not really."

"Do you think this is real or another of the princess' dramatic episodes. Though they usually involve a vehicle." Canned laughter followed.

"It looked real to me, but then I was three tables away from the actual event."

"Come on, Sara, are you being coy about this because you want the glory on your social media account, or maybe you think this is a good thing?"

Claire whispered, "Fuck off, it isn't happening. "

The door to the apartment opened, and she switched off the TV. She looked at the message screen on her phone, none from Soph.

"You are never going to believe this…"

"I don't." Claire ground her teeth.

"I didn't say what the thing was."

Claire snarled. "If it's about Soph and her 'kiss,' it's all over the TV."

Jean walked closer to her. "You look angry, why?"

"Why? Why? Because she gave me some lame excuse to meet her at that fucking restaurant, and all the time she was with that woman. What was I going to be, chopped liver!"

"I think it's a good thing, if it's true," Jean softly replied.

Claire looked at her. "A good thing, she's a bloody servant. All she does is take the calls and anything else the royal family needs. How can she be fit to be a royal wife?"

Jean dropped the bags she held onto the wooden floor. "I like you; I really do. I've put my career in jeopardy…well, it's screwed now because I didn't get this scoop. You! All you can do is bemoan someone else's position in life. I'm leaving." Jean headed to the door.

"What do you mean, about your job?" Claire looked at the paper bags on the floor.

"I'm a reporter, Claire. You know that. This is the scoop of the decade for this family."

Claire frowned. "You were only using me to get the scoop on the royal family?"

"I wish it was that simple. Goodbye, Claire." Jean opened the door and left.

The soft whisper of the door closing, sent a chill down Claire's back.

†

Abby walked through the walled garden and hesitated at the gate that gave her entrance access to the castle grounds.

She looked at the gate and knew she had to make her apologies, her mom was right, the Princess would have to take the brunt of her stupid reaction to…God only knows what she was thinking last night.

She grasped the handle and tried to open it, but it didn't budge. Releasing it, she then tried again, still with no joy. *What the heck.* Then she heard a voice on the other side of the wall.

"How difficult is it to open a damn door?"

That voice made Abby smile, and she released the handle. "Try again."

"Abby?"

"Yes."

"I was coming to see you."

"I was coming to see you."

The door opened.

They stood on either side of the entrance.

"I'm sorry."

"I'm sorry, too."

"You have nothing to be sorry about. I overstepped the mark," Abby quietly replied.

"So did I in asking you to marry me. I just wanted to say everything is cool."

Abby wasn't sure what was most important to her at that moment. "Why me?"

"It's not important now. Abby, be happy. Find that person who will love you and make you happy." The Princess turned back from where she came.

"Will you find happiness if you are forced into a marriage of convenience?"

The Princess stopped. "It's expected of me. What else am I trained for other than to do my royal duty?"

"You are a wonderful woman in your own right. Perhaps you should make the emotional decisions yourself, not someone who thinks they know you."

A wonderful shining gaze caught hers. "Thank you, Abby. My life is going to be bereft without you." She continued her journey toward the Castle.

"I kissed you because…" Abby turned back toward her home.

"I'm sorry, I didn't catch that?"

Abby's body turned into a statue.

"Please, Abby? You began this line of conversation."

Abby considered the words carefully. "Because I love you."

†

Sophia turned the handle, it didn't move. "How difficult is it to open a damn door?"

"Try again."

"Abby?"

"Yes."

"I was coming to see you."

"I was coming to see you."

The door opened.

They stood on either side of the entrance.

"I'm sorry."

"I'm sorry, too."

"You have nothing to be sorry about. I overstepped the mark." Abby said.

Seeing Abby again made her feel better. The look in those sympathetic eyes took her breath away. In fact, they had since the first day they met. "I did, too, in asking you to marry me."

Abby shook her head.

"Why me?"

"It's not important now. Abby, be happy. Find that person who will love you and make you happy." She turned back to where she came from.

"Will you find happiness if you are forced into a marriage of convenience?"

"It's expected of me. What else am I trained for other than to be a royal?"

"You are a wonderful woman in your own right. Perhaps you should make the emotional decisions yourself, not someone who thinks they know you."

Sophia smiled. "Thank you, Abby. My life is going to be bereft without you." She continued her journey toward the castle.

"I kissed you because…" Abby softly said.

Sophia turned. "Because?"

Abby didn't move or say anything.

"Please, Abby? You began this line of conversation."

"Because I love you…"

Sophia felt like someone had hit her hard. She was punch-drunk and staggered.

Abby moved to her side. "Are you okay?" She placed a hand on her shoulder.

"Yes." Shrugging off Abby's hand.

"I'm sorry." Abby moved away.

Sophia grasped Abby's hand. "If you love me, marry me?"

Abby dropped her gaze. "You don't love me, Princess."

Sophia gulped back the bile that threatened to choke her. "I think, I might…love you. I know for sure I do love your presence in my life."

†

Eons seemed to pass as Abby tried, but couldn't understand what was happening. She was in a walled garden with a Princess. Who had asked to marry her. How wonderful could that be in life for anyone—the fairytale! Except she wasn't just anyone.

"Abby, I know you want both parties to be in love before you say yes."

"I already gave you my answer, Princess."

"I could do the whole 'I love you, Abby' if that's what you want. I will not, out of respect for you. Love can grow out of a friendship."

"Friends, perhaps. Out of necessity, I don't think so."

"No! You are more than that."

"Really, why?"

"I indicated…"

"Indicated?" Abby closed her eyes. This was a foolish discussion.

"Abby, stay please. At least give me a chance to make my case?"

"Typical."

"What do you mean?"

"It's all about you. Why should I even consider getting involved with you romantically? Princess, find someone who can be a doormat…goodbye."

Abby walked away and heard a sob but didn't turn. She opened the gate to return home and then couldn't help herself as she turned. Her heart was on fire as she saw tears streaming down the Princess' cheeks. Then she said, "For the record, Princess, when I said I loved you, I was ten years old, apparently. I do wish you a wonderful, fulfilling life—with the next commoner you ask to marry you." She walked through the gate to the field, crossing to her farm, and closing the gate firmly behind her.

†

Sophia stood in the walled garden, unsure what to do. She needed someone to talk to about this. Closing her eyes, she couldn't think of anyone who was independent who could give her a true perspective. "Damn."

Her phone rang. “Yes?”

“Soph, what’s this bullshit about you getting engaged to a commoner? Absurd, right?”

“Claire, I’m busy right now. Catch up later.” Sophia drew a deep breath, ended the call, and began a slow walk back to the castle.

Chapter Eighteen

Abby settled in and clipped the seat belt. She'd chosen the window seat, at least then no one would bother her by wanting to get by going to the toilet. Her thoughts were angst-driven. This trip to the US had been emotionally draining. How was she going to tell her mom what she had found out without causing her pain? The original trip had been for a couple of weeks, maybe three. It had extended to five weeks. *God, Davy will be annoyed with me.*

The senior flight attendant called them to observe the emergency message. Abby watched it, though her mind was filled with so many thoughts. One in particular took precedent...*Did you find a wife, my Princess?*

She closed her eyes as the plane took off.

†

"Charlotte, can you change my schedule tomorrow? I need a day on my own."

Charlotte Debussy nodded. "Absolutely, Your Highness. Is there anything else?"

"No, no, I don't think so." Sophia hadn't initially wanted Rupert's PA, but after a genuine talk together, Charlotte was exactly what she needed. Her help and insight in the last few weeks had bordered on brilliant strategy for a person in her position. She even felt that her reputation was salvageable.

"I heard on the grapevine that Ms. Ranger is due home this morning."

Sophia turned to her PA. "Really, I hadn't heard. Abby isn't a member of the royal household, so why would I be informed?"

Charlotte furtively looked at her tablet.

"I guess not. Abby is such a lovely woman; everyone here adores her. She never has a bad word for anyone and will help people out, even if it's a hardship for her. She might not officially be a member of the royal household, though she certainly is to everyone who works here."

"Even Henry?" Sophia watched as a slight smile creased her PA's lips.

"Hmm, Henry perhaps not, but he definitely misses her."

Sophia nodded, turning to the window in her office that overlooked the entrance to the walled garden. "Abby is a rather special person."

"Yes, she is. I'll catch up with you later this afternoon—after your visit to the children's home and the hospital kids' ward."

Sophia nodded. As she heard Charlotte open the door, she spoke. "Charlotte, will you help me hatch a plan to speak with Abby before she leaves the airport?"

"I don't understand?"

"Abby is important to my life, too. Maybe more than I ever knew. I think you knew that when you mentioned Abby."

Charlotte shut the door. "Your Highness, what are you asking?"

"Help me make Abby my wife?"

Charlotte's grin was so wide it reminded her of books she had read as a child, except the smile was from a cat.

"Do you mind if I say right now, I'm wetting my pants." Sophia glanced at the woman's white linen trousers. "Figuratively speaking, I mean. Wow. We will need help, especially from the media. It needs to be low-key, or Abby will probably freak."

"I don't understand."

"Princess, it's an event. A positive one, and our small country could do with a great love story. Who better than the media to facilitate that?" Sophia frowned. "Orchestrated by you, of course."

"True. Abby will not like the media in her face. God, I hate it, and I was born into that life."

"Abby will forgive you. You are our Princess. We all forgive you."

Sophia pulled at her bottom lip, thinking. Then smiled. "I have, I hope, a close friend who has a trusted media contact. Let's arrange that, shall we?"

"Claire, right?" Sophia's eyebrows rose. "Sorry, Princess, you don't have many close friends. Besides, who else of your friends is going out with a media hound? Not sure that she is …"

"Correct. We don't have much time. Organize this, please."

Charlotte grimaced. "Yes, Princess. Will you contact your friend direct?"

Sophia pondered that question for a few moments, but Charlotte answered herself before she could answer.

"Better leave it to me. Then you can honestly say you had nothing to do with the arrangements."

"That's incorrect. I am, by default, with this conversation, culpable. I shall speak with Claire. Then you can do your…whatever we need."

Charlotte nodded. "As you wish, Princess." She left the room.

Sophia looked up to the heavens. *Abigail Ranger, I hope you understand and will forgive me one day.*

†

Abby walked wearily toward the exit to the airport. Hopefully, someone was here to meet her. Her mom didn't drive outside of the farm these days. Abby's mind was overloaded with so many emotions she figured her head would burst at any second. Hanging her head, she drew a deep breath and slowly exhaled.

"Abby."

Abby looked up and saw the woman she'd had a date with, if you could call it that, months ago. "Jean?"

"Great. You remember me." Jean walked closer, barring her way out of the airport.

Abby frowned. "Well, it was a memorable night." *That night, I shared a meal with my Princess for the first time.*

"Really, I thought we didn't hit it off. Never mind."

Abby frowned, "Are you going somewhere nice?"

"Hardly. It's work-related."

"Oh."

"I did tell you I was a reporter, right?"

"I don't really recall…"

"Suffice to say, I am. A small news sheet, mostly online, you will never have heard of it, *The Truth Is Out There*."

Abby knew it more by reputation than from having read it. A scandal sheet. Always some poor soul under scrutiny. "Well, I'd better let you get on with your mission." Abby gave a curt smile.

"I don't need to leave."

"Oh, why?" Abby felt like she was in a surreal dream.

"Abby, you are the news. Did you or didn't you kiss the Princess Royal before you left?" Abby frowned. "Hey, that's an easy question, and the answer is yes. Abby, you will never go to a café without someone watching you and taking a photo, living in this country."

"Ridiculous, that was weeks ago." Abby retrieved the bag she had placed on the floor when Jean turned up.

"I know there is a life span for most things, but royalty and a commoner, true magic publicity. People love it and are salivating for more. No matter what you do now, Abigail Ranger, your life is inextricably linked with Princess Sophia."

Abby was frozen to the spot.

†

Claire took Sophia's hand. "Is this really what you want?"

"Yes."

"If she finds out, she will probably hate you." Claire watched several expressions traverse the Princess's face. *It wasn't good.*

"We will ensure she doesn't."

"Soph, I love you. Are you sure? It helps my relationship with Jean big time. I don't want it to cost you forever. If you've taught me one thing in the last few weeks, it's to be yourself and do better."

"Glad to help."

"Why her?" Claire watched her best friend's tense body language.

"Stuff is going on."

"Soph, stuff is going on all the time with you…you are our Princess."

"I don't know why. Other than she makes me happy."

"How?"

"Ridiculous question, of course."

"Yep, sorry. Why does she make you happy?" Claire insisted. Her hand was squeezed so hard she was sure when Soph released, it would drop off.

"She is real."

Claire raised her eyebrows. "Real, what does that make the rest of us, artificial lifeforms?"

"I'm sorry, Claire. We are superficial. We both know it. Abby is the real thing. I don't want her to be involved in that world."

"You asked her to marry you?"

"It was a reflex reaction to what my father asked of me."

Claire sucked in a breath; this conversation was bringing clarity to her brain. It didn't happen often. *Soph was right, they lived a superficial life.* "He asked you to marry Abby?"

Sophia frowned. "No, of course not…well, not exactly."

"What does that mean?"

"Nothing, nothing really."

Claire watched Sophia gazing out of the window, then moved to stand next to her. People below on Main Street were milling around, going about their business.

"Soph." Claire took the Princess' hand. "We go back a long way. Can't remember when we weren't friends." Sophia turned and smiled.

"You could have asked me to marry you. I'd have said yes." Claire sucked in a silent breath.

Sophia shook her head. "You and I married? God, we'd be divorced within a week."

Claire laughed. "True. Though the sex might have been great." Sophia raised her left eyebrow. *Such a subtle action, but it told its own story.*

"It's been a hell of a time over the past few years. Good and bad. I'd rather have you as my best friend, in my corner if things go wrong with my future wife," Sophia quietly said.

Claire considered the words for a few moments, then chuckled. "Hell yeah. Can you imagine? When the spouses get mad at us, and we need someone to have a quiet drink with, you can count on me."

They both laughed.

"Well, in your case, Claire, silence isn't usually the description that goes with you and drink."

"Oh, bloody right. So, what's next?"

She watched as Sophia straightened her body posture. It was one of those actions that only royal people do. There was no other explanation.

"I'm going to make a spectacle of myself. Want to join me?"

"I wouldn't miss it for the world."

They hugged.

†

Abby looked around the airport. As a provincial one, it wasn't usually busy. There was a commotion to her left, and she glanced in that direction. There seemed to be something important happening. "Is this you?" She turned to Jean.

Jean shrugged.

"I'm going to the bathroom. Will you safeguard my luggage?" Abby felt like her feet had wings as she sped to the restroom.

"Sure."

†

"Fuck," Jean softly said. She looked at the entourage that had spooked Abby. A rather large family gathering. The Ting Tone Party Girl had Jean fishing for her phone. "Hey?"

"Everything going okay?"

"No!"

"No?

"Claire, Abby is like a frightened rabbit. She's in the restroom. This is cruel."

"Babe, I'll be there in five minutes."

"Do you have the cavalry?"

"Count on it."

The call ended.

†

Abby stood in front of the mirror in the restroom. She'd desperately wanted to stay inside the cubicle, but it was busy, and that would have been selfish. Nothing worse than wanting to relieve yourself, and there was no cubicle available. What did she do now? Gazing at the mirror, she saw a tuft of hair out of place, a pale complexion, and a scared expression.

"Did you see the paper this morning? They say she's due home today. I wonder if *she'll* turn up." Two women entered the restroom, speaking excitedly.

"Why wouldn't she? She loves our Princess. Our Princess is gorgeous. I hope it's true about the kiss."

Abby bit her lower lip.

"You are such a romantic. Did the Princess kiss her back, though? That's the question everyone is asking."

"I'd hate to find the answer."

"Why?" The woman began to put lippy on at the mirror, close to Abby.

"I want to think that the dream we all have of falling in love and marrying a princess or prince is still achievable. Call me sentimental."

"Yeah, you are. Probably all publicity, got to be."

The door opened to one of the cubicles. "Sorry, I'm desperate."

Abby tried to move away from the mirror but felt glued to the spot.

"Hey, sorry, were you first?"

Abby shook her head.

The woman stood against the basin. "What do you think about our Princess' newsworthy story?"

Abby swallowed hard. "I think even our royalty should have some privacy."

"Oh, an old-fashioned royal fan."

Abby sighed. "If you were working out a romance or any other problem, would you want some privacy?"

"Yes, but I'm not a royal. Royalty is fair game. We pay for them in our taxes."

Another cubicle came free, and the woman took it.

Abby, for the first time since this situation began, knew which direction in life she should take.

†

As Sophia entered through the airport doors, it was like finding an alien world. Photos were being taken by numerous photographers. She'd usually had two or three following her since Rupert's death. Prior to that, she'd hardly been taken notice of unless she'd done something stupid. This appeared different. *Ah, Claire's friend's influence.* There was a cavalcade of questions buzzing around her. *Are you going to meet her after her trip? Was the kiss real? Who is she? Are you in love? Do we have a new Princess-in-waiting?*

Sophia sucked in a deep breath. "It was an overzealous fan. I'm happy being single." Sophia had always scoffed at security, but right now, she felt it might be prudent in the future.

She looked at Claire, who raised her eyebrows.

"Guys, let the Princess through. If you aren't taking a flight or picking someone up, you get lost."

"Subtle Claire, as always."

"Hey, what are friends for?"

Sophia smiled. "Quite." She squared her shoulders. "Are these Jean's people?"

"Not sure."

Sophia rolled her eyes. "Great, what do you know?"

"We are requested at the restroom. "

"What the hell?"

"Sorry. Jean says Abby will not leave. Got spooked by a large party arriving fifteen minutes ago."

"Who the hell stays in a restroom for that long?"

"Someone who might be scared."

Sophia, for the first time in ages, thought that Claire might have said something that made sense. "I guess the restroom it is."

Claire chuckled. "This is going to be one hell of an event for the royal family. An airport bathroom."

Sophia gave her a shake of the head. "If it works out, Claire, you are not going to be my wedding planner."

Claire laughed as they closed in on the restroom. Jean was standing outside, two pieces of luggage at her feet.

"Thank goodness. The cavalry."

Sophia raised her eyebrows. "The cavalry?"

Jean gave a half pass at a bow. "Well, you are, aren't you? Unless Abby has diarrhea or something like that, she for sure is avoiding everyone." Jean placed a hand to her mouth. "Crap…oh no. Damn. Should I even be speaking right now?"

"It's not the 50s. Soph doesn't mind, right?" Claire turned to her with a hopeful expression.

Sophia didn't answer. She placed a hand over her eyes as the light from the photos being taken blinded her. "Keep them at bay." She pushed open the door to the restroom.

Abby was easy to find, holding onto the water basin. Sophia's heart felt saddened at the misery her body language gave off. At the same time, she was happy. How extraordinarily odd her emotions were about this woman. Abby completed her in ways that didn't make sense to her or perhaps even to the universe.

"Abby." A frightened deer expression crossed the woman's face. "I wanted to say welcome home."

Abby opened her mouth, but no words emerged. Then she found her voice. "Why are you here?"

Sophia moved closer. "I was worried that you might have been picked up already."

"We said goodbye weeks ago. Why are you here? Is that why there are reporters?"

One of the doors opened from the stalls. "Oh my god, it's her." There was a shriek. "Diana, it's our Princess!"

"Really. Are you sure?"

"Yep, you know I love our Princess; she's gorgeous. She's talking to the woman who looked sad at the basins."

"Does she look like the blurry photo on the front page?"

"Ann, I told you they were in love. This is wonderful."

Sophia frowned. "Abby, I think we need to go somewhere more private. Do you agree?"

Abby nodded and released the basin.

Sophia nodded, walked ahead, and opened the door. "After you." Abby gave her a wan smile.

As they emerged, there was a lightning glare that would have given a thunderstorm a run for its money.

"Princess, is she the one?"

"Princess, when will you announce your betrothal?"

Sophia didn't look at Abby as she moved ahead of her. *Crap, this is totally wrong.* "Sorry, can't answer those questions."

"Is she the one?"

"Do you love her?"

The questioners turned to Abby the more they asked.

Sophia turned to Abby. "I'm sorry."

†

Abby looked into the eyes of the Princess. She was doomed one way or another. She wasn't foolish enough to think that with her background, this story would be a non-event. Nope, Jean was right. With the media these days, it might end up a mega story online, even if it didn't merit the attention.

"Abby, I'll leave now." Sophia turned away.

"My Princess, Sophia." Abby dropped to her knees. "Will you marry me?"

†

Princess Sophia Osric stared down at the woman who had quite literally blown her mind. Is this happening? No, surely not. Abby is more sensible than becoming involved with me, for goodness' sake, even if it's why I'm here and what my father wants. She placed a hand on Abby's shoulder. Those innocent, expectant, pale brown eyes entranced her. Mentally, she shook her head. I need to do this for the country.

"Yes."

The paparazzi must have had the national grid on high alert because so many lights lit up the airport; it was incredible.

"A kiss for good luck," one reporter shouted, and then it became a chant.

"I think you can stand now, Abby."

"Thank you, Princess. My knees were beginning to ache."

Sophia took Abby's hand. "I think you can call me Sophia. After all, we are engaged." A red hue covered Abby's cheeks. "The reporters want their pound of flesh. Alas, I can't stop this," she whispered and pulled Abby close and gave her a chaste kiss.

There was uproar in the area, wolf whistles, cheers, laughter, and general congratulations greeted the action.

Sophia gave Abby a smile as they moved apart. "I think we need to go somewhere private." She saw Claire pushing forward from the throng of news reporters.

"There's a private room the airport admin say you can use." Claire ushered them toward a room to their left, opened the door, and pushed them inside.

"Thank you, Claire." Sophia gave her a heartfelt smile.

"Any time, my Princess." Claire winked and shut the door.

Inside the drab utilitarian environment, Sophia sighed.

"I guess this isn't how you ever expected to be asked to marry?" Quiet words came from the woman she had forced into this situation.

She turned and gazed at Abby. "Oh, I don't know, it's certainly unique."

Abby nodded.

"You can say you had a moment of madness and go home."

"I thought this was what you wanted. Don't you want to marry me?"

There was a puppy dog expression on Abby's features, and if her protocol regime hadn't stepped up to the plate, she'd have wept.

"I think I asked you first?"

Abby nodded. "Yes, you did." She dropped her gaze for a moment, then looked up. "It isn't too late for you to say you made a mistake."

Sophia smiled. "The baying wolves outside the door probably expect that. They have little respect for me. I don't blame them."

Abby tentatively touched her hand. "From my perspective, baying wolves wasn't the impression. Adoration and happiness were."

"Abby, you are so…so naïve." Sophia stepped away. Abby clutched her hand.

"I know. But I'm not walking away if you want to make this work?"

"Do you want this?"

"You did say your life is going to be bereft without me, is that true?" Sophia nodded. "Mine is too. I've thought about you all the time I've been away."

Sophia's heart raced at the reply. God, I hope I don't make this woman's life hell. Being a royal wasn't exactly an easy life.

"Abby Ranger, you may regret this. Welcome to what it means to be royal." She took Abby's hand, kissed her cheek, and opened the door. "We need to inform Papa."

Lights flooded them, and the questions were overwhelming.

Chapter Nineteen

Abby sat in a window seat of the Crown Prince's private parlor in Osric Castle. She watched as her new fiancée talked to her father, who looked less than happy with Sophia. He kept looking over at her and shaking his head. *Guess I'm not the right person he expected. He knows she's lesbian. What was he expecting, a token male to make the masses happy?*

"Abby, are you sure you want to be part of this family?"

Abby looked at the Crown Prince. Then to Sophia, her expression deadpan.

"I thought I was already part of the family."

"What do you mean?"

"The Ranger family lineage has lived here for the last three centuries. I'm almost part of the family in today's terminology."

"Interesting, I like that. If you agree to marry my daughter, there are obstacles that you would never have experienced in your lifetime.

"True." Abby stood and walked to her Princess and took her hand. "There are a lot of new experiences we will have over the years. For all of us."

She saw Sophia smile. Her heart doubled its pace.

"I'll take whatever fallout there is." She faced the Crown Prince. "Do you approve our union?"

"Yes." He held out his hand, and Abby took it. "Welcome to the Osric family."

Abby smiled, "Wow, that was easy. Now I must tell my mom, maybe not so easy."

The crown prince chuckled, and Sophia clutched her hand a little tighter.

"Then I think it only fair that as a 'family' we inform your mother of the good news."

"She'll be pleased, Mom had the idea I might want to spread my wings a bit and see other countries."

"Can't let that happen, can we, unless you are with me," Sophia softly said.

Abby looked at Sophia, and her heartbeat increased. *Is this really happening? Am I marrying my Princess?* "No, we can't."

There was a knock at the door, and Henry entered. "Sir, we have a problem."

"A problem, what is it, Henry?"

The thin man shuffled on one foot to the other. "The phone system is overloaded. We can't cope."

Abby turned to Henry. "I can help…" She was pulled gently to face Sophia. Her expression said it all.

"Henry, then don't," Sophia replied.

"Sophia, we need communication," the Crown Prince declared.

"Oh, I don't know, a few hours without a link to us can't be so bad, Papa."

Abby watched the looks between father and daughter

"Sir. If Abigail could…"

"Abigail Ranger is my future daughter. You are the first to know outside the royal family. Today in particular is very special, and you expect her to work on the switchboard?"

Abby cringed at the Crown Prince's tone. *God, I hope I don't ever piss him off.*

"No, no, of course not, sir." Henry turned to her. "Congratulations, Ms. Ranger."

"Thank you." Abby dropped her gaze as her cheeks heated up.

"Good, it's time to see your mama, Abby. Henry, deal with this situation as I know you can."

Henry left the room with a tinge of pale green crossing his complexion. Abby, at that moment, felt sorry for Henry.

"I could help…" A glacial stare encountered hers. "Mom, right. Let's go and see Mom." She rushed to the door.

"Hey, not so fast. What about me?" Sophia looked perplexed.

"Sorry, Princess." Abby held onto the door handle as if it were an escape lever.

Sophia frowned. "Are you okay, Abby?"

Abby's heart began to beat even faster than when she had kissed her Princess. *This is going to kill me. I'm a fool, I can't do this.* Her thoughts changed dramatically as Sophia took her hand. That simple touch made her world right itself.

"If you want to tell your mother on your own, that's okay. I'll deal with Papa," Sophia whispered.

Abby allowed the millions, if not billions, of euphoric sensations, flood her senses. "We will all go; it is the right thing to do."

Sophia gave her a look she hadn't seen before, making her toes curl. Then a kiss to her cheek sealed her fate.

"Good. Papa?" Sophia turned to her father, who was jangling a clock chain on his suit vest.

"I'm ready," he grumbled.

†

Jenny sat with a cup of tea entwined between her fingers. Abby would be home soon. She had news from the trip that she only wanted to share in person. Taking a sip of the tea, Jenny grimaced. "Damn, I've let it go cold."

The phone in the hall rang. Abby always scowled at the old instrument. She was a daughter of new technology, not the old landlines. Jenny stood, left the kitchen, and picked up the receiver. "Hello?"

"Is this Abby Ranger's mother?"

Jenny frowned. "Yes. Is there a problem?" Her stomach did several somersaults. *Something had happened to Abby.*

"What do you know about her relationship with Princess Sophia?"

Jenny bit her bottom lip. "Pardon me. Who are you?"

"A member of the public, interested in their relationship. Is it true they are getting married? When did you know?"

Jenny rammed the phone down on the cradle. What was going on? That kissing situation was weeks ago. There hadn't been any publicity for at least two weeks. She heard footsteps on the gravel drive and walked toward the door. She hesitated to open it after that phone call.

She was a foot away from the door when it opened, and Abby stood in the entrance.

"Oh, darling." Jenny threw her arms around Abby, tears in her eyes.

"Mom, Mom, what's the matter?" Abby held her close.

"Nothing, nothing at all. I'm so glad you are back."

Abby smiled. "Me, too. I have a surprise for you."

Jenny raised her eyebrows. "Well, you said…"

Abby moved to one side and held out her hand, exposing the others behind her.

Jenny gasped. "Your Highnesses."

"Jenny, please, we have known each other for a very long time. I told you, in private, Claude is perfectly adequate."

"Princess Sophia."

Sophia moved past her father and Abby, taking Jenny in her arms. "Sophia, please, as my father said in private. You do like me, don't you?"

Jenny thought it was a very strange question as she was released. "Yes, of course, you are my Princess."

"Nothing more than that?"

Her mind was preoccupied with the odd situation. "Princess, sorry." She turned to her daughter. "Abby, what's going on?" Jenny enfolded her daughter in another hug. "I've been counting the days until you returned."

Abby smiled at her mom. "I asked Sophia to marry me, and she accepted."

The silence appeared to go on forever. The Crown Prince coughed.

Jenny found her voice. "Well, why didn't you say that immediately?" She hugged Abby even closer. Then she looked at the Princess and opened her arms to enclose her in a group hug.

"Ah, a great feminine moment. Now, do you think I can get a round of golf in this afternoon?" The Crown Prince chuckled.

Jenny released their children and faced him. "I'm sure we wouldn't want Your Highness to miss out on a round of golf."

The Crown Prince smiled. "Excellent. Welcome to the family, Jenny." He kissed her cheek. Turning to head out of the doorway, he switched back. "Tonight at dinner we can celebrate and discuss…hmm, whatever it is we need to discuss." He rapidly left.

†

"Sorry, Papa was never very relaxed with 'emotional events.'" Sophia shrugged.

"I know. I have been around for all His Highness' events at home. We go back a long time." Jenny grinned. "Let me make us tea, or should we have something more potent?"

Abby chuckled. "Not for me—the potent kind. I need to speak with Davy and check out the situation on the farm."

"Davy has been a wonderful manager. He is the ideal candidate to take over the role full-time."

Sophia watched as perplexity crossed Abby's face. Was there something she was unhappy with? Although it was true that, with their engagement, everything was going to change for Abby. She took Abby's hand, and that dark cloud disappeared. "Abby, go do your stuff, and your mama and I will gossip until you return."

"Gossip?"

That frown again. *I love this woman.* Sophia moved to smooth the crease on her forehead and dropped a gentle kiss on her lips. "Time for you to find Davy. I'll see you at dinner."

Abby flushed, nodded, and headed out the door.

Sophia turned to Jenny, who simply wrapped her in a hug.

"I'm glad you found each other. You will not regret it," Jenny softly said.

"I know." Sophia enjoyed the warmth of the hug. *I hope Abby doesn't regret it.*

†

"Mom, I'm home. I'll get a shower before we head for dinner at the castle." Abby grinned as she sped inside the house. She made for the lounge where her mother would be watching her soap, but she wasn't there. "Mom?"

The TV wasn't even switched on. Puzzled, Abby went to the kitchen and found her mom sitting, holding a teacup. She appeared oblivious to Abby's arrival. "Mom, are you okay?"

"Oh, darling, sorry. What did you say? What time is it?" Her mother's expression was strained.

"Mom, it's ten to six. I thought you'd be ready for our dinner at the castle. What's wrong?" Abby touched her shoulder.

"Oh, I have a headache." She stood.

Abby wasn't entirely sure her mom was being honest, and that wasn't like her. "Don't you want to go to dinner at the castle?"

"Truthfully?" Abby nodded. "I was hoping to have you all to myself tonight. You said you had news from the trip."

Abby sighed. "I'm so sorry, Mom. I was so excited…"

"Yes, and you should be, you became engaged today. To your Princess no less. I'm selfish, and I'm so sorry. We will catch up on your trip tomorrow."

"I let my own life take priority over…"

"My darling, this is right now, and it certainly takes priority. The past is in the past."

"Well, you might not think that when I tell you…" A gentle finger was placed on Abby's lips.

"For you, I will move heaven and earth to see you happy." Her mom winked. "I've always wanted to know what a family dinner was like behind those closed doors."

Abby laughed. "Me, too." She returned her mom's wink.

"Go get a shower, darling. Don't forget you have a fiancée to look nice for."

Abby was halfway to the door and turned. "Yes. I do, don't I?" With a wide grin, she left the room and took the stairs two at a time to reach her bedroom.

†

Henry had never in his thirty-five years of service with the Osric family felt so frazzled. From one call to another, there were continuous questions about the Princess, ranging from congratulations to pure animosity. Even the hanger-on cousins and times-removed family, who felt they had been betrayed in not being told personally, recognized there was a serious romance. *Well, who knew*! He wanted to scream at them. He didn't. His traditional respect for the hierarchy, however unpalatable at times, kept his mouth firmly closed.

He entered the kitchen area. It was six-thirty; dinner had been scheduled for eight. Yet the number had not been finalized.

"Henry, mate, you look pale, what's up?"

He cringed at the Australian's familiarity. No matter how many times he asked, the man refused to be formal. "I'm perfectly fine. Is everything in order for dinner?"

"I guess. Want to tell a fella how many to cook for?" He grinned; his wispy beard quivered.

For the first time since Sam died, he wanted to laugh, but he refrained. "The Prince has arrived home from his golf round. The Princess is in her office."

"Ah, so two for dinner. I'll get on with that."

"At the moment, I'm unsure."

A raucous laugh greeted his statement.

"You think it's funny?"

"Henry, mate. The fact you don't know. When you know pretty much everything that goes on in this place, even to the number of bed bugs resident who don't pay their way, astounds me. Want a cup of tea?" The burly man switched on the kettle.

"That's your answer to everything, I suppose, a joke?"

"Nope. On the other hand, when you've had a tough day and can't have a stiff drink because you are working, tea is the next best thing, I find." Darrel shrugged. "Mate, it's up to you."

"Tea would be welcome…thank you."

"No worries, mate. Have a seat." Henry sat in the first chair he came to at the long staff table.

"Do you like working here, Darrel?"

"Never a dull moment since I came. Sure I do. I like things to change a little but not too much to upset the apple cart."

Henry scratched his left eyebrow. "It's been chaos since Prince Rupert died. His Highness isn't the man he was, and the Princess…" he sighed.

"I like her." Darrel poured hot water into two mugs. "Can't be easy living in the shadow of an older brother who couldn't or didn't do any wrong. Heard she was a bit of a non-conformist."

"I'd prefer not to comment."

"You don't like her? She'll be your boss one day. Isn't she by proxy now?"

Henry frowned.

Darrel dropped a mug of tea next to Henry and scooted into a seat next to him. "Are you leaving when she takes over? Got to say, mate, you look the type to leave the job feet first. No offence."

Henry wrinkled his sharp nose, unsure if it was the proximity of the man or his questions that affected him. "The Princess, according to tradition, is not next in line. Tradition is that it falls to the next male in the line of succession."

"Aw fuck, man, not some incestuous has-been. Damn, I feel for the girl." He sipped his tea.

Henry, for some unexplained reason, thought that his drinking action was quite charming. The language, however, was another story. "If you want to keep your job, please refrain from such language here in the castle."

Darrel gave a hearty laugh. "I like you, Henry. Pardon me, but it's more likely you will lose your job than she will. Her dad loves her. I bet he's moved mountains to have her take the family legacy. It's a whole different ball game now, mate. Females aren't the silent little women behind closed doors anymore."

"I highly doubt it. I'm sure I would have been party to meetings about this."

"Mate, people with money and titles only let the help know what they need to know. Haven't you watched those British series about them? Fucking great, some of them. Anyway, he's a dick if he hasn't changed things, and if he hasn't, I'm happy to resign now."

"What tosh!"

"Tosh? What the hell does that mean? Is it even a word?"

Henry heard that taunting wild laugh and, today with the day he'd had, enough was enough. He turned to Darrel. "You have no bloody idea about me, or my age, and you never will. If it was up to me, you'd be gone tomorrow." He retreated to the door. "Tosh means rubbish." He left the kitchen with that wild laugh following him.

†

"Princess, I wonder if you could spare a moment."

Normally, she would have waved Henry away and arranged another time. His downtrodden expression stopped her. "Is it a sensitive matter?"

Henry looked down at his highly polished shoes. "Yes."

Sophia mentally rolled her eyes. "My office then." She headed to the door halfway down the main corridor. As they entered, she motioned for him to sit.

"I'd rather stand, Princess."

Sophia nodded, "Well, I know we are both busy people, so how can I help?" Sophia pushed around her favorite Mont Blanc pen on the ink blotter.

"I would normally have talked with your father about this. However, he has given you the household affairs as part of your portfolio, and it is to do with this and I…"

Sophia held up her hand. "Henry, get to the point."

He withdrew an envelope from his jacket breast inside pocket and handed it to her.

"What's this, a ransom demand?" Sophia chuckled as she ripped open the envelope and withdrew the pristine white linen paper. Her smile died as she read the contents. She looked at Henry and then back at the letter.

"No, not a ransom demand," Henry quietly replied.

Sophia took her chair at the desk. Then she steepled her hands together close to her mouth. "Indeed, not a ransom demand. Is it because of recent events?"

"I'd rather not say."

"Henry, you've been here all my life. I remember you helped me when I fell off my bicycle, and Rupert ran off laughing. My knee was bleeding, and I cried. You picked me up and carried me to the kitchen and dressed my wound."

"Princess, you were five years old; I'm surprised you remember."

"You remember, why shouldn't I. So why leave now?"

"I need a new start. Samuel's death has been hard for me."

Sophia frowned. "I accept that. I even understand. Rupert's death has left a hole that never will be filled."

"I must give three months' notice. I have done so. Will you accept my resignation?"

"Do I have a choice?" Sophia stood.

Henry remained silent.

Sophia placed the letter on her desk. "I guess I have no choice then. You had better begin an employment campaign to replace you."

"Me?" Henry looked like a startled deer in headlights.

"Of course, who better to find a replacement than the man who is an integral part of the Osric family?" Sophia held out her hand. Henry hesitantly clutched it. "Oh, the wedding is going to be in three months. Call it your swan song." Sophia passed him and left the room.

As she headed for the dining room, the doorbell rang. *I'm here, what the hell.*

†

Abby held her mom's hand as they rang the bell to the front door of the castle. For both, this was odd; they didn't have a clue how else to enter. Maybe the kitchen entrance.

The door opened, and Sophia stood there. Her beauty took Abby's breath away.

"What's this all about? I thought you would have just come to the dining room."

Abby felt small at the comment. They were not family yet. "My mom…"

"Jenny, come inside, you look cold." Sophia took Jenny's arm, and they entered the house. Abby stood there a few moments and followed.

As Abby entered, she looked around the hall entrance. It looked the same, but for some reason it was different. One day, she was probably going to live here, and it made her stomach roll.

"Are you coming, or are you waiting for the public tour?"

Abby looked at the speaker; the words hurt. "Princess, I'm right behind you."

"Good." Abby watched as her new fiancée was nice to her mom. *Great. Not even civil to me.* She followed

"Abby, Jenny, how wonderful." The Crown Prince stood, moving to welcome them as they entered the dining room.

"Oh, Your Highness, it's good…"

"You are shortly going to be my daughter-in-law. Call me Papa, Dad, Father, Claude, whatever. Make it less formal." He slapped her on the back.

Abby grimaced. "Okay."

The Crown Prince went over to her mom. "Jenny, welcome to the family. Not that you haven't always been part of it. Adeline loved you. I'm so glad that now it's going to be official. Who would have thought?"

"Not me," Jenny replied.

"Sit, everyone, sit. Dinner will start shortly. We can get acquainted. Plenty of drink and appetizers to keep us going."

Abby watched Sophia as she sat at the other end of the table, pretty much the farthest you could get. There had been no intimacy between them, not even words. The opposite, in fact. *I'm out of my depth. This was a bad idea.*

†

Sophia discreetly glanced at Abby. She didn't look happy; in fact, she looked miserable. That could have been jet lag, but she was certain it wasn't.

"Princess, Chef Darrel has produced a new menu for this evening. What choice do you prefer?" Henry handed her a pristine white card.

Sophia stared at the man, who in the past, she had selfishly accepted as always being there and taking care of everything. Now she had the prospect of him not being around. "Those options are, Henry?" She turned the card over in her hand.

"Truffle compote or prawn salad as the entrée. Chicken a la Darrel or beef Wellington. The desserts are iced champagne or," he turned to Abby, "as a tribute to your upcoming nuptials, Abby jelly roll."

Jenny laughed. "Abby, you have a dessert named after you. How lovely."

Abby smiled at her mom and nodded.

"I will have the new items on the menu this evening, Henry. Thank you."

He nodded and took the orders from the rest of the table.

Sophia watched as Henry recited the dinner order for everyone. Her attention was focused intently on Abby. She couldn't hear the words. Abby spoke so softly to Henry.

"Drinks anyone? In fact," her father headed to the small bar area in the room, "Henry, before you go, will you do the honors?" Her father produced a magnum of champagne from behind the bar.

"Papa, allow me." She turned to Henry. "Is that okay with you, Henry?"

Henry blushed. "Yes, Your Highness." He left the room.

"I do know that this task I can take care of without a hitch." She proceeded to uncork the bottle.

†

"It was a rather marvelous dinner, don't you think, darling? Even a pudding named after you. It was delicious. He's quite a joker, Chef Darrel. Poor Henry doesn't know how to handle him at all." Jenny Ranger giggled as Abby held her arm and they navigated through the walled garden to home.

"Yes, I'm sure," Abby quietly said.

"I can't believe that we will be part of the royal family. My daughter is marrying a princess. Your dad would be so proud."

Abby frowned. As they headed closer to the farmhouse, the dim lights from the kitchen and hall lights greeted them.

Jenny giggled even more. "Do you think I had too much champagne?"

"Maybe a little. It was a celebration, though, so not a problem." Abby steered her mother to the front door, and she unlocked it. "Home, Mom."

"Yes, it is, and I wouldn't want to be anyplace else." Jenny smiled.

Abby smiled. "I know what you mean."

Inside the house, Jenny turned to Abby. "Will you have time to talk about your trip tomorrow? You've left me in suspense since you said you had something that you could only tell me in person."

Abby's stomach lurched. The engagement had deterred her from something equally as important. Especially for her mom. "Breakfast for sure."

Jenny grinned, then hiccupped. "I think it's bedtime. Good night, darling." She hugged Abby and slowly went up the stairs.

Abby watched until she reached the landing. She walked into the kitchen and drew a glass of water. Her mind was filled with chaotic emotions.

She doesn't love me. She never even kissed me goodnight or touched me. She took the seat farthest away from me. I'm a convenience. Damn, I fell for her when I was a child, and I still feel the same. I don't want to be an unloved doormat. She switched off the light and headed for bed. Her body at least told the truth; she was exhausted.

†

Sophia strode confidently to the Ranger farmhouse. As she did, she was struck by the feeling that here in this place was where she should be. *I like it.* She lifted her hand and tapped on the ancient door knocker. The door opened seconds later.

"Princess."

Sophia's heart throbbed. She turned and faced the woman who was her betrothed. "Abby." Abby didn't move. "Do you think I've woken your mother?"

"Mom sleeps like a log until her alarm goes off. At seven-thirty."

"Abby, I want your thoughts on a problem I have." Abby stared at her so hard she was sure she'd turn to stone. "Of course, if you are busy. You must be going somewhere to open the door so immediately." Sophia turned toward the path leading back home.

A strong but gentle hand settled on her left forearm.

"I'm a farmer, we get up early. If I can help, I will." Abby gave a small smile.

Sophia was lost. How was it this woman gave her a smile, and suddenly, all her problems faded to obscurity. "Henry gave his notice last night. I don't want him to go."

"Isn't that a selfish reaction?"

"Yes." Sophia sighed.

"Then tell him that. Tell him you care. Henry will respond."

"I did tell him. I said he could only leave once he'd organized our wedding."

"That must have been a tense situation for you both." Sophia had a suspicion Abby was secretly smiling, though you couldn't tell from her expression.

"That's why I need your help. How do I deal with him? You know. You work here."

As soon as the words left her mouth, she wished them away.

Abby removed her hand from her arm. "I'm afraid I don't comment on my fellow workers. Though technically, he isn't." Abby gave Sophia a slight smile. "You need to find someone that views the world the same way as you do, because I certainly don't." She moved back inside the house and was about to shut the door. "Don't worry, I'll be the bad person in all this for your media friends. Find someone else for your advice bureau; it's out of my league. Goodbye, Princess. I need to work. I'm just a farmer after all."

Sophia looked like a voyeur as the door closed.

"Fuck." Sophia stood at the closed door for what seemed an eternity as tears welled up. Then she held her head up and marched back to the castle.

†

Abby shut the door on the Princess and leaned back against it, fully expecting her to rap on the door, guessing she'd want more of an explanation. She hadn't. *Guess I know my place.* The sound of footsteps on the gravel path indicated the Princess was leaving. At that moment, Abby allowed the whole Princess, engagement, and breakup to finally take over as she slid to the floor and wept.

Chapter Twenty

Henry gazed around the apartment he'd shared with Samuel and, for the first time, smiled. They had loved and enjoyed it so much in the time they had been together. It had taken a brash Australian to remind him that life must go on, and he still had time to find a life and, perhaps in the future, love again.

He glanced around one more time to ensure everything was where it should be. Samuel had been a little messy. In the early days, it annoyed him. Then it became part of who Samuel was, and he'd loved everything about the man.

He opened the door and left. He would miss living here; in fact, he had never thought of living anywhere else. He'd had the notion that once he retired, he'd live in one of the tied cottages overlooking the river. Not going to happen now.

He descended the back stairs, constantly looking for any imperfections from the staff in their cleaning regime. As he reached the staff corridor, he could hear singing, nothing he had heard before, but then he wasn't up on the new music. It was pleasant though.

He smiled and walked toward the kitchen where the voice emanated from. As the door opened, he was startled.

"Henry, do you have time to have a meeting?"

He could imagine his features did a few U-turns as he recognized the voice.

"Princess, I always have time for you. How can I help?"

"I've been jilted."

†

Jenny Ranger blinked several times as her alarm indicated it was seven-thirty. Groaning, she pulled herself out of bed. Since Paul's death, it had been hard to even sleep. The drink she had the previous evening helped. Abby's outgoing attitude and compassion had helped her realize that you must go on, no matter how much you loved someone and wanted to be with them even in death, and she'd certainly wanted that in the first year of her husband's death. She had even found an ally in her grief, the Crown Prince. He'd found her one day, crying in the walled garden. She'd always considered him far above her and aloof to his employees, more so since his wife died. Princess Adeline had been his savior in so many ways. She'd found that out in their conversations. That day, he just sat next to her and held her hand, until she stopped sobbing.

The smell of bacon cooking, well overcooking might be a better expression, had her eyebrows twitching. She quickly pulled on her work clothes and headed for the kitchen.

"Hey, darling, I love you, but usually I make breakfast," Jenny said as she entered the kitchen with a smile and looked at Abby flipping bacon in the frying pan.

"Thought I would do it today. Any objections?"

Whoa, must be a menstrual cycle day.

"No, looking forward to it." She saw Abby hit the bacon with the slicer so hard the fat from the pan went ballistic. *Hmm, not good.* She went to the kettle for a brew.

"I can do that. Mom, you just sit. It will be three minutes."

"Okay." Jenny wanted to smile, but she didn't. It had annoyed her husband that Abby was so focused, giving timetables on her actions, and she was always spot on. She'd never had the heart to say he was similar. *Doesn't fall far from the tree.*

"Mom?"

"Yes, darling?"

"I ended my engagement to the Princess."

"Oh." Jenny swallowed the multiple questions she wanted to ask, knowing there was only one important one. "Dare I ask why?"

"She doesn't think of me as anything other than the help. She doesn't love me, Mom. I love her so much. This isn't fair. I just want the pain I feel to end."

Jenny stood and walked over to the range. "How about I stop you pulverizing the bacon, god knows what you would do with the eggs." She took the spatula from Abby. "Make us a decent cup of tea and we'll work it out. Sound good?"

Abby nodded, and, snuffling, she handed over the implement." I love you, Mom."

Jenny heard the soft, muffled cries. She wanted so badly to hold her daughter and say everything was going to be okay. How could she though? Life wasn't all okay. There were no guarantees in life. Damn, there were so many obstacles, some so hard to overcome that you felt like giving up. She almost had, until the Crown Prince had simply given her hope that there were still things worth living for. Sometimes you need someone to care enough to put you on the right track. That's what Abby needed now.

"Abby, do you love her?"

"Yes. It doesn't matter, Mom; she's way beyond my pay grade."

"She has a different life from you, that's true. If you did choose to marry her, you would live a different life from what you do now. Sophia lives the life she was born into. From my dealings with the aristocracy, it's very hard for them to accept any other life, no matter how hard they try. Do you want that life? Better yet, are you prepared to just love the woman with all the baggage?"

"I thought I could. She just thinks I'm the help. I don't want to be a symbol. When I marry, Mom, I want that person to love me for who I am.

Jenny slid a plate of bacon and eggs to her daughter. The bacon was rather crisp; the eggs, thankfully, had been saved from being pulverized. "Eat your breakfast, darling. Things always seem better when you have a full stomach. That's what my mother used to say, and your dad did, too. They were always right." As she plated up her own breakfast, she wondered if she was telling her daughter a lie. "And…"

"Yes?" Abby looked at her expectantly.

"I love you no matter what you decide. Worst-case scenario, you are stuck with me." She placed her plate on the table and walked over to her daughter, enveloping her in a tight hug. Then she kissed the top of her head.

Abby sobbed. "I need to tell you about the trip."

"Darling, that can wait. Maybe at dinner."

†

The Crown Prince had made two phone calls immediately, one after the other; his head was reeling, not to mention the pain he had in his chest. "I haven't even had my first coffee." He stormed out of his room

†

"Princess, do you mind if I ask a personal question about you and Ms. Ranger?" Henry was hesitant. Though the Princess did not have the temper of her late brother, she tended to skirt a difficult issue, and he didn't know which was worse.

Sophia frowned. "As I'm the one asking for your help. It is fair that you are privy to some. I will give some personal information regarding myself and Abby."

Progress. Henry nodded. He was sitting opposite her, a polished teak coffee table between them. She was seated in a high-backed, sage green, buttoned, leather armchair. It had been the Princess' mother's favorite chair. In the early days of Princess Adeline's death, Sophia would simply sit for hours in the chair. It had taken a battalion of servants to drag her out of it on the day of the funeral.

"What is the question, Henry?"

"Why Abigail Ranger? You could choose from so many other women in your," he cleared his throat, "class."

Sophia gave him a glacial stare and rasped, "You think Abby is out of my class?"

"Do you?"

"I certainly do not!"

"Maybe you need to indicate that to Abigail. I'm sure she's overwhelmed by this situation. Even someone in your circles would be."

Sophia frowned. “I’ve asked her to marry me. Isn’t that enough?”

Henry smiled. “Yes, for most people. Princess, you are not most people. Abigail certainly isn’t part of your circles.”

Sophia pulled her legs up and sat on them. Henry could recall the teenage Princess as clear as day, doing the same thing. “I’m not sure what you want from me, Princess?”

The silence resonated in the room; even their breath couldn’t be heard.

“Henry, you have known me all my life. I respect your opinion. Please tell me how to fix this.”

Henry almost expired at the statement. Kind words had been few and far between since the Princess had left for university. She had found a crowd, or perhaps a person, who had influenced her in a different way. He allowed a few seconds to pass before he answered.

“I can’t, Princess.”

There was a shuffle on the chair opposite him. Hell, I wish I could do that. If I did, my legs would be in spasms for days.

“Of course you can. You always have! How is this different?”

“If Abigail is indeed the woman you want to spend the rest of your life with, only you can fix it.”

“This is ridiculous. I haven’t even slept with her. How would I know?” Sophia unfolded her legs and stood. “Thank you, Henry.”

“I guess that means my termination is sooner than expected?”

“Termination? How ridiculous. You are family. I was just…I’m sorry. If you want it signed in blood, you are here until my tenure is ended.”

Henry smiled. It was like going back years to when the Princess had been kind and thoughtful. "Then perhaps you need to be more intimate with Ms. Ranger, and you can both decide if you are the perfect pairing."

"She doesn't want to see me again. I'm not a farm person. I don't know how to make her talk to me."

Henry was sure the groan he gave could be heard in every room of the castle.

"Princess?" Those intelligent blue eyes caught his eye with a laser beam.

"Yes?"

"Abigail Ranger is not a toy. She is not a trifling item to play with."

"I am not playing, Henry."

"Are you sure? If you wanted to marry Abigail for her, you should have simply talked and figured things out. Or is there another reason?"

The Princess frowned. "My papa instructed me to marry a commoner."

Henry wasn't surprised at the reason. He had thought that the Princess might be stronger to ignore such a request. "Then I come back to the original question. Why Abigail Ranger?" Several expressions crossed the Princess' features before she replied.

"She fits me somehow. I don't know why. When I'm with her, I feel like my life is enriched for her being in it. I am bereft when she isn't around."

"Princess, have you told her that?"

"Not really. How ridiculous."

"Then perhaps you should. To engage with a royal family takes a tremendous amount of courage. To accept an offer of marriage means only one thing—Ms. Abigail Ranger may, in fact, love you for who you are. Have you thought of that?"

"No." She frowned, then glanced away. Then stared at him intently. "I'm such a fool, Henry." She strode to the window. "I need to make this right." She turned and headed for the door. "Thank you." She grasped him in a hug. "I'm glad you are in my life, Henry Torvois."

She left the room.

He stood for a few moments and contemplated the rather odd conversation he'd just had with Her Royal Highness. Then he smiled. "Samuel, you were right all along. Our lovely Princess needs someone who completes her. I believe she has found that in Ms. Abigail Ranger."

†

Sophia strode with determination to the Ranger farmhouse. Now was not a time to prevaricate or rethink anything. No, right now, her goal was defined. As she entered the walled garden, she stopped for a moment, looked around, and smiled. *I think you would approve, Mama; I know you would.* Exiting by the door Abby used, she walked until the farm loomed in front of her. It was like encountering an event from a fairy story. Maybe this was her fairy story. She had always known deep inside that there was someone who would complete her life. Sucking in a deep breath, she raised her hand to the door knocker. She almost fell backwards on the gravel as the door opened. Gaining her equilibrium, Sophia sucked in a deep breath before speaking.

"I know you don't want to see me again, Abby." She dropped her gaze. Mama, please help me. You must have had difficulties with your relationship with Papa?

"Correct, I don't." The door began to close.

Sophia raised her hand and pushed against the door. “Please give me one final chance, Abby. I know I probably don’t deserve it.” Sophia frowned; her hands were balled.

“Princess, I think you have said enough between us for a lifetime. When I said it was over, it is. I’m tired of being hurt.”

The only word that connected was “hurt.” Sophia took a step away from the door. *How did I hurt her? She hurt me. S*ophia waited for a reply. It was like waiting for paint to dry. She took a huge breath, “I love you.”

“Really, well, I wouldn’t know that.”

Sophia wanted to strangle this woman and, at the same time, hug her close. “I’m not good at saying personal things. Help me out here?”

“No, this is all yours, Princess.”

The door moved more to closing than opening.

“Okay. Why didn’t ‘I love you’ mean enough?”

“Anyone can say that. Do you mean it?”

Sophia gulped, *Listen to your heart, darling.* Stunned, Sophia looked around her.

“Princess, are you okay?”

‘Of course, yes. Abby.” Sophia wasn’t exactly sure what she was going to say next.

“That’s my name. At least we can agree on that.” Abby gave a wry smile.

“At least we can do that.” Sophia felt a weight had lifted from her heart. “Abby, can we find a middle ground?”

“Us? Are you sure it isn’t you?”

“What do you mean?”

Abby stepped out of the doorway and closed the door after her. “I’m an ordinary woman. I work for a living. I love my family, and I’m happy with that.”

“Your point is?” Sophia was out of depth.

"I love you…"

"Well then, it's going to work."

Abby dropped her gaze and then lifted her head. "Exactly all about you. You never let me finish."

Sophia bit her bottom lip. "I'm sorry, please continue."

Abby caught her eye, and they locked gazes.

Mama, I don't want to lose her. What do I do?

"We have no future as a couple. You don't speak, or touch me, as a person who is in love."

"I can do that, let me try."

Abby sighed. "I shouldn't have to tell you; it should be instinctive. You don't love me, Princess. Spending the rest of our lives together needs friendship and love, especially with your lifestyle. We are lucky we came from a background of parents who loved us for who we are. It's important today."

Sophia was lost for words. Everything Abby said was right.

"What will you do now?"

Abby shrugged. "I need to concentrate on the farm. I also need to return to the US shortly."

"Why? You have just arrived back?" She saw a sadness cross Abby's features.

"It's a family situation."

"Maybe your mama could go? "

"My mom isn't fit enough or emotionally able to make the journey." Abby turned to the door, her hand on the handle. "Princess, I hope you find your perfect partner." She opened the door, entered, and closed the door behind her.

Sophia watched in fascination. It was surreal. Abby had been simply Abby. One of the reasons she loved her. Did she though, or were her feelings more love for someone she respected rather than an emotional connection that meant they could be a loving couple? What was this family problem that meant Abby had to leave the country again?

†

Abby's tears fell as she closed the door on the only woman she had ever loved. There had been friendships and minor liaisons in her life. Nothing had quite been enough for her to commit to anyone. She was the epitome of the ridiculed virgin on TV. Her heart wanted to agree to anything the Princess wanted. That way, at least she would be in her life. Her mind, however…. Wiping away tears, a heavy load on her chest kept her seated. She listened for the gravel to crunch, but silence greeted her.

†

Sophia stood contemplating what to do next. She could pass her problems on to others as she had in the past. Closing her eyes, she groaned. *I'm a terrible person. Abby deserves more than someone like me.* She looked at the castle looming in the background. Then she turned her gaze to Abby's home. A farmhouse, a different upbringing, hardly ready to be thrown feet first into the royal forum.

She sank down next to the closed door and leaned her back against it. I'm going to be waiting for you, Abigail Ranger, until you open the door. Because I think you and I are a great couple. We, or probably I, need to know how to make it work.

†

"I'm looking for the Princess?" Henry glanced around at the staff before him. Stupid question, really. They were unlikely to know. If he didn't, they would have no chance.

"Mr. Torvois, one of my juniors, mentioned he saw or thought he saw the Princess at the Ranger's farmhouse."

Henry sniffed the air. "Thank you, Malcom. At what time was that?"

"I saw him a few minutes before this meeting. He said it was on his way to work. Twenty minutes perhaps."

"Thank you."

Henry contemplated his next move, and then a voice interrupted his thoughts.

"Better make sure there are no people taking photos, mate."

"What do you mean?"

"Just the princess is a great Sheila."

Sheila, for god's sake, this man is infuriating. "Her name is Princess Sophia, not Sheila."

"True, not Sheila. Being Princess has privileges we mere mortals only aspire to. Perhaps she deserves a little privacy, especially as it's the home of her new fiancée." Darrel turned to the others in the room. "Am I wrong?"

Several heads nodded, but no one spoke.

"For once in her life, let her make some decisions on her own. I figure Abby will be good for her; she's one of us."

Everyone in the room gave positive hums and ahs.

Henry sighed. He looked around the room at the people who, for the most part, had been involved with the family for as many years as he had. "Thank you for your help." He turned and was about to leave the room.

"We all think it's a great thing, the Princess and Abby. What about you, Henry?"

"I agree." He left the room and then received a call.

†

Sophia stood, smoothing down her dress. There were only two ways this was going to go. She would leave or stay. Most would say she was a fool for even having any thoughts on the subject. She was Princess, after all.

She rapped on the door and listened for any sign of life. The silence settled around her, and a sense of foreboding engulfed her. Her phone rang. She reached inside her pocket and glanced at the caller's ID. The message was simple but effective. She ran as fast as she could back to the castle.

Chapter Twenty-one

"Henry, my father?" Sophia advanced toward her father's bedroom suite. Henry held her back. "What's the meaning of this?"

"The doctor is inside. He didn't want to be interrupted."

"My papa was perfectly well yesterday."

"Your Highness, he has had what the doctor believes is a minor heart attack."

Sophia pushed against Henry. "Then it is imperative I see my papa. You can't stop me, Henry."

"I cannot, Princess, however…" he withdrew his phone and held it out to her.

She grasped the object. Then she saw her father, and he spoke. It was a recording.

"My darling, please don't get angry with Henry; he is merely doing my bidding. I need you to be strong." Sophia glared at Henry.

"What is this?" she angrily asked.

Henry stopped the message.

"Please listen, Your Highness." She nodded, and he began the message again.

"I need you to be strong for not just me, but most importantly for our people. Our people need strength right now, after Rupert's death. They want good news, my darling, and you have given them that with your engagement." Tears streamed down her face. "I love you." The video ended.

Sophia turned to Henry, his expression bland. The color of his skin was another thing. It was altogether ghostly.

"Did my father expect this?" Her sobs almost overwhelmed the words.

"I don't know. Your Highness, he sent this to me shortly after Prince Ruptert died. Perhaps your father is right. You can bring light back to our principality. It's been hard for everyone, with the COVID-19 virus, Prince Rupert's death, and now this."

"How can I contemplate being happy when Papa is sick? Why isn't he already in a hospital?"

"The doctor has called the ambulance. It is His Highness' wish that you take care of the principality until he is well again."

Sophia blinked rapidly. "I don't know how to do that, Henry."

Henry nodded. "You have a very professional staff at your fingertips. They are at your behest."

"Thank you." Sophia sighed. "Will you help me?"

"Yes."

Sophia hugged the man hard. "Will you arrange a meeting with…whomever I need to see to keep the principality moving forward, tomorrow?"

"Yes, of course, Your Highness. "

Sophia groaned. "I'm not sure Abby is talking to me right now. Papa's feel-good vibe might not work on that front."

Henry nodded. "Then perhaps you will have to make it happen by the soft approach of an apology."

"How did you know it had anything to do with me making an apology?"

"Your Highness, I've known you from the day you were born. Really, a farmer's daughter and a royal princess hardly coexist in the same social worlds. Though you could make a royal demand."

Sophia bit her lip. "Royal demand? Henry, what do you mean?"

"The farm belongs to the royal family. I can give instructions for you to veto the arrangement we have with the family if Ms. Ranger will not cooperate." Sophia gripped Henry's arm.

"I can't do that!"

"As of now, you can do what you want. Your father has passed you that right."

Closing her eyes, she reviewed the options in her mind. None that felt good came to mind. Sophia stared at the door that separated her from her papa. Sighing, she leaned against the wall, waiting.

†

"Abby." Jenny Ranger shouted as she pulled on her shoes at the front door. She grabbed her overcoat and dragged it on. "Abby."

"I'm here, Mom, what's the problem?"

Jenny bit her bottom lip. "I'm needed at the castle. The Princess needs to speak to me. I'm sure I won't be gone long." Abby groaned. "Darling, I'm sure it doesn't have anything to do with you."

"Mom, don't go. I'm sure it's just a foil for her to make me do what she wants."

"Oh, my goodness. How cynical." Jenny shook her head. "I'm going if for no other reason than to find out what she wants."

"She wants only what suits her."

"Abby. You do realize what you are saying?"

"What?"

"You don't trust the woman you love and are engaged to."

"We are not engaged. I told you this morning."

Jenny frowned. "Why?" She opened the door and frowned. "We will talk about this later. Right now, I want to know why our Princess needs to speak to me urgently. I heard on the grapevine His Highness has been taken to hospital."

Jenny opened the door and glanced back at the distressed expression on her daughter's face. "Darling, you wanted to concentrate on the farm, and the chickens need to be cleaned out." She left the house and headed for the castle.

†

Henry paced the hallway. In all the years he had served the Crown Prince and his family, this was as hard to bear as Sam's death. Tears welled, and he brushed them away.

"Hey, mate, how are you doing?"

Henry wanted to be angry at the words. Instead, he sighed and faced the head chef. "I've had better days. You?"

Darrel nodded. "He's going to be okay, mate. Hell, he's a highness and they get all the best health privileges, right?"

Henry focused on the lopsided half-smile Darrel gave. "I want to be there at his side. The doctor insisted that it wasn't necessary for the next twenty-four hours."

"I'm sure Her Highness will keep you informed."

"That's the thing, Her Highness won't, can't. His Highness decreed that she take care of the principality."

Darrel frowned. "Ah, mate, she won't do that and not see her father when he's sick. I'm sure she'll…"

"She's a royal. They look at emotional things differently than the rest of us. When it comes to the principality, she will do as instructed."

"I always thought this royalty crap was about money and prestige. They didn't give a damn about the regular people." He touched his chest.

"The Osric family came from farming roots. Perhaps one day I will give you the history."

"I'd like that, mate. Is there anything that I can do for you to help?"

Henry didn't care if he wasn't alone as tears slowly fell down his cheeks. The large man at his side pulled him into a bear hug.

"Got you, mate."

†

Sophia sat at her desk waiting for Jenny Ranger. She checked her watch. There was a knock on her door. "Enter."

Jenny Ranger appeared. Sophia knew instinctively that there wasn't going to be a problem.

"Princess, you said it was urgent?"

"Yes." Sophia's voice croaked, "My papa has had a heart attack."

Jenny moved forward to within a foot of her. "Oh, Your Highness, I'm so sorry. His Highness is a very fit man for his age, and you have excellent doctors. I'm sure he will be okay."

Sophia drew back her shoulders. "They say he has had a mild heart attack. Jenny, he can't die. I'd be alone."

"You will never be alone, Your Highness. You have your people and, I'm sure, extended family."

There was a silence that extended between them.

"You never mentioned Abby?"

"She told me that you and she had had a difference on being engaged."

"We did. I intend to make things right with Abby."

"Abby is a very empathic. Perhaps you should have asked her…"

Sophia gulped back her tears.

"Perhaps." Sophia cried.

Jenny pulled her into her arms. "It will all work out."

†

Abby knew she was wearing the already-worn carpet out in the lounge, as she paced incessantly. The biggest thing on her mind was why did the princess ask for her mom? Okay, they hadn't exactly been on good terms, but she was the Princess' go to when she had a problem, at least in recent months. "I've messed everything up. "

The sound of the door opening had Abby racing to the hall, where she stopped dead.

"Princess?"

"Your mother gave me the key."

Abby frowned. "Why?" She watched as the Princess hesitated. "Is my mom okay?"

"Yes, yes. Why would you think anything else?"

"Well, she isn't here, you are…Princess, what do you want?"

"My papa has had a heart attack."

Abby saw tears in the Princess's eyes. All she wanted to do was engulf her in a hug. She restrained herself. "Why aren't you with your father?"

"I was…informed I am to represent my father in the principality."

"He's your dad, Princess! I wouldn't leave one of my parents for anything when they were sick!"

She watched several expressions cross the Princess's face. "What does Henry think?"

The woman before her wiped her eyes. "Henry was following my papa's instructions as I do. This was a bad idea." The Princess turned toward the door.

"I'm sorry." Abby didn't know what else to say. "Whose idea was it?"

"Your mother said you might be empathic. Obviously not."

"I'm sorry. What about your friend…friends?"

The silence between them became awkward.

"Abby, do you dislike me so much that this isn't the right option? You are my fiancée in the public's eye."

"We both know it won't work. You are hardly going to get up at four in the morning to prepare breakfast before I go to work on the farm. Hey, tell me if I'm wrong."

Sophia nodded. "Would you be willing to attend royal social events at any time of the day?"

They gazed at each other.

Abby felt like her brain was overloading, then blurted out, "How do we make it work for everyone?"

"We spend more time together. In fact, she said we should live together in the same place and see what happens." Abby raised her eyebrows, and the Princess laughed. "Your mother approved."

"When would this be?"

"Your mother said now. I came prepared."

Abby simply stood, not quite sure she understood the situation, next best thing, keep busy. "Do you need any help with your belongings?"

"So glad you asked." The Princess opened the door.

Abby groaned. "How much stuff do you own? It's almost as much as you left at the hotel."

"Is that a problem?"

Abby shook her head and walked toward the Princess' possessions. *She has more clothes in one suitcase than I have in my closet.*

†

Sophia sank into the chair Abby pulled out for her in the kitchen. She watched as Abby began to prepare the tea she'd promised. "Abby, thank you."

"You are welcome, Princess."

Sophia looked around the sitting room. A few months ago, she would have scoffed that she'd agree to live in such basic conditions. Right now, being here with this woman made perfect sense.

"I'm glad you are in my life, Abby. Sometimes I feel lost and strangely alone. Though not when I'm with you. Do you think this time we have together will decide our collective fate?"

Abby chuckled. "Sounds a bit melodramatic to me, Princess."

"Yes, it does." Sophia smiled. "We are though. Melodramatic. Or at least the situation we are in. Don't you think?"

"Perhaps." Abby placed a mug of tea, then brought milk and sugar jugs and placed them in front of her. "I don't even know how you like your tea."

"I guess you wouldn't." Sophia picked up the mug and sipped the contents. "Hmm, nice and strong."

Abby nodded, adding milk and three spoons of sugar to her mug, then drank from it.

"Whoa, three sugars. That would keep me wired for hours. I guess we are finding things about each other, and that's a good thing, right?"

Abby nodded and frowned at her mug.

"You know, it isn't just me that's a problem. How do you think I feel when you constantly call me Princess. It isn't very intimate."

"I'm sorry. What else do you want me to call you? You are my Princess."

"Yes, yes, but for god's sake, Abby, if I'm making love with a woman, I'd prefer her not to call me Princess."

Abby dropped her gaze, continuing to stare at the mug in her hand.

Sophia wanted to scream and saw Abby's cheeks redden. "Abby, how do you see me other than as a royal princess?"

A huge frown wrinkled Abby's forehead. Sophia's heart felt the pain she was sure Abby was feeling in the conversation. It is way out of her wheelhouse. Damn, it's out of mine, too. This was ridiculous. Regardless of her father's fate, this stupid wish of his for me to marry a commoner at short notice will not work!

"Abby, thank you for taking me in. I will leave tomorrow. You were right, I should be with my papa. I allowed so many opinions to cloud what is important. This engagement has barely been reported. Merely a hiccup in the media, and we can go on with our lives. A good one, I hope." Sophia smiled and drained the tea in her cup. "Which room shall I take?" She stood.

Abby scrambled out of her chair. Her expression was stoic.

Sophia watched as Abby drew in a breath, and her chest heaved. *Oh god, I'd love to touch those breasts. Stop, stop. Slap yourself five times and forget it.* Sophia gently tapped the back of her hand five times.

"If you give me some time, I will prepare your room with fresh bedding and towels. You know where the sitting room is. I'll let you know when it's ready."

Sophia nodded. "Thank you." Abby stared at her intently. *Does she want a tip?* Sophia fled the room.

Outside the room, she frowned. "Fuck!" Then withdrew her phone and called Claire. It went straight to voicemail. She tried again, still the same. The third time, she gave a voicemail. "Hey, Claire. Lots of things are happening here. Call me when you get this." Sighing, she headed for the sitting room.

CHAPTER TWENTY-TWO

Henry stood outside His Highness' rooms. He had performed his duties as the Crown Prince had requested. It had not, in his opinion, been correct. Disallowing his daughter's access when he was sure it should be the reverse. What was he to do now?

†

Jenny sat next to her best friend and toyed with her drink. "Mary, my Abby loves the princess."

There was a chuckle. "Well, of course she does; everyone in the household, at least the older ones, knows that. Do you remember when she came home looking like she'd been to the swimming pool?"

Jenny raised her eyebrows. "It was almost her downfall."

"Princess Sophia was a bonny child that was for sure. Abby was brave though, wasn't she? Especially as she was coming down with the flu when she rescued the little princess from the fountain?"

"Yes, she was. It turned into pneumonia. The doctor said it was touch-and-go; we'd know in forty-eight hours. Her dad never left her side." Jenny wiped the tears that welled. "Paul said we had to watch over our special 'princess' to ensure she knew we were there fighting her corner."

"Jenny, I think they are meant to be."

"Perhaps. Although."

"Yes?"

"They might just be souls that need to pass by each other this time around."

"Why do you say this, Jenny? It isn't like you."

"Abby will do anything for Her Highness, as we know, to the point of death. I'm not sure Her Highness feels that way about Abby." Jenny began to cry.

Mary hugged her. "Jenny, maybe this connection they have will work out. I hope so, we could all do with some good news."

Jenny allowed a smile to cross her lips as she disengaged from the bear hug. "I hope so. How about we watch *Bridgerton*?" There was a tiny giggle from her friend.

"I thought you'd never ask. I'll get the tea and scones."

†

Abby threw down her phone on the coffee table. Her eyes travelled to the drivel she was watching on the TV, an idiot reality show about real estate in Los Angeles. Who had that kind of money?

"Abby, is something wrong?"

Abby was startled by the voice. She turned quickly. "No."

"I'm sorry I left you for so long. I didn't realize I needed sleep."

Abby simply stared at the Princess. How wonderful would her life be if she could have this woman in her life forever? Her body became alive as soon as she entered her personal space.

"Abby? Is something wrong?"

She walked the few feet between them and took the Princess' hand. "I called Henry. He believes His Highness' heart attack is mild." Her hand was clasped so tightly she thought the circulation might be compromised.

"You are my star. Thank you, Abby."

Lips hovered milli-inches from hers. Then she simply kissed her. Abby's whole world spun out into the universe as her Princess kissed her back.

When they came up for air, Abby began to move away, and a delicate hand stopped her.

"Will you call me Sophia, please, before we kiss again?"

Abby bit her bottom lip, and the Princess smiled. "It's not difficult, Abby."

It wasn't the words that made her speechless; it was the sheer delight in knowing that she was going to kiss her Princess again. "Sophia…" Speech was irrelevant as her lips were captured again, and they sank into the sofa.

†

Sophia stroked Abby's corn-colored hair; it threaded through her fingers like silk. "Your hair is amazing. I wish mine felt like this. What products do you use?" Abby's eyebrows furrowed.

"Normal stuff from the supermarket for flyaway hair. I really don't give it much thought." Abby moved out of Sophia's arms to sit opposite her.

Sophia grinned. "Abby, you are just so…gosh, I don't have the words. Please never change."

Abby shrugged. "Wasn't planning on it. Well, at least…"

Sophia moved, capturing Abby's lips, and allowed the magic of the moment to overwhelm her. When they released for air, Sophia couldn't think of anything better than having Abby as her consort. "Abby, we seem to be like a revolving door when it comes to us. If I'm mistaken, please tell me?"

Abby shrugged. "A revolving door works."

"I've asked you to marry me, you've asked me. We have both broken it off." Sophia sighed. "We've both said we love each other." Sophia stopped. A part of her didn't want to know the answer to her next question. She swallowed hard.

"Yes."

"Abby, I need to confess something." Abby's eyebrows furrowed big time. "I'm the next in line to the principality if I marry a commoner. If I don't, according to my papa's instructions, one of my male relatives will take the title. I've always been prepared to be the sister of the next Crown Prince. Then my wonderful idiot brother, whom I adored, dies. Under other circumstances, I would have called that inconsiderate. You probably don't understand." Sophia glanced down at the coffee table in front of her. It was adorned with table mats of cats. Sophia attempted to stand; Abby stayed her hand.

"I do, I really do. Tell me about Rupert."

Sophia kissed her lightly. "I loved Rupert so much; he was all the things I wanted to be. God, he used to be livid when I didn't meet the expected protocol. He and Henry tried so hard to stop me from making a mockery of myself. I did it out of sheer…who knows. Maybe I missed my mama. My whole life was dictated by men. I hated being at boarding school. Most of the girls talked about their mothers and what their advice was. I did not have that role model."

Abby drew her close and kissed the top of her head. "Hey, take a breath. Remember, I love you, and your family does, too. Isn't that worth everything?"

Sophia felt the world that had landed on her shoulder disappear. "You love me, for me?"

"Hey, after this afternoon, what's not to love about you?"

They relaxed into a slow, intimate kiss. When they broke apart, Sophia sighed. "Abby, my life is so much more when you are in it. I'm not sure if I've ever told you."

"Princess…" She gave Abby a frown. "Sophia, you bring me to life. I don't want to be anywhere else but with you. I've always felt that from the first moment I saw you."

Sophia laughed softly. "That helps big time."

Abby stared directly at her. "When did you know you loved me?"

Sophia was taken aback at the question. Then her phone rang. "Doctor, yes, I understand. Can I visit?" She nodded several times. "I will be there." The call ended.

"Abby." They both stood at the same time. Inches apart. Sophia gently touched Abby's lips.

"Yes?"

"Do you mind if I do this on my own?"

"Sophia, he is your father. I wouldn't expect anything different. Whatever happens, always remember I'm here, no matter what."

Sophia stared at the woman who made her world simply worth living in. *God, she is the woman I'm going to marry.* "No matter what, right?"

Abby nodded.

Sophia drew a deep breath, leaned forward, and kissed Abby. A simple kiss, but it gave her strength. "No matter what."

They headed for the door, and Abby held it open. There was an expression on her face that puzzled Sophia. "Is something wrong?"

Abby shook her head." Go, see your father; he needs you now."

"Yes." She smiled. "I'll be back, we are owed at least a weekend together, without interruptions. Before our life is taken over by Henry and protocol for the wedding. You are going to marry me, still?"

"Later." Abby gently pushed her toward the door. Sophia smiled and left. Halfway up to the walled garden, she turned back and looked at Abby. She was standing just as Sophia had left her. Her heart wanted to return to those strong, loving arms. Family and duty overpowered that thought, and she headed toward the garage for her vehicle.

†

Abby watched her princess leave, and her heart hurt. *I'll take just a few minutes of your day anytime. Even though I'm not sure you love me.* She closed the door and then searched for her phone.

CHAPTER TWENTY-THREE

Sophia strode into the Mercy Hospital entrance and headed for the main desk. Heads turned as she walked inside. Hmm, maybe I should have perhaps brought Henry or Abby to shield me from any interference. Not to mention calling ahead and not having to wait behind two people ahead of me. There was a soft cough behind her, and she turned.

"Your Highness, we were not told you would be visiting."

Sophia gave the man, who appeared to constantly wring his hands as he spoke, a smile.

"I'm sorry. I should have called ahead."

The man shook his head, his wiry hair curled around his forehead. "No, please, no apology necessary. I will take you to your father's room."

The woman in front of her spun around. "His Highness is sick? Oh no!" the voice shrieked, echoing off the walls. People in the vicinity stopped what they were doing and watched.

Sophia swallowed hard. "Don't worry, just a precaution only." She gave her practiced smile and turned back to the man. "Please, let's go."

The man hurriedly pointed to an elevator to their left, and she walked ahead of him toward it. The clicking of her high heels was the only sound in the area, which was bizarre because there were people teeming everywhere.

"I'm sorry, I didn't quite get your name?"

"Drake, I'm the administration manager for the reception."

"Nice to meet you, Mr. Drake." She followed him into the elevator and watched as he pressed the button for the eighth floor.

The benign music in the small confines of the metal box they traveled in had Sophia cringing. She gave Mr. Drake a tight smile. He was still wringing his hands. It reminded her of a book, and she suppressed a giggle. He appeared exactly how she would imagine a present-day Ebenezer Scrooge would look. *Maybe he needs to change professions and become an actor; he'd do great in the Christmas pantomime season.*

The elevator lurched, and the doors slowly slid open.

The pungent smell of cleaning materials and a sterile environment greeted her.

"Your Highness, if you allow me, I will talk to the nursing staff and inform them of your arrival."

Sophia nodded. "Thank you, Mr. Drake, for being extremely helpful. I will not forget this."

The look of devotion in his face caused a bubble of laughter to rise, but she fought it down. This was her life now, and she liked it. She slowly walked in the direction Drake had gone. Her eyes glanced into rooms that were fitted with so much equipment it was hard to decipher if a human being was inside. She stopped at a room just before the reception desk, where a nurse hovered over someone she could vaguely see in a bed. The nurse was fully masked. She moved closer.

"Princess, Senior Nurse Blackwood is the acting nurse manager for the ICU. She will take you to His Highness' room."

"A pleasure to meet you." The woman gave her a direct gaze, her expression fake. Years of faking being polite to people you don't like had made her an expert in detection. Mr. Drake scooted back down the corridor.

"Mr. Drake, thank you." The man turned, bowed, and grinned. Sophia was sure his face would split. Then she turned to the woman. "Nurse Blackwood, may I see my father?"

The woman glared at her, then huffed and motioned for Sophia to follow her. A room at the end of the corridor greeted Sophia. The blinds were drawn.

Nurse Blackwood opened the door, and Sophia stifled a sob as she saw her papa. Entering the room, she sped to her father's side. "Papa." Weary eyes caught hers, and she clutched his hand and placed a kiss on his cheek. Then softly cried, "Papa, why?"

Those exhausted eyes suddenly became alert. He drew Sophia closer and whispered, "When we are alone."

Puzzled, Sophia turned. Nurse Blackwood was settled against the wall. There was something not quite right about how the woman looked at her. Then she realized. *Fuck, all my people know of me is as a party animal*. She withdrew from her father and stared at the nurse. "Thank you. I need private time with His Highness."

"His Highness needs constant monitoring."

Sophia wanted to rip into the woman who was looking at her smugly. "Then why was he unattended prior to our entrance?"

"Sophia," her father croaked.

"There was a shift change."

"Really?" Sophia glanced at her watch. "Nurse Blackwood, I'm sure you have other more pressing duties that require your attention."

"I'm happy to be here until the next shift takes over."

Sophia moved to within inches of the woman. "Is there something you wish to address with me?"

"Why would you think so?"

Sophia's phone pinged for a text. She glanced at the caller ID, expecting Claire.

I might be a bit slow, but you should have taken Henry or me with you. I hope it wasn't too dramatic to get to see your dad. A xxx

If she thought Mr. Drake's face split when he smiled, hers must surely match it.

She glanced at the woman in front of her and replaced it with her tutored smile. "It really doesn't matter. I'm sure you can allow me a few minutes of private time. There is, after all, lots of sophisticated equipment monitoring my father."

"A few minutes." Scowling, the nurse left the room.

Sophia returned to her father's side. "I'm so happy to see you, Papa." She snuggled gently into him. "I love you so much."

"My darling, you bring me to life when I really feel like giving it all up."

"Please don't say that. What would I do?" She gently squeezed her papa's hand. "Though I understand, Papa, Rupert's death has been heart-wrenching." His tired gaze caught hers, and she felt his pain. "It's hard for me, too. I can't help feeling this isn't real, and the last few months are a dream."

"I have often thought the very same thing. Yet, we are here today, suffering our loss and the ever-changing landscape we and our people must endure."

Sophia sighed. "All I want right now is for you to be well again, Papa. Nothing else is important to me." Though she spoke the words, and they were true, Abby's image invaded her mind.

"Are you sure about that? What about a certain Ms. Ranger?"

Sophia shook her head. Could her Papa read her mind? "I'm not sure what you mean, Papa?"

"Of course you don't." He smiled weakly.

"Ab…Ms. Ranger and I are happy together."

"I hope with benefits."

"Papa! Really, it isn't the Dark Ages when the lord of the manor takes any wench he wants." She smiled. Abby was highly unlikely to agree with that kind of arrangement.

"True, and a deplorable tactic it was, too. Though if it hadn't happened, we wouldn't be ruling this principality."

"Can we save the family history lesson for a better time? Papa, what have the doctors said? Even Henry isn't here at your side. I do not understand that at all."

Her father looked around the room and grimaced. "My darling, you need his guidance now. Henry is the most capable person I know who can help you in the coming weeks whilst I convalesce.

"He could still have been with you. Few people know of your current health situation. I didn't hear anything on the radio news when I drove here, and surely there would be something. Perhaps because it is a Sunday. I have often gotten away with a few misdemeanors they would have been interested in, except it was a Sunday." She closed her eyes and hoped her father wasn't listening.

Her father chuckled and kissed her hand. "Oh, I'm sure they knew."

"Papa, the doctors are insistent that you don't exert yourself."

"I must have told you how much you are like your mama. My darling Adeline was strong-willed, beautiful, and knew her mind, even knew mine."

Sophia heard the slurred words as her papa's eyes closed. There were beeps from the machines around him. No one immediately turned up.

She raced to the nurse's station. "My father needs attention." Sophia was thankful the dragon nurse wasn't in the area.

A woman barely out of school almost fell out of her chair and headed for her father's room.

Sophia followed slowly, thinking about her father's situation. She wanted so desperately not to be alone. Then a voice spoke her name, and the hairs at the back of her neck stood on end. She looked in the direction of the voice and knew at that moment that everything was going to be okay.

"Henry. Excellent, now I know my papa is in good hands."

"Your Highness, thank you. Which room, please?"

Sophia pointed to the room, "I will be right behind you." She watched as Henry moved like lightning to her papa's room. She turned back to the elevator.

"Princess, how are you doing?"

That slow, sexy voice, yes, sexy, turned her on for sure, but also soothed her. "Abby. What brought you here with Henry?" She moved closer to Abby.

Those broad shoulders shrugged. Sophia wanted to latch onto that strength and just be held by Abby, wanted to allow the world to float away for at least a minute or two.

"I decided that my Princess needed support, as did her father. I decided Henry should be here by your side. He did not need asking twice."

Sophia moved to within inches of Abby. "I will never forget this act of kindness, Abby." She stroked Abby's arm and smiled. Then whispered, "Later."

Abby smiled. "Later, I like the sound of that."

"Princess, this is an acute unit. Only essential personnel are allowed here. Who is this person?" Sophia almost jumped out of her skin.

Turning, she gazed at the dragon nurse. Yes, that was the appropriate description of the woman. The corridor walls began moving closer together in a suffocating threat. Then strong fingers threaded through hers, and she turned to look at Abby. Right there, right now, maybe it was an epiphany. With Abby by her side, she could do whatever was required of her in the future.

"This is Ms. Abigail Ranger. A friend. I want to add her and Mr. Henry Torvois to the list of visitors to see my Papa. Does that answer your question, Nurse Blackwood?"

"You do realize his Highness is very sick."

"I'm his daughter, who better to know his condition?"

"Well, this must be a first from you. Don't you usually spend most of your time partying and drinking? It must be an embarrassment for His Highness to have you alive when Prince Rupert is dead."

Sophia wasn't sure who was most amazed by the vitriolic words, herself or the woman speaking.

"How dare you!" Abby softly spoke. Yet the words had a power that demanded notice.

"How dare I? Don't tell me you are one of her party friends? We deserve so much more than wasters heading our country."

Abby unclasped Sophia's hand and moved within inches of the nurse, who didn't look the least bit intimidated.

"If I hear any more hurtful words from your mouth, I'll personally see to it that you need to see a dentist."

Sophia suppressed a giggle but kept her best bland look. Nurse Blackwood, this time, did appear rattled. Without another word, she stormed down the corridor.

"Well, I hope I never upset you, Abby, because you certainly put the dragon nurse in her place."

Abby frowned. "Oh no, did I go over the top? I'm so sorry, I didn't want to embarrass you."

Sophia shook her head. Then she looked around, and there wasn't anyone in their vicinity. She gave Abby a snatched kiss and winked. "Definitely later."

Abby blushed, shuffling her feet.

"Abby, please come see Papa. I'm sure he will be happy to see you."

"Oh, I don't think I want to intrude. I just thought Henry might be a welcome sight for His Highness."

"Is that all?" Sophia softly asked. She watched a puzzled expression soften Abby's features. "I understand, Abby. I suspect you have a lot of work to catch up on. I have selfishly taken over your life recently. Turkeys, chickens, cows, perhaps?" Sophia smiled and took Abby's hand.

"Yes, turkeys and chickens for sure." Abby grinned.

"I will expect the grand tour of your…estate, Ms. Abby Ranger." She bowed her head. "At a time suitable to you."

A cough behind them dragged their attention to Henry, who was standing at the entrance to her father's room.

"Is something wrong? My Papa isn't getting worse…"

"No, Your Highness. In fact, he is in good spirits. He asked if you were going to return."

"Yes, immediately." Sophia turned to Abby. "Thank you." She was about to head for her father's room when Henry moved closer.

Henry stood for a few moments and then spoke. "You might as well admit that she's the one."

"Pardon, Henry?"

He moved closer to Abby. "Our Princess will give you a run for your money, that's a certainty. It will be worth it. Though I know you've worked that one out yourself. Sometimes dreams we have as children come true, Abigail." He smiled and headed back to His Highness's room.

CHAPTER TWENTY-FOUR

Abby drifted back to her old mud-covered Land Rover, and opening the door, she settled inside and stared out of the windscreen. Henry's words floated in her mind. *Sometimes dreams we have as children come true.* What did that mean?

Then she thought about her anger towards the nurse. Damn, I was over the top. Maybe I need to apologize. She shuffled in her seat. No! There was no need to say the things she said. If that's good bedside practice, she needs to find another profession. Drumming her fingers on the steering wheel, she sighed.

"I need to see Mom." Switching on the engine, she headed for home.

†

Jenny Ranger wondered how Abby and the Princess were getting on. She fervently hoped that Abby would put her shyness aside and contemplate taking Her Highness seriously. Her daughter's stubbornness had been a point of contention in the family, especially as a teenager. Only her dad could ever get her to do something she resisted. That option wasn't on the table anymore. Paul had been such a caring man. He'd understood Abby so well. Both of their girls.

The screech of wheels on the gravel drive near the kitchen doorway drew her attention. She knit your brow and peeked out of the window. "Abby?" The dusty Land Rover, her late husband's favorite vehicle, stopped, and Abby alighted from the SUV.

"Oh no, what's wrong now?" She rushed to the door and opened it as Abby was about to reach for the handle.

"Whoa, Mom, do you have second sight?" Abby chuckled and entered.

"No. I thought you were with Her Highness?"

"I was. She's with His Highness at the hospital. I left her and Henry at his bedside."

Jenny paled and placed a hand to her mouth. Abby shook her head.

"He's doing well. I took Henry there after the Princess left the farm. I figured they both needed him there."

Jenny heaved a sigh of relief. "Thank goodness, we've had enough tragedy this year."

Abby nodded and wrapped her in a bear hug. The hug went on for what seemed like minutes but was only a few seconds.

"Are you okay?"

"Yes, more than okay. I need to ask you some questions. Can we talk?'

Jenny felt her heart lift. Her daughter's smile lit up the shadowy corridor.

"Of course. I'm intrigued."

†

Abby smiled as her mom placed a hot mug of tea in front of her, and then she joined her at their kitchen table. She sipped the tea, wrapping her hands around her favorite mug. The words on it had always made her smile: *I'm the biggest mug around. I dare you disagree with me, teacup!* Her dad had bought it for her. Mom always insisted they drink from teacups, until her dad had given her the mug when she was twenty-one. Almost two decades later, it was still the best birthday present she had ever been given. Although the words had faded after many washes, they would never fade in her memory.

Her mom gave her a fake cough to draw her attention. "Sorry, Mom. I was miles away."

"I could see that. You wanted to talk?"

Abby took another sip of the hot tea, catching her mom's gaze. "I'm going to ask Her Highness to marry me again." Abby was sure her mom was about to expire in front of her.

"Oh my god, Abby. I only left you and the Princess alone for less than twenty-four hours." Jenny gushed. "Of course, if you are sure and really love her."

"I do love her. I think she loves me, too. But..."

"But? There should be no but, Abby. How can there be?"

"The Crown Prince has asked her to marry a commoner, or she loses the chance to be our next head of state. I was wondering…"

"No, no, Abby, don't wonder." Her mom stood and walked around the table to place a hand on her chest. "Here, Abby, here. The heart will always win out. The only thing you must feel is, is she the one?"

Abby clutched her mug and became pensive.

"I bet you wish your dad were here now instead of me."

Abby's eyebrows took off to the moon. "No, no." She looked at the knowing expression on her mom's face. "I miss Dad more than I say. It isn't that. I don't…"

Her mom wrapped her in a tight hug. Then kissed the top of her head. "My wonderful Abby, I miss him, too. Though you do know he wouldn't approve."

Abby sighed. "Yes. He wasn't a royalist. I don't understand why he kept doing the traditional stuff. I asked him once."

"What did he say?" Her mom took her hand and squeezed it.

"He met the love of his life. Who loved the royal family. She gave him another focus. Her life became his. Nothing else mattered." Abby watched as tears ran down her mother's cheeks. "I'm sorry, Mom."

"No, no. There have been times over the years that I wondered if he regretted his decision. I now know the answer." She wiped away the tears."

"Henry said something I didn't understand at the hospital."

"Really, what?"

"Sometimes dreams we have as children come true. What does that mean?"

"All about context, I'm sure."

"He seemed to imply that I've expressed a situation about myself and Her Highness getting together. I never have. At least until recent times."

"I'm sure you are overthinking this. He was talking about when you were a child."

Abby raised her head and glared at her mother. "I said what as a child?"

"Darling, it doesn't matter."

"It does to me. Especially as Henry mentioned it." Abby sharply replied.

"Henry probably said something out of context."

"Mom, you've said that twice. What does he know that I don't? Or can't remember."

Abby watched as her mom sipped her tea, then faced her. "You have always loved Her Highness, Abby. We almost lost you when you saved her from the fountain in front of the castle."

Abby frowned. "I don't remember that."

"You were twelve, Her Highness was six. You had a heavy cold. Didn't stop you from getting chilled to the bone to save the Princess. It was touch-and-go whether you survived. All you kept asking in your fever, 'Is the little Princess safe?'"

Abby bit her bottom lip. *Surely, I'd remember that*. "I really don't recall. Why is that?"

"You were sick for a few weeks afterward. Abby, why does this matter?"

"Because you and Henry know and maybe others. I don't want to be a laughingstock."

"Love, no one is laughing. We all love you and think it's wonderful if your dream comes true. Your dad would have had a sweepstake on the date."

"Dad thought it was a good idea?"

"Well, he figured if his Abby wanted something, she would get it in the end."

"He would have hated having a formal dinner at the castle. Can you imagine him all dressed up?"

Jenny grinned. "Well, you do take after your father in that respect."

Abby laughed and drank from her mug. "If it goes how I hope it does, I'll need a lot of help."

"Oh, Abby, you will have a whole royal staff to assist you."

"Mom, I'm excited."

"Excited is the start of something wonderful, love."

Abby's expression sobered. "We still haven't talked about my trip and the news I have."

Her mother smiled. "There has been a lot going on in a very short space of time. It can't be that important."

"It is important, Mom, very. It should have been the first thing I told you before allowing my own interests to take over."

"Then tell me now." Jenny smiled as she lifted her teacup to her lips.

"Beth had a baby a few months after she arrived in America."

A choking sound emanated from her mother, and Abby ran around the table and held her mom. "Are you okay? I'm sorry. I should have…"

"No." A hand was waved in her face. "Tell me more."

Abby didn't want to say anything as she saw her mother's anguished features.

"Abby, tell me." Jenny clutched Abby's hand tightly.

"I've got a sketchy story for the first three years. Beth travelled around a lot. When COVID hit, she was near a small town in Oklahoma. Beth and her child were taken in by a local ranch owner to help in the kitchen. She contracted COVID weeks before they found a vaccine."

Her mother moaned. Abby blinked back tears as she spoke. The first time she heard the story, she had run to the bathroom and burst out crying. "Shall we take a break?"

"No. Please, Abby, continue." Tears streamed down her mom's cheeks.

"Beth…died of breathing difficulties a week later." Abby drew in a shallow breath. "She's buried on the rancher's property in his family plot. They didn't know anything about her background." Her hand was gripped so hard she thought the blood would stop.

"What about Beth's baby?"

Abby gave a weak smile. "A girl. Jennifer." Her mom sobbed. "She's being taken care of by the rancher. His name is Charles Leeston. He has no family of his own."

"Have you seen her?"

"Not yet. I saw a lawyer in New York who told me to get together various official documents to prove who I was, and that Beth was family. He's waiting for me to give the green light, and he will set up a meeting."

"Your dad was right all along, "Jenny sobbed. "He knew something was wrong when she left, but she refused to say. I always thought Beth was wayward."

Abby gently placed an arm across her mom's shoulders. "I'll contact the lawyer tomorrow. Do you want to travel with me?"

There were a few moments of silence between them. "I want to say yes, but…"

"I know." Abby nodded.

"I have a granddaughter, and you have a niece, Abby. Out of tragedy there comes hope."

Abby watched her mom become more excited. "How about I brew us another pot of tea?" Abby didn't wait for a reply and moved toward the kettle. Switching on the machine, she contemplated what to do. Sophia needed her. Her mom wanted to see her granddaughter even if she hadn't said as much, and then there was the farm. *I can't be in three places at once.* Davy would take over the farm; that was a given. Then how would she choose between her family commitments and her own life with Sophia. She wiped her forehead.

"Your dad always wanted grandchildren."

Abby sucked in a deep breath. Decision made. "I know."

†

Sophia smiled as she left her father's room. Then her attention was caught by a woman crying, seated on a chair outside the person's room she had tentatively investigated earlier. *Damn, it can't be good.* Walking closer, she was sure the woman was familiar. Then the elevator door opened, and she stopped dead in her tracks. Claire's parents.

"Your Highness. It is good to see you." Claire's mother rushed over and hugged her tight.

"Baroness, I'm not quite sure…"

"They say my baby will not survive." The words were engulfed by sobs.

Sophia frowned, then caught the glance of the woman in tears beside the room… *Jean.*

Her heart did so many somersaults, she thought maybe she should be attached to an EKG machine. Pulling gently away from Claire's mother, she focused on the room, which was filled with nursing staff.

"Who is the relative here?" Nurse 'Dragon' Blackstone growled out. Their eyes clashed.

"I'm her mother, and this is her father."

Baron Demeter clutched the outstretched hand of his wife.

"You can enter. You will need masks."

Sophia watched as Claire's parents followed the nurse. She wasn't sure what to do.

"I guess I won't see her before she goes."

The sad words reached Sophia, and she looked at Jean. "What happened?"

"COVID, the new strain. You know Claire. She doesn't give a damn about protecting herself from the virus. She appeared okay when I left her. I should have known. She was coughing." Jean began to cry.

Sophia took the seat next to her. "I don't think this is the end, Jean. Claire is made of hardy stuff. Didn't you see her parents? Scary, right?"

Jean nodded. "I love her. I want to spend my life with her."

Sophia sighed. For the first time in her life, she knew what those simple words meant.

"Then let's tell her."

"It's only family. I'm hardly that."

"Oh, well, I guess I need to use the royal card." She stood and held out her hand. "Jean, let's tell Claire how we feel."

†

Abby stood in the hall of the castle. Sophia had said she wanted to speak with her urgently. Closing her eyes, she allowed the whole world around her to disappear. It had been a godsend on several occasions when things overwhelmed her. She wasn't like her sister, who had been very selfish, at least in her eyes. The thought of Beth agitated her even more. She should be with her mother, mourning Beth. Opening her eyes, she considered going back home. The world stopped turning as she watched her Princess descend the staircase. Sophia was dressed in a simple, light beige blouse that opened at the neck, revealing perfectly smooth, slightly tanned skin. Abby had to cross her legs as she reacted to the sight; she had kissed the breasts teasing the onlooker.

"Abby, have I got a lot to tell you." Sophia appeared to glide down the rest of the stairs and then stood before her. "I'm so glad you are here." Abby was engulfed in a tight embrace, and then soft lips captured hers for a few seconds.

"I'm glad to be here. I have some news, too." Abby felt like a fool for not saying something clever instead of repeating what Sophia had said.

"Let's go to my office." Sophia grabbed her hand, and they entered the third door in the hallway.

Abby meekly followed. That and holding hands with her Princess wasn't a shabby thing. Once inside the room, her hand was released, Sophia headed for the large desk, and sat behind the chair. Abby stood, pretty much where Sophia had left her.

"Abby. My best friend, Claire, is in serious condition, on the same unit as Papa."

Abby frowned. "I'm sorry to hear this. Will Claire be okay?"

"Yes, yes. I hope so. Though I do not know for sure. If we all want it to happen, it will, right?"

"Sometimes." Abby, now more than anything, wished she had left for home to console her mom.

"Abby." Sophia stood and walked around the desk and stood inches from her.

"Yes, Sophia." Abby was once again engulfed in a hug.

"I love you, Abigail Ranger." Tears fell, and Abby shifted so that she could comfort her Princess.

"I love you too, Sophia." She held the small shoulders closer. "I'm sure Claire will recover. What is her illness?"

"COVID, another new strain. I told her she needed to take better care of herself, but she insisted that COVID was a fiction." A deep sob followed her reply. Sophia shook her head. "I can't blame her or others for thinking the same thing. It didn't affect any of my family or friends."

Abby sucked in a deep breath, and her eyes filled with unshed tears. "Then you were very fortunate. What have the doctors said about Claire's condition?"

"They called her parents and said the situation was dire." Sophia sank her head on Abby's broad shoulder. "I don't know what I will do if she dies."

Abby didn't have a reply. This was a big thing in Sophia's life, but the way she was acting was like it could simply be waved away, and everything would be as it was. Life wasn't easy; situations happened, and you had to deal with them.

"Abby, I did a good thing at the hospital. Do you recall that reporter, Jean something or other, who attached herself to Claire?"

"Yes."

"She was there at the hospital. They wouldn't allow her to see Claire. She wasn't family. I made that happen. I thought if it was you outside my hospital room and they wouldn't let you in to see me, that would be unconscionable." Sophia kissed her cheek.

Abby's heart lifted. "How about I call Henry at the hospital. He will inform us of any changes to your father and Claire."

Sophia smiled. "You are a very sympathetic woman. Why are you still available?"

"Maybe I'm elusive." Abby chuckled. "Though I thought I wasn't."

Sophia grinned. "Elusive, I like that. A challenge."

Abby dropped her gaze. Then she looked directly into blue eyes that entranced her. "Life is the biggest challenge."

Sophia frowned. "Indeed, it is. I recall earlier that you had news. I took over the conversation. I'm sorry. Please tell me."

"I think this is a conversation for another day, Sophia. Too much is going on in your life now."

Sophia pulled away. "Abby, something is always going on in my life. It isn't going to change. Perhaps it may get worse. Please, Abby, tell me."

Abby kissed Sophia's lips. "You need some rest; it's been a heck of a few days."

"Abby, you are being evasive. What is your news?"

Abby frowned. "Family stuff. Nothing for you to worry about. I love you. Please try to get some sleep."

"You would confide in me if it was important?"

"Sleep well, Sophia. Good night."

"I thought that we…"

Abby placed a kiss on her lips and moved away. "Later," she whispered as she left the room.

Abby retreated from the castle as fast as she could and headed for the garden entrance to the farm. Her steps felt like lead as she headed home. She had just lied to the love of her life.

†

Sophia was frustrated because she had hoped to spend, if not the night with Abby intimately, at least to be surrounded in her embrace. Why was Abby so sad? *She is right, of course, as usual, it is all about me. I need to address this.* Pacing the room, she was interrupted by a resounding knock on the door. "Enter."

Charlotte entered. “Your Highness, the news media is inundating the switchboard about the Crown Prince.”

Sophia glared at the woman. “Make something up, that’s your job, right?”

The woman dropped her gaze and softly replied, “It isn’t wise to make up a story, Your Highness.”

Sophia hissed through her teeth. “You are right, it isn’t. His Highness has had a mild heart attack. He is well taken care of. We expect him home in a few days.” She perched on the edge of her desk.

“Thank you. All the staff wish His Highness a full recovery.”

“Yes, I’m sure. Is there anything else?”

“We had planned to discuss your diary for next week. However, it is understandable if you don’t want to currently.”

“No, I don’t want to.” Charlotte turned away. “But that isn’t my answer. The world goes on even though situations may change, and I must continue my duties.”

“I’m sure people would understand if you couldn’t make some of the meetings and events.”

“They might. My papa, on the other hand, would not think of it. Tradition and all that.”

Charlotte nodded. “Traditions change or can.”

Sophia sighed. “Perhaps. I’d like to ask you a question if you don’t mind?”

“You may ask whatever you want, Your Highness.”

“You’re aware of my relationship with Abigail Ranger from the farm next door.”

“Yes.”

“What do you know about the family?” Sophia realized as soon as she spoke that perhaps this wasn’t a wise conversation. *Too late*!

"The family has been tenants of your family for centuries, not sure how many. Jenny is the current legitimate tenant of the farm title. They bring daily produce to the kitchen. Sometimes it's hard to remember that they aren't part of the royal household."

"Oh, pretty normal then." Sophia slipped off the desk and turned to the window.

"Well, they have had their fair share of tragedy in recent years. Abby's father died of COVID. The youngest daughter left abruptly to travel five or six years ago, and she hasn't returned. They don't talk about themselves much, at least not in a gossipy way. I'm sure I don't need to tell you this though." Sophia closed her eyes, thankful that the woman in the room with her couldn't see her expression.

"No, no, you don't." Her reply sounded hoarse to Sophia, but apparently it wasn't noticeable to the PA.

"Shall I arrive at nine am?"

"Yes, and thank you, Charlotte."

The door creaked open and then shut with a whisper.

Abby's words now swam in front of her. *Then you were very fortunate*. "I'm so sorry, Abby."

CHAPTER TWENTY-FIVE

Sophia paced her office. The local tabloids on her desk were full of her father's illness. The more inventive gave odds on his survival and, of course, who would inherit the title. Then, of course, her picture was front and center, mostly unflattering images when she'd been drunk or obnoxious to a reporter. Nothing in the past had bothered her, and in some instances, it was a correct representation. Privilege and a royal title had a habit of diluting all the bad reports, and people seemed to be forgiving. *If the worst scenario happened, am I ready? Damn you, Rupert, you had all the training. I can't even get the woman I love to agree to marry me. How the hell can Papa expect me to be the Head of State on his demise?*

A knock on the door made her jump. "Enter." Her heart soared as Abby entered.

Sophia wanted to run over and be engulfed in a bear hug that only Abby gave. Instead, she smiled. "Thank you, Abby, for indulging me and interrupting your daily routine." Abby didn't move farther into the room; she just stood by the closed door. *Absolutely bloody beautiful, even if a little austere.*

"Princess, your PA said it was urgent. Your father isn't worse?"

Sophia shook her head. "No, I have been reliably informed by Henry that he will be home tomorrow."

"Wonderful." Abby smiled and then looked down at her feet. "Your friend?"

"Thank you for asking. Claire isn't out of the woods yet, but apparently, she has turned a corner for the better. I will be visiting them both this evening after normal visiting hours have concluded."

"I'm glad. There has been too much sorrow in the past few years." Abby caught Sophia's gaze.

Sophia closed the distance between them. "I'm a selfish, entitled, spoilt, going-on arrogant, not to mention a royal princess." She saw Abby's eyebrows hit the roof. "We both know it. Hell," she waved a hand at the desk with the newspapers. "The tabloids are having a field day. On how I can possibly take over from my papa."

"Princess…" Sophia placed a finger on Abby's lips.

"It wasn't a question, Abby. It is a fact. I'm not able to take over from my papa. Even when it is time. I may never be."

"I'm sure you will have gained many years of experience under your father's tutelage before that time occurs."

Sophia smiled. "I love your positive view…except."

Abby frowned. "Except?" Sophia gently touched the furrowed lines.

"Without you by my side, I will be a hollow vessel doing my duty."

"I don't understand?"

"It's simple, Abby. I love you and I want you to be my wife." Abby's eyes flared. "I know you probably think I'm the most selfish person you have ever met. For you, Abby, I'll do my best to be good enough." Sophia shrugged with a slight smile. "I'm sorry, I am an entitled bitch who hasn't taken the time to learn about your family." Abby frowned, and Sophia smoothed away the creases. "Truthfully, I don't care about your family. At least they may hate me, or like me, or just put up with me. It doesn't matter. I care about you and how you feel about me, about us. I'm asking you to be my wife with all the crap that goes with being related to my family house." Sophia sucked in a deep breath, waiting for a reply.

The silence stretched between them. Abby's expression was nondescript.

Sophia wasn't sure if she had heard the words. "I guess my pitch wasn't good enough. Thank you, Abby, for pandering to me. I promise not to…"

Abby engulfed her in an embrace that would stay with her for the rest of her life. Then those luscious lips kissed hers.

When they came up for air, she stared into heaven. "I do love you, Abigail Ranger."

Abby released her and dropped to one knee. "I love you, Sophia Osric. Please accept my offer of marriage."

Sophia knew, at that moment, this was her future. "I think I asked first."

They both laughed.

"Yes."

"Yes."

Sophia held out her hand and pulled Abby toward her. "My PA said to me today that if I didn't take you off the available list, she definitely would try."

Abby blushed. “I don’t think I’ve even had a conversation with her.”

Sophia laughed and gently kissed her lips. “You are a very special woman, Abigail Ranger. I’m honored that you want to attach yourself to me, with all my faults.”

“I have faults, too.”

Sophia nibbled gently at Abby’s lips. “I’m sure you do. Abby, I must ask this, it’s tradition.”

“Okay.”

Sophia grinned. “Are you a virgin?” The red that stained Abby’s cheeks was delightful, but she saw anxiety too, and that wasn’t her intention. “I’m sorry, Abby, in today’s world, that’s a total no-no question. I don’t even know why I asked.”

“Are you?”

Sophia laughed as she snuggled into Abby’s neck. “Nope.”

“So, why ask me?”

“I was being silly. Hey, traditionally, you couldn’t marry the heir or heiress to the principality unless you were a virgin.”

“Is that still a tradition or prerequisite?”

“Of course not. Abby, these days no one abstains from sex if the right person at the right time turns up, even if it’s just a one-off.”

Abby moved so that they were face-to-face. “I have.”

Those two words staggered Sophia. “You are a virgin?”

“Yes.”

Sophia was blown away. She moved to look directly into Abby’s eyes. “I…I’m lost for words.”

Abby shrugged.

“Have you never fallen in love or wanted to experience lovemaking with anyone?”

"Sometimes. I'm not a cold fish. I just wanted the person I loved enough to marry to have that gift.

"Gift, my god, Abby. This is the decade or several decades where…fuck. Sorry, wrong word. "Sophia shook her head. "I don't even know what to say." She grasped Abby's hand and kissed it.

"Do you still want to marry me?" Abby's expression was pensive.

Sophia drew Abby's head closer and kissed her gently. "I think the question is, do you still want to marry me?"

Abby smiled. "Every second of every minute to infinity."

Sophia cried.

"I'm sorry, did I say something…?"

Sophia dragged her close and ended the sentence with a long kiss. When they came up for air, Sophia smoothed Abby's furrowed brow. "I will promise you, Abigail Ranger, if you marry me, I will love you until infinity.

A knock on the door drew them apart.

"Sorry, I have duties."

Abby whispered. "My Princess, you are always going to have duties. Have a wonderful day."

"You have duties, too. Perhaps, if you aren't too tired, you might accompany me to see my papa and Claire this evening?"

"I will never be too tired to accept a request from my Princess. What time?"

"Pick me up at eight-thirty?"

Abby grinned. "Yes, my Princess."

Sophia laughed, drew Abby close, and kissed her. "I love you."

"Glad to hear that." Abby walked toward the door and opened it. "Ms. Debussy, her Highness is expecting you." She disappeared.

"Ah, the Women's Guild. They do know it's me presenting the trophy and not my papa?"

"They will when you get there." Charlotte looked down at her tablet.

Sophia smiled. "I like that. However, there is another matter that we may need to ponder."

"Princess?"

"Abigail Ranger and I are unofficially engaged. How do you see this playing out on social media?"

†

Abby sat at the end of her bed as numerous situations, going through her head, made it ache. The choices were going to be even harder. Did she just leave and not tell Sophia why? Her mom had been insistent that they keep the situation low profile. She sank backwards and lay on the bed. *I need a doppelganger*. She closed her eyes.

Her phone rang.

"Hi?" Abby listened intently.

"Thank you. I will be on the next available flight."

She disconnected the call and sat upright. "I need to tell Sophia."

†

Jenny Ranger arrived home and placed the groceries she'd bargained for at the castle on the floor. Abby's favorite coat and boots were still in the hall. She glanced at her watch; it was ten-thirty.

"Abby?" The silence went on for a few seconds. "Abby, are you here?" Jenny went to the kitchen. No one was there.

She went to the kettle and checked if it needed water. Refilling the kettle, she switched it on.

The door opened, and Abby appeared. She didn't look happy.

"Hey, darling, what are you doing here at this time of the day?"

"Mom, stuff is happening."

Jenny frowned. "Well, I know that when you aren't out doing farm things." Abby's expression became gloomy. "Darling, stuff might be good and bad. Tell me."

Abby sank into the nearest chair. "I've booked a flight to the US for tomorrow."

"You had news from the lawyer?"

"Yes. Mr. Charles Leeston has agreed to meet me. On his terms. I need to be there in three days. The lawyer said it's best we go immediately in case he changes his mind."

"He can't do that; we are family."

"He can apparently. I need to do this for the family."

Jenny wrapped her arms around Abby. "It's probably good that you and the Princess have gone different ways."

"That's just it, we haven't. In fact, we are engaged for real this time, Mom. How do I tell her that I have to leave? She will probably think I'm cutting loose again."

Jenny held her daughter, who began to cry. In all her years, she had never come across a dilemma like this. "Have you told her of our situation with Beth and the child?"

"No. I was going to, and then, well, the situation happened with the Crown Prince."

Jenny held her daughter tighter, then gently withdrew a little to lift her chin so that they looked at each other.

"Abby, this is a momentous occasion, getting engaged for anyone but to a Princess. You need to do what is right for you, not the family. Beth's daughter will wait another few months. I'm sure Mr. Leeston will understand if you explain your circumstances. Or perhaps I could go." As Jenny said the words, her heart dipped. The thought of flying was torture. She hated flying.

"I made the decision to continue Dad's quest to find out what happened to Beth. It's important I follow it through. I will speak with Sophia. I'm sure she will understand."

Jenny nodded. Her heart warmed that Abby called her Sophia, not Princess. "A good idea, and now those chickens?"

Jenny hugged Abby, and they both laughed.

"Yes, those darn chickens."

†

Charlotte Debussy couldn't contain her excitement for another second. She gave the biggest whoop of joy she was capable of and, although alone in her small office, she was sure it could be heard around the whole castle.

With a wide grin, she began typing an official announcement, and an hour later, it had been approved via email by the Princess.

She looked it over one more time, finger poised over the send button to the world media.

Princess Sophia Osric and Abigail Ranger Announce Engagement

Her Royal Highness Princess Sophia and Abigail Ranger are delighted to announce their engagement. The couple have been dating for a short time, though they have known each other since they were children. Abigail Ranger is an Agriculturist.

The engagement took place at Osric Castle yesterday.

The couple plan to marry as soon as His Highness the Crown Prince can attend.

Media Contact: Charlotte Debussy Public Relations Officer, CDebussy@osric.com

"Looks good." She pressed send.

Sitting back in her chair, she now had to find out as much background as possible about the Ranger family. "They won't have any skeletons in any cupboards, or we would have known about it by now."

Her email began to go ballistic.

Grinning, she opened the first one. "I love my job."

Chapter Twenty-six

Abby received a text from Sophia asking if she was still able to accompany her to visit the hospital. A no-brainer, she'd attend regardless of what was going on in her world. She looked down at her attire and shook her head. *How can a princess love me*? The words revolved constantly in her head as she arrived home. Without even a hello, her mom dragged her to the TV.

"Abby, you made headline news."

Abby frowned and looked at the TV screen. Sure enough, an image of Sophia and a grainy one of her were paraded on screen.

"Looks like it."

Jenny Ranger chuckled. "You are famous, my darling. How does that feel?"

Abby once again looked at her work gear and wondered, *Why me*? "Well, at least it's in the open now."

You are so selfless." They both watched the evening newscast. Lots of videos and images of the royal family, the recent tragedy of Prince Rupert, and the Crown Princes's ill health were all featured.

"I need a shower. I'm going to visit the hospital with Sophia after hours."

"I thought you had an early flight in the morning?"

"Yep, but Sophia doesn't know that." Abby walked toward the door, and the words from the TV struck like lightning.

Tomorrow, her Highness and her new fiancée will be live for an interview.

She turned and looked at her mom, who shrugged her shoulders

"Damn, don't I have any say in this?" She left the room abruptly. She was angry more with herself than about not being consulted. She should have spoken to Sophia sooner.

†

Sophia stood beside her Jaguar. She was reminded of another occasion not so long ago, and it made her smile. The crunch of the gravel on the driveway drew her attention to the person who moved closer. Her heart skipped several beats.

"Abby, I know you must be tired, but I'm grateful you want to attend with me." Abby stopped a few feet away. Sophia was puzzled. "You do want to accompany me?"

"I do," Abby replied.

"Great. It's a momentous time. We go as an engaged couple officially. Papa will be so pleased." Abby didn't move. "You will need to get in the car, Abby, or are you going to make us both walk?" Sophia laughed.

Abby spoke. "I saw the TV news tonight."

"I know. Charlotte is doing a great PR job."

"How do you know that I'm free for an interview tomorrow?"

Sophia frowned.

"The presenter said that we are going to do a live interview tomorrow?"

"If that's what she's arranged, great."

"I was never consulted."

Sophia smiled. "Trust me, it's great publicity for the country and us. Abby, is this a problem?"

"Actually, yes. I told you I had family issues."

Sophia nodded." Yes, but you indicated they could wait."

"I have a flight booked to the USA tomorrow at six am. At least the first flight."

Sophia didn't reply immediately. *She's only just come back home. What could be so important?* Then she stared at Abby and gave a tight smile. "Are you jilting me?" The old-fashioned term had her smiling inwardly. However, it did motivate Abby, who closed the distance between them.

"I would never do that. I love you."

The impassioned words flooded Sophia. "It's almost nine, and after our visit to the hospital, I'm sure it will be close to midnight. I think it best that I go alone."

"I made a promise, and I never negate a promise. I want to support you, Sophia."

Sophia wasn't used to feeling bad about someone else's self-sacrifice, but right now she felt like the worst person in the world. There was only one thing for it. She reached for Abby and dragged her into a kiss.

When they came up for air, Sophia rested her head on Abby's shoulder. "I love you, Abby, and I will absolve you of your promise this evening if you tell me why you are leaving so suddenly."

Sophia caught Abby blush from the corner of her eye..

"I'd rather spend the next few hours with you. I will be away for at least ten days, and it will comfort me."

Sophia snuck a sweet kiss. "Then we must go so that you can at least get a few hours of sleep before your trip."

"Thank you, but being with you is as good as any rest."

Sophia grinned and opened the driver's door. Abby smiled and went toward the passenger door.

†

The visit with her papa and Claire had been better than Sophia expected. Both had been tired, Claire more so. Her papa was happy that they had resolved their issues and were now officially engaged. He had declared that once he was home and fit enough, there would be a magnificent engagement party. Sophia had watched Abby's expression turn from pleased to trepidation. Her love was not a party girl, and that was just fine with her. Claire was drifting in and out of sleep, but at least it was a good sleep. Abby did not have time for her friend. Claire was a good friend when she didn't drink too much. Sophia had been surprised that Abby had conversed convivially with her friend.

Now she sat facing her steering wheel as Abby climbed in next to her.

"They both look better," Abby said, buckling in."

"Yes, Papa more so. Claire will take a little longer, I believe."

Abby placed a hand on hers. "They will both be well by the time I return."

Those words defeated Sophia. "Abby, if I asked you not to go, what would you say?"

Abby frowned. "It's only ten days."

"I guess I'm being me. Selfish as always." Abby took her face between her hands and kissed her.

"Never, I'm glad you want me around. I need to tell you why I'm leaving. Shall we go for a coffee somewhere?"

Sophia sighed. "Abby, it's a quarter after eleven. Don't you need at least a few hours' sleep?"

"Nope, if I can have more time with you."

Her heart soared in her chest. "How can I resist that. I know a place." Sophia snatched a kiss and then set the car in motion.

†

Abby was pleasantly surprised when they turned up at a tired-looking cafe. As they entered, a nun came out of nowhere and greeted Sophia.

"This isn't your usual time of the day, Princess." The older woman chuckled. Then she gazed at Abby.

"Ah, now I know why. This must be your new fiancée. Many congratulations to both of you."

Abby smiled. "Thank you." She watched as Sophia nodded.

"Thank you, Sister."

Their appearance was finally beginning to be noticed by the others in the room, and before they had time to take a seat, there was thunderous applause. Abby halted, trapped in the sudden accolade. Then Sophia took her hand.

"This way, Abby. I did say your life was never going to be the same again."

They took a seat in the far corner of the room.

Still in a state of surprise, Abby looked around the room. The vast majority of the customers were what you would call less than wealthy.

"Out with it?" Sophia chuckled as she touched Abby's hand on the table and threaded their fingers together.

Abby bit her lip. "I guess I wasn't expecting that."

"Oh, you will be getting more and more as the days go forward. When the wedding is announced, it will go into overdrive."

Abby was speechless.

"Abby, all you have to remember is that I love you. Now I can say the coffee here is delicious, or tea if you prefer. Sister Cathleen makes a mean dark brew that would put hair on your chest. Though I'd rather it didn't in your case."

Abby laughed, and Sophia grinned.

"How do you know this place?"

Sophia shrugged. "A while ago, I came across it when I was under the influence of alcohol and needed to have a huge amount of caffeine at a godforsaken hour in the morning." Sophia paused and looked around. "It saved me that day. I've been a semi-regular ever since. If you are hungry, I can recommend…"

"I need to explain why I'm leaving."

"Of course."

"My sister, Beth."

"I wasn't aware you had a sister?" Sophia closed her eyes, a slight lie. Then she felt a strong hand grasp hers.

"I would not expect you to know. She left for America for a great adventure six years ago."

"Abby, I should know at least if you have siblings."

"Sophia, my sister died of COVID three years ago." Abby's voice softened. "As it turns out, she died a week after Dad. Ironic, really."

Sophia gripped her hand as tears glimmered in her eyes. "I…I don't know what to say."

"It's okay, Mom and I came to terms with Dad's death. Beth is a different matter."

"Your mama must be devastated, poor Jenny." Sophia stood. "Coffee or tea, Abby?"

"Tea, I prefer tea." Abby absently replied.

"I will be back." Sophia moved like lightning to the counter. In what seemed like seconds, she was back.

"Well, that was quick."

Sophia shrugged, "I guess they know me, and now they know what you like to drink. It will be easy when we come here again."

Abby nodded and took Sophia's hand. "I like the sound of that." Sophia didn't take the seat opposite. Instead, she dragged the seat next to Abby. "This is even better."

Sophia glanced around and put a chaste kiss on Abby's lips. "I know."

Abby's heart was beating as hard as with any exercise she had ever encountered, and hauling bales of hay for hours was hard to beat. "I guess I should continue."

Sophia snuggled closer. "Let's just enjoy being together while the drinks arrive."

"No way I'd disagree with that." Abby welcomed the warmth of Sophia's body close to her. She stroked Sophia's silky hair and wondered if her hair was spun with gold like the story of Rapunzel.

A woman who could give Methuselah a run for his money approached the table.

Abby immediately broke contact with Sophia. As she did, she heard a small growl from her fiancée. "Hi."

"I wanted to personally wish you both a healthy and loving marriage."

Abby stood and dwarfed the woman. "Thank you. I'm sorry, I don't know your name."

The old woman began to shed tears, and Abby bit her lip. "I'm sorry, is there anything wrong?"

"No, no. It's perfect. I remember our dear Princess Adeline saying the same thing. She was such a lovely, caring person." Abby's hand was taken and dragged down with a surprisingly strong grip to allow the old woman to whisper to her. "Our Princess will be hard work but worth it. She loves you. Exactly what I told Adeline when she courted the Crown Prince."

Abby was about to speak, but the old woman moved away, and their drinks arrived. Abby regained her seat.

"You are already a favorite, Abby." Sophia took a sip from her drink.

"Maybe." Abby took the mug of tea and drank from the dark liquid after adding a dash of milk. *Whoa, that's nice.*

Silence settled between them for a few minutes.

"Beth had a baby shortly after she arrived in the US. My dad tried to keep up correspondence with her, but she never answered. He never stopped. Then COVID hit, and Dad was desperate to know that Beth was okay."

Sophia drew Abby closer.

"Dad had people looking for her, and eventually someone found a clue."

"Is that why you left before?"

"Yes."

Sophia took Abby's hand and squeezed it gently. "Go on, please."

"Eventually, it came to light about the child. I had to come home, but I had all the details of who Beth's daughter was living with and the circumstances. I've been working with a lawyer to be allowed access.

"That's why you have to go now?"

"Yes. Worse possible timing, I know. It's important to my family, especially Mom."

Sophia sighed. "We are engaged. What is important to your family is now important to mine."

Abby couldn't prevent the tears from falling. "I don't know what to say."

"Just say you love me and you will return to me."

Abby looked deep into Sophia's eyes. "I love you."

"Let's take you home. You need at least a couple of hours' sleep. Ten days, no more, right?"

Abby nodded. "Ten max."

†

Sophia hadn't wanted to let Abby out of the car, but she understood family came first. As she garaged her car, she now wondered why there hadn't been any reporters following them or attempting some kind of interruption when they left the hospital. There hadn't been anything at all.

"I can't be as important as I thought I was." She smiled. Then she withdrew her phone and called her PA. A groggy voice answered. "Charlotte, cancel the TV interview. Abby can't make it."

"Princess, it's great PR for you both and the royal family."

"I know, but Abby will be on her way to America."

"America?"

Sophia was pretty sure her PA was now out of bed.

"I don't like to ask, but has she had second thoughts?"

She couldn't blame Charlotte for thinking that, since she had done the same. "No. It is a private family matter that I neglected to inform you of."

"Will you be seeing her off at the airport? We could use…"

"No!"

"I will cancel the interview, Your Highness. Is there anything else I can help you with?"

"Maybe tomorrow at our morning meeting, you can tell me why I'm not being followed by reporters. Goodnight, Charlotte."

Sophia walked a few yards to the entrance to the castle and looked around her. The fountain was in its glory with colored lights skimming off the water. Ever since she was a child, it both scared and comforted her. She turned and withdrew her key to unlock the door, but was surprised when it opened as she was about to insert the key.

"Henry?"

"Your Highness."

Frowning, Sophia walked inside. "Do you ever sleep?" She passed him and then looked at his attire. He wasn't in his usual immaculate suit but in a rather colorful robe with matching slippers.

"Not when I'm needed."

Do I need him? Sophia contemplated that all of a few seconds. "Abby's going to the USA early morning."

Henry nodded his head. "I know. Her mother informed me this evening."

"Do you know the reason?"

"Yes. Jenny has told, in confidence, a few of the staff."

Sophia sighed. "I guess that's okay then. I'll retire now, Henry. Thank you for your concern."

"I wasn't concerned, Your Highness, you were in safe hands with Ms. Abigail Ranger. You always have been. Good night."

Sophia ascended the stairs, contemplating Henry's words. Indeed, she was safe with Abby. What did he mean, I always have been? Darn, I must be tired, thinking about stuff that isn't relevant.

CHAPTER TWENTY-SEVEN

Abby was dog tired as she sat in a cab that was taking her to the Leeston ranch. Having had only a few hours of sleep prior to setting off on this journey, she had endured four flights to reach Oklahoma City. Then a three-hour train ride took her to the town closest to the ranch. She'd arrived at ten am, and now, as she glanced at her watch, it was almost one, and she was only a short distance from her destination.

"This is the Leeston-Adair ranch."

Abby blinked the sleep away as she stared at the large iron gates with the name above. "Thank you."

"Mr. Leeston is a good guy. Very generous." They went through the open gate.

Abby nodded. "Good to know."

"Are you friends? Can't quite place your accent. Not English exactly, but you have a lilt of foreign." The driver chuckled. "Sorry, you know Americans, we have no clue, everyone outside of the US is a foreigner and speaks different."

Abby laughed. "Not English, but they have a lot of influence from that part of the world. My dad was Irish, and I live in a place you will not have heard of. It's a spec on the map."

"Sense of humor, I like that here."

Abby struggled to hold the conversation even though it wasn't difficult. "Are you from this region?"

"Born and bred. I love the seasons here. We have all four. Like you probably."

"Yes, but it can be havoc if the weather changes before you expect. I've lost a few crops to extreme weather fronts in recent years."

"Ah, a farmer."

They turned a bend and suddenly a building appeared: a single-story homestead that seemed to go on forever. It was elegantly functional, Abby figured. Her mom would love a place like this.

The car stopped, and the driver turned to her. He had a wonderful, welcoming smile she had missed when she had begun the ride.

"Call me when you need a ride back to town, though I doubt you will. Charles takes care of his visitors well. This is my card." He thrust the small white object into Abby's hand.

"Thank you. How much do I owe you?"

The man grinned, "Taken care of."

Perplexed, Abby frowned. "I don't understand."

"If you weren't welcome at Leeston-Adair, then those gates would have been shut tight. Have a good stay."

Abby climbed out of the car, still unsure. Her bag was deposited next to her. The driver climbed back into his car and sped away as she stood there speechless.

She looked around her, and for the first time in a while, she was afraid. She was in a foreign country, she hadn't booked into her hotel, and she was in a place miles from anywhere. Plus, did her phone even work out here?

A deep voice spoke. “Ms. Ranger?”

Abby turned, and the gravel on the drive protested with a minor dust bowl. “Yes.”

A man, probably in his late sixties with a weathered complexion and cool grey eyes, stared at her. Looking her over, he smiled. “I’m Charles Leeston. I can see the family resemblance.”

Abby’s fuzzy brain literally had her unable to respond.

“Please, you must be tired. Let’s go inside, and we can talk.” He took her bag and walked ahead.

Abby soundlessly followed.

†

Sophia twirled her pen around her fingers. A trick she’d learned in boarding school, it helped her when she was nervous. Almost thirty-six hours after Abby left, Sophia was wondering if she’d ever come back. Yes, she understood the reasons, but still she was anxious.

There was a knock on her door. “Enter?”

Charlotte appeared, holding her tablet as if it were a comfort blanket. It made Sophia smile and think about her own toy that merited that description. That dog-eared bear that had been with her all through her school years was even more cherished now. The stories that bear had been told over the years. *Gosh, Abby might not want to marry me.* She smiled. “Charlotte, I don’t have any appointments for another hour?”

“True, Princess. I was wondering if you might want to brainstorm the news release for Abby leaving the country. The paparazzi rats are baying at the gates.”

"Of course, the gentlemen and women of the press need their pound of flesh." Sophia sighed. "Sit."

"Thank you, Princess."

"It's a private family matter, as you know. How would you recommend I respond?"

Charlotte grinned. "Glad you asked." She flicked her finger over her tablet.

Sophia had to admit that Charlotte was becoming an invaluable member of her staff. Nothing seemed to phase her. "Great, tell me."

"Well, His Highness is coming home tomorrow, and we can shift focus to that event. Plus, your engagement so far has been low-key. Not many of the foreign press have taken it up so far. Not exactly sure why that would be." She frowned. "A bonus for us. I thought we could do an article on Abby's family roots here, and that her family has been on these lands as long as the Osric family. I figure if we release several short articles over a period, Abby will be back home. Ten days, you said, max?"

Sophia nodded. "Yes."

"When she comes home, we can have a grand engagement party, and the world will know her background for real."

"Abby isn't a party animal."

Charlotte gave her eye-to-eye contact. "She's marrying you, Your Highness. Party girl or not, Abby will have to attend social functions with you. Unless…"

"Unless what?" Sophia glared at her PA, who didn't flinch.

"This isn't real."

The three words struck Sophia like a bomb. She was lost for words. Her phone trilled. "Yes?"

"Having a bad day?"

"Abby! Where are you…no, I know that. I mean, how are you? God, it's good to hear your voice." Sophia sank back in her chair and cradled the phone close to her ear.

"Are you alone?"

"No, let me…"

"Princess, talk to Abby about my suggestion. Her word will be sacrosanct. I apologize for my earlier words."

Sophia didn't have time to speak as Charlotte left the room. "I am now. How are you?" A soft chuckle greeted the question, and Sophia felt her world was right on track again.

"Tired. It's hard work getting to places, even though they say the world is so much smaller now. Tell that to my body clock."

"I love you." Sophia wasn't sure why the words spurted out. Except it was true.

"I love you, too. I'm going to stay overnight at the ranch. Charles is a nice man."

"Have you seen your niece?"

"Nope, she's in school. That's why I'm staying overnight. I don't think I can keep up with the travelling right now, or I'll sleep through something important. How is His Highness?"

"Coming home tomorrow, and he looks well. It was a wake-up call. Though he seems happier than he has been since Rupert died."

"Your influence, I'm sure, Sophia."

Sophia smiled as she cradled her phone closer. "Maybe." The silence stretched between them. "Are you falling asleep on me?"

"Truthfully, yes, but I wanted to hear your voice."

"I love you, Abby. Go to sleep. You will be back soon, right?"

"Absolutely. I love you, my Princess." The call ended.

Sophia gazed at her phone and wished she was with Abby.

†

Abby had been given a room that was three times the size of hers at home and an en-suite. *I'm going to hate leaving here.* Her first thought was to contact the woman she loved. Sinking into the bed that had a wonderful, crocheted cover with numerous patches of wonderful colors, she commenced her call.

Five minutes later, it couldn't have been more, she settled on top of the bed. Her eyes closed, heralding much-needed sleep. Then there was a tap on the door.

"Hello?"

"Miss Jenny is home now. Mr. Charles thought you might want to know. They are in the parlor."

Thank you, yes." Abby raised her tired body up. *I can do this.* Abby straightened her crumbled clothes, opened the door, and headed down the polished wooden hallway. Her stomach lurched incessantly as she reached the door to the parlor. "God, I could do with some support right now." Tears glistened as she knocked on the door and heard a loud, "Enter." She walked inside.

Charles Leeston stood and smiled.

Abby had always thought she was a good judge of character, and she felt that this man was the genuine article, as her dad would say. She dashed away the few tears that had refused to stay put. "Hello, again."

Charles nodded and waved her forward, "Come meet Jennypenny." There was a delightful giggle from the child in the room.

"Granchy, who is this?"

"I was telling you…" He turned to Abby and shrugged.

Abby simply watched as the child moved closer. Her heart was beating overtime as the child reached her.

"Why are you crying?"

Abby wiped away the tears that continued. "You look so much like someone I love."

"Oh, who is that, Granchy?"

Charles Leeston moved closer to them both. He then lifted Jennifer into his arms. "I told you this is someone important. This is Abigail Ranger, and she is your mother's sister, your aunt."

Abby watched as Jennifer frowned.

"Remember what I told you that your mother's family do not live in this country."

"Yes, Granchy."

"Well, Abigail has travelled a long way to meet you. I think it is polite to welcome her here, don't you?" Charles slowly placed Jennifer next to Abby.

The child held out her hand. "Hello, Abigail, and welcome to the Leeston-Adair ranch."

Abby took the small hand in hers, wondering if, at six years old, she had been that cultured. She certainly knew a person who had been. "Thank you, Jennifer."

"Come sit, Abigail, you can chat with Jennypenny until dinner is called. I'll leave you to it."

"Granchy." Jennifer grabbed his leg.

"This is your aunt, Jennypenny. You are safe. Isn't that true, Abigail?"

"I'll be on my best behavior." Abby nodded toward Charles, and he smiled.

Charles kissed the top of Jennifer's head and left the room.

Jennifer moved away and hid behind the most imposing chair in the room.

"Charles, your Granchy is a nice person. He helped my sister…your mom when she was alone."

There was no noise or movement from behind the chair.

Abby sat in a chair opposite. "My dad, your grandfather, never stopped looking for your mom. That's why I'm here."

"Was she lost?"

Tears fell at the tentative question. "Perhaps. She found a wonderful place here for you."

Jennifer peered around the chair. "Mommy said that one day I would meet my real family."

Abby considered that for a few moments. It was what she and her mom wanted to hear. "Jennifer, you have a family here with Granchy. I just wanted to meet you."

Jennifer scooted around the chair and stood before her. "Do I have a grandma?"

Abby blinked back her tears. "Yes. If Granchy approves, we can have a video chat with your grandma tomorrow."

The little girl gave a whoop of delight. "Granchy loves me; he gives me everything."

Abby shrugged. "Great. So, tell me about yourself. I want all the details; do you have friends?"

Jennifer giggled. "Of course I have friends. Do you?"

Abby allowed her nervousness to dissipate. "Yes, I do."

Jennifer grinned, sat on the sofa, and pointed to the place next to her. Abby obliged.

"My best friend is a girl called Pinky."

"Pinky, what an unusual name."

Jennifer giggled. "It's not her real name. She's called Rita, but she loves pink."

"Ah, I get it, a nickname."

Jennifer turned her head a fraction. "I don't know that, I'm only six." Abby stifled an all-out laugh.

"You definitely remind me of your mom right now."

"Why?"

"She was a very precocious six-year-old, too."

Jennifer frowned. "What is preco…precon?"

"Precocious, very intelligent."

"Can you tell me stories about my mom?" Jennifer scooted closer.

"Yes. We lived on a farm, and your mom was always getting into scrapes…."

†

Sophia walked into the Women's Guild and was greeted with enthusiastic applause. Aggie Rice, the chairwoman of the guild, shook her hand and motioned for her to sit. Charlotte took the seat next to her.

"Thank you, Your Highness, for taking the time to speak with us today. I know you must be very busy, especially now with the engagement. Congratulations from all of us." Applause threatened to raise the roof.

"Thank you for having me. This is my first appearance since the news became public."

Even more applause. Sophia dropped her gaze. *Damn, am I glad I don't have a hangover.*

"Do you mind if we ask how you met your fiancée, Ms. Ranger?"

Sophia glanced at Charlotte, who rolled her eyes. "Her family have lived on the Osric lands for as many years as we have. Truthfully, I may have met her years ago and not known. We recently connected when I needed help."

A voice in the room spoke up. “Yes! It’s like something out of a storybook.”

“Abigail is definitely worthy of a fairy tale.” Charlotte nudged her slightly.

Several voices asked the same question. “When will the wedding be?”

In truth, Sophia didn’t know. She and Abby hadn’t gotten that far. Getting engaged had been one drama after another. “

“Sorry, Your Highness. Ladies, please, enough of the personal questions.” Sophia smiled at Aggie Rice. “Ladies, it’s time to show Her Highness some of the things we do for worthy causes. Who wants to start?”

Sophia looked at Charlotte, who spread her palms. Ten minutes and they were done.

†

The day dragged on incessantly, and Sophia was sure she was in a surreal world for not being a better person in her earlier life.

“Your Highness, do you mind if I add one more stop?”

Sophia groaned.

“I know it’s been a long day. Will you trust me?” Charlotte stared at her.

“Then can we go home? I’m seriously hungry. The nibbles at lunch, at that so-called upmarket restaurant, were barely edible.

Charlotte laughed. “You will like this, I promise.”

“Ten minutes tops, okay.”

Charlotte nodded, then instructed the driver to continue, and they sped off.

Sophia glanced at her social media pages as the car sped towards their next destination. The engagement was trending slowly in Europe. She saw a post from Claire.

Working through the COVID shit. Got my best girl next to me. There was a photo of her and Claire, which had been photoshopped big time.

Oh no! Claire, you promised to keep a low profile. She flicked through several other feeds. One thing Charlotte had taught her was to check certain feeds daily and others only if she wanted a punch in the stomach. Some of the evil trolls would say anything to get a hit. As she glanced at a few of those feeds, the stupid, totally incorrect media blasts about her and Abby had her wondering if Abby did social media. *God, I hope not. She'd freak!* Glancing at another feed, one she thought was, if not positive about her, at least not hateful.

Princess gets engaged; Princess is left in the lurch as new fiancée departs for a trip abroad. Either the royal publicity department didn't know this, or it was sudden. Maybe the fiancée has had second thoughts.

"We are here."

"Sure, whatever."

"Are you okay, Your Highness?"

Sophia looked up from her phone and saw their destination. "Charlotte, this is."

"Yes, your Highness."

Sophia climbed out of the vehicle, heading for the building in front of her. She looked back and smiled.

†

Abby wasn't sure who Charles was talking to when he mentioned it was time for bed. Glancing at her watch, she saw it said six-thirty.

"Granchy, do I have to go? I want to speak with Abby some more."

Charles frowned. "Jennypenny, this is your aunt. You will speak more respectfully."

Jennifer's bottom lip trembled. Then she glared at Charles. Abby couldn't stop the tears falling at the next words. "Love you, Granchy." She grinned at Abby. "Aunt Abby, will I see you for breakfast?"

Abby nodded." Yes, I wouldn't miss it."

Jennifer, with a cheerful goodnight, kissed Charles on the way out.

Charles walked slowly over to the small bar in a corner of the room. "What can I get you?"

Abby sighed. "Honestly, when you said it was time for bed, I figured you were talking to me." She laughed. "I don't drink much."

Charles laughed. "How about an early nightcap. I recommend it." He rubbed his chin. "I will pour you a glass of water, and you get some rest."

"Thank you, Charles. However, I will risk a vodka and soda."

"That I can do."

A few minutes later, Charles walked across and handed her a tall glass. Abby smiled and sipped the liquid. He then settled into a chair opposite her.

"What do you think of our Ms. Jennypenny?"

Abby grinned. "I love the nickname, rather James Bondish."

Charles gave a deep chuckle. "Absolutely. I love the Ian Fleming books." He took a drink from his shot glass. "Beth approved. In fact, she once confided that her dad would be jealous that I thought of it first."

Abby took another sip of her drink. "Dad loved the Bond movies, too." She hesitated. "Beth was always a person who did what she wanted. My father was devastated when she left. Then, when she never got in touch, it was his mission to find out why."

Charles gave her a hard stare, then a smile lightened up his eyes. "Before your sister died, she did indicate why she never contacted the family."

Abby sucked in a breath that threatened to choke her. She sipped more of the drink, but it didn't help as she coughed.

"Abigail, are you okay?"

"Yes, yes. Please, Charles, tell me more."

"Beth said she loved a person at home. It wasn't the right time, she'd been told, for their relationship to be public. She decided to apply for a green card. She said she was going to make her lover aware that it wasn't all about him, that she had choices. Beth found out she was pregnant a couple of weeks into her trip."

Abby gasped. "I don't understand. We loved her; she could have told us."

"Perhaps you were close to the father. Before you ask, she never said who he was."

Abby knew her body was calling for sleep, but her brain wouldn't give in yet.

"Did she give any indication of who the father was, other than what you've already said?"

Charles shook his head. "All I'll say is she loved him. I'm sure it's quite like I loved my wife. As far as I know, she never dated anyone while she was here."

Abby felt her heart breaking at her sister's dilemma. Who would know who was dating her sister at that time? Beth never had many friends. She was basically a loner. "This is a lot to take in, Charles." Abby stood. "Do you mind if I head off to bed? It's been a long couple of days."

Charles stood and nodded. "We have breakfast at seven-thirty. Though if you sleep in, I'll smooth it over with Jennypenny." He smiled.

"Thank you, Charles, for your kindness, and especially to Beth and Jennifer."

"It's been an honor and pleasure, believe me. Both young ladies have brought a lot of pleasure to an old man."

Abby left and returned to the bedroom she had been given. Her head was in a spin. Groaning, she collapsed on the bed. *It wasn't the right time she'd been told for their relationship to be public.* Why? Maybe he was married? Dad would have been upset for sure, but not to the extent that he wouldn't welcome her and his granddaughter home. It didn't matter how many times she pondered what the words meant; there wasn't an answer, not right now. Her eyelids drooped. Then she simply allowed the tiredness to overtake her, and she was out for the count.

†

Jenny Ranger smiled warmly as she opened the door to Princess Sophia. "I wasn't expecting you, Your Highness. You must be so busy."

Sophia smiled. "Yes, but I will always make time for my future mother-in-law."

Jenny chuckled. "Sounds rather strange, but lovely."

"Good to hear. I've had a long day of meetings and answering lots of questions about myself and Abigail. All I want now is to have a decent meal, and a glass of wine wouldn't come amiss."

"I can certainly feed you, but the wine might be a bit of a problem."

Sophia shook her head, "No, Jenny, it's okay. Chef Darrel will have my meal waiting when I arrive back."

Jenny frowned.

"Why am I here?" Sophia softly asked, and Jenny nodded. "Charlotte must have realized I needed to have a break from royal business. She didn't say where we were going, but when we arrived, it was a welcome relief.

Jenny grinned. "In that case, I shall make sure young Charlotte gets an extra portion of our free-range eggs for her breakfast. She is a very astute person."

"Yes, yes, she is. I didn't like her when she worked for Rupert, but now…now she's invaluable."

"Well, if you won't eat, how about a cup of tea, and then I'll send you off home?"

Sophia chuckled. "Tea it is. Abigail would probably have offered the same. She must take a lot of her wonderful traits from you."

"Oh, I doubt my daughter would thank you for saying that."

"Why?"

"Let's have that tea, and I'll share a family story or two."

"Wonderful, I need stories of Abigail. It will make me feel we are closer."

CHAPTER TWENTY-EIGHT

Two weeks later.

Abby listened to Charles and Jennifer chatting away on the porch below her bedroom, well, more Jennifer than Charles. The weeks she'd spent at the ranch with Charles and Jennifer had been at times sad but also extremely fulfilling. The one thing she knew as she zipped up her suitcase for her return home was that this was Jennifer's home. To wrench her from Charles and his love and those around her would be cruel. Explaining that to her mother would be hard, but there was a caveat. Charles had agreed to travel with Jennifer to see her grandmother next month. Their discussions over dinner regarding Jennifer's future had been remarkably cordial.

Charles had expected her to want to take Jennifer home, and truth be told, that had been her intention. Now, after spending time there and getting to know not only Jennifer but Charles and everyone around him, she had changed her mind. Jennifer was more Charles' kin than her own. They had both begged Abby to stay longer, but she refused. It would be nice to stay longer, but her heart needed to see Sophia, her mom, and her home.

She pulled the case off the bed and looked around the room. *I'll be back.*

†

"Shall I make the arrangements for you to greet Abigail when she arrives at the airport, Your Highness?"

Sophia considered the question carefully. "No."

Charlotte raised her eyebrows. "This would be a good publicity moment, especially as your fiancée has been away several weeks. People would expect you to be there."

"I don't care what people say, Charlotte. I've been the dutiful daughter, the dutiful Princess, even the dutiful fiancée in the last two weeks. Do I get a day off?"

Charlotte looked down at her tablet. "Her flight is due later today?"

Sophia glared at her PA. "Don't you think, I don't know that."

"Yes."

"I'm sorry, Charlotte."

Charlotte smiled. "We know that the media will be there. I know you probably prefer a private connection. I can arrange that."

"No. Let the media miss out on the reunion."

"Your Highness, they will think you don't care, and the conspiracy theorists may be proved right that the engagement is a sham."

Sophia sucked in a deep breath. "Abigail and I are meeting when she gets off the plane, but not here. I booked a flight to Paris," she glanced at her watch, "in two hours. Abigail is disembarking in Paris in four hours' time. We shall travel back home together."

Charlotte gasped. "I…I book all your flights. I don't understand?"

"Charlotte, I'm a big girl. I've been booking flights across the globe since I was fourteen. Abigail and I will have private time together. The French love a romantic tryst and can be very discreet under those circumstances."

†

Abby winced when the trolley carrying her luggage squealed like a pig as she moved along the customs line. The man behind her scowled at her. He had been moaning incessantly about the bad flight from New York, the flight attendants, food, and anything or anyone that he could. The flight had been two hours late, so that wasn't exactly untrue.

"Do you have to make that noise? It's very disturbing."

Abby turned to the man. "Do you think I have a choice?"

He stared at her and grimaced. "No need to be nasty."

"Nasty…god, that's saying something coming from you," Abby grumbled.

The man, who was taller than her, glared. "What do you mean by that?"

"I was across from you the whole flight. I've got to say I didn't know there could be so many things wrong with a flight that didn't fall out of the sky." Although she hadn't meant to say it too loudly, there were a few people nearby who laughed and even agreed.

"What the hell do you know?"

"I don't. I'm just a tired passenger wanting to go through the formalities so I can go home. What about you?"

"I'm going to send in a complaint about the airline and staff."

"What the heck are you saying? The staff were wonderful."

"They were all queer. I didn't want to eat anything they gave me."

Abby seethed. "They were lovely and very attentive. Besides, they don't prepare the food; they just reheat it."

"I thought you'd say that, you are probably one of them." There were a few gasps around them.

Clasping her hands around the suitcase trolley lever, Abby sucked in a deep breath and remained silent.

"Thought so. Touched a nerve, right? Bet the only person meeting you is a TV dinner and a cat." The man grinned.

A couple behind the man spoke. "That is totally out of order. Man, can't you just shut up and keep your bigoted opinions to yourself?"

The man turned to confront them, and Abby just wished she were home.

A customs officer approached them, "I'm looking for a passenger by the name of Abigail Ranger?"

Abby was taken aback for a moment or two. "That's me."

"May I see your passport?"

She grabbed the document and passed it over.

He grinned. "Her Highness will be happy. She's been waiting a long time." He gave her back her passport. "Please, Ms. Ranger, follow me." He opened one of the ribbons, separating areas for her to walk through.

"What's going on—why is she getting special treatment?" The obnoxious man spluttered.

The customs officer looked him over for a few moments. “Because she’s engaged to a Princess. Sir, if you want special treatment too, come this way.”

The man walked behind Abby.

“Oh no, sir. That line is for VIPs only. We need to check your bags thoroughly.” He pointed to a red line, which was longer than the one he was in. “That way, please, sir.”

Abby ignored the noise from the obnoxious traveler. Her only thought was that Sophia was here and that was all she wanted.

†

Sophia was sure she had broken some protocol rules when she had arrived and sought out the airport management to arrange for Abby’s VIP status. She had been too late for the message to be relayed to the aircraft, but customs had been alerted. She had never felt this nervous about anything.

When the door opened and Abby stood in the doorway, it took a lot of strength not to run over and enfold her in a hug. *Oh, what the hell.* With her arms around Abby’s neck, she kissed her full on the lips, regardless of anyone looking. “I love you.” There was a slow chuckle that throbbed through Abby’s body.

“I love you, too.”

Sophia released her grip and stared into the eyes of the woman who made her life complete. “I’ve arranged for a room at the airport hotel. We have three hours before our flight home.”

Abby frowned. “Why? If we only have such a short time, by the time we get there and sign in and get settled, we will be coming back?”

"I've already booked in," She withdrew the keycard from her pocket. "The hotel is ten minutes on the link from the airport.

Abby smiled. "You want to take the public link?"

"Actually, I have a car waiting for us. It will take even less time. Is that bad of me?"

Abby shook her head and smiled. "Lead the way."

Sophia laughed. "That's my Abby."

†

Abby lay in Sophia's arms on the rather nice, comfortable sofa in the large room they had entered. She wanted to ask if this was a bit over the top, but frankly, right at this minute, she didn't care. This was what she had been missing in the time she'd been away, being close to the woman she loved.

"Want to tell me about your trip?"

"I did tell you. We talked almost every day." Abby was given a passionate kiss in return.

"Sure, but not about details."

"It was intense but rewarding if you know what I mean."

"No, not until you tell me."

Abby moved so that they faced each other. "Meeting my niece for the first time was emotional. So was finding out a little bit more about why my sister left so suddenly. I still can't get my head around why she cut us off."

"Why did she?"

"Something about how we were too close to Jennifer's father."

"And are you close to her father?"

"Not a clue. I was always busy helping Dad with the farm. Mom might know who her boyfriend was back then.

Though she hasn't said anything since I mentioned Jennifer's birth. At least in that respect."

Sophia traced a finger over Abby's lips. "Now you have found her, are you bringing her home?"

Abby frowned. "Charles is her family right now. From the time she was three years old, he's been the only family she's had, and he loves her so much. To take her away from him would be cruel for them both."

"Will your mother agree?"

"No." Abby bit her bottom lip.

Sophia snuggled closer to Abby's body. "Then together we shall persuade her."

Abby sucked in a deep breath. How had her world collided with this woman? "It's not your problem, Princess."

Sophia shook her head. "When you call me Princess, you send me to a less familiar group. I love you. Abigail Ranger. Your problems are mine. Just as…well, perhaps you won't want…"

Abby kissed the rest of the words away. "I do for eternity."

Sophia's watch began buzzing.

"Time to go, the flight leaves in fifty minutes."

Abby stood and pulled Sophia with her. "You did say that together, we talk to Mom?"

"It's in the bag, my love."

Hand in hand, they left the room.

†

The reporters on their return had been taken off guard when Sophia and Abby had arrived together. Officials had escorted them via a private exit. A car had been waiting, and what might have been a horrendous experience for Abby had turned out to be a damp squid, publicity-wise. Sophia allowed herself a small smile.

"Wow, I thought we would have to go through all those reporters waiting in airport arrivals. Did you arrange this?" Abby grinned.

Sophia shrugged. "In a way. Charlotte made the arrangements. Though she wasn't happy. Charlotte loves a publicity opportunity."

Abby stared at her. "I would have been okay."

"You've had a long journey, and it's been an emotional trip. If I could spare you another delay in returning home, then it makes me happy."

Abby smiled, cupped Sophia's face, and kissed her gently. "I love you."

Heads close together, Sophia whispered, "I love you, too."

Hands clasped together, they sat in virtual silence for the rest of the journey.

As the car drew up outside the farmhouse, the front door opened, and Jenny rushed toward the vehicle.

"Mom is happy to see me." Abby smiled as she exited the vehicle and was engulfed in a hug.

Sophia watched the exchange. Though happy, it was sad too. Her mama's hugs were barely a phantom memory.

The car driver pulled Abby's luggage from the boot and returned to the vehicle.

"Princess, shall I take you to the castle?"

Drawn out of her reverie, she answered. "No, I shall walk home from here." Sophia stood beside Abby's luggage.

Abby rushed forward. "God, I'm so sorry, Sophia, I totally forgot about my cases." Abby frowned.

Sophia moved to within inches of Abby and stroked a light finger over the frown. "The driver took them out of the car. I'm just standing guard. Kind of ridiculous." She grinned.

Abby engulfed her in a bear hug she would never forget. The melancholy she had felt a few minutes earlier vanished instantly. She was never more certain than at that moment that this woman was her life compass. Without her, she would be adrift in the sea of life, never finding home.

"Cup of tea, girls?" Jenny Ranger asked.

"Yes," they said in unison and entered the house.

†

Abby had left to shower, leaving Sophia with Jenny. Jenny's questions in the last two hours since they had arrived had primarily been about her granddaughter. Understandable. Abby had dutifully told her mother about Jennifer and the family she was living with. When Abby explained about her decision not to pursue Jennifer's return here, she held Abby's hand as tight as possible for support. It wasn't her right to interfere. Jenny had been upset and blamed Abby for putting her life ahead of bringing Jennifer back to her rightful family. There were sharp words, but not anything Sophia would lose sleep over. However, this family dynamic seemed like a volcano had erupted. Abby had left to take a shower, and Sophia was left with Jenny glowering over her teacup.

I should probably go. Then again, I should stay a little while and wait for Abby to return. Fuck.

"Jenny, I thought that was rather harsh, the words you exchanged with Abby."

Jenny didn't look up from her fascination with the cup. "Jennifer should be with her family. It isn't Abby's decision. It's mine!"

Hmm, never heard her speak so violently. "I understand, Jenny. I'm not family and don't want to interfere. In the time I've known your daughter, she has never done anything that would hurt anyone. She goes out of her way to help, even sacrificing her own life choices. God knows I didn't want her to go to America immediately after we became engaged."

Jenny looked up through tears forming, but she brushed them away. "Selfless doesn't mean she can make this decision alone."

Sophia nodded. "Great word, selfless. I wish I could be half the woman Abby is. I'm so far out of her league in the empathy stakes, I keep pinching myself she's agreed to be my wife."

"My daughter…" Jenny began to cry.

Sophia bit her lip and wondered if she should call Charlotte to give her advice on what to do. Instinctively, she pulled Jenny into a hug. "Abby makes great decisions. I should know, she's going to marry me. Can't say I'm the best prospect with my background."

Jenny sniffled. "Abby has always loved you. From the moment she saw you and later pulled you out of the water fountain when you were six. Abby almost lost her life. She ended up in the hospital with pneumonia."

Sophia scratched the side of her neck. "I don't recall the event at all."

"Of course you won't remember." Jenny smiled. "She sent you a bear when she recovered, saying her princess needed the comfort from the ordeal."

Sophia sucked in a silent breath. "I remember the bear."

"I'm sure it's a distant toy long thrown out."

Sophia shook her head. "Actually, I still have it. I always thought it was a present from Rupert, and he never denied it."

"You were all children, and Abby was just a commoner. Why would he say otherwise if you liked it, when he was the one who pushed you in the fountain?"

Sophia swallowed hard. *Why hadn't anyone told her*? "I need to check on my papa. Please tell Abby I will call her later." She walked to the door. "Jenny, trust Abby; she would never do anything that would hurt you. Give her time to explain all the circumstances." Sophia left the room.

†

Abby drew in a deep breath as she ascended the stairs. *God, I hope Mom isn't too upset still*. Her one positive was that Sophia was here with them. When she walked into the kitchen, she glanced around, but only her mom was there.

"Did Sophia leave?"

"She had to check on His Highness."

"Yes, of course." Abby nodded as she sank down in her chair at the table.

"Do you want something to eat?"

Abby gazed at her mom, who didn't look happy. "No, thank you for asking."

"Her Highness said she will call you later."

Abby smiled. "Great." She moved the chair a little.

"Tell me everything. Her Highness said I needed to know the full story."

"Mom, I would never hurt you intentionally. I accept that not bringing Jennifer home is hard to accept, but …"

Her mom waved a hand. "Abby, your wife-to-be is right, I need to trust your judgement. I do, my darling girl, I do. I just want to meet my granddaughter in the flesh." Her mom began to sob.

Abby stood and enclosed her mom in a deep hug. Several minutes later, she released her. “You will meet Jennifer, Mom. I invited Charles to our official engagement. He’s bringing Jennifer with him.”

“When is this?”

“Actually, next month.”

“Darling, I’m sorry for my behavior. I know better. I love you. Jennifer is so lovely, and the image of Beth at that age.

“Yes, she is the image. Jennifer is looking forward to meeting you. I don’t have to tell you that, though, she’s said it in our video calls.”

“Tea, then tell me what you haven’t on video.”

Abby grinned. “For you, Mom, anything.”

CHAPTER TWENTY-NINE

Marrying a princess had many challenges, not the least of which was the lack of privacy whenever Abby left the farm. Congratulations for sure, but lots of personal questions she wasn't going to entertain. Today was extra special. Tonight, they were going to have an engagement celebration. Just a small event, with close family and friends. She had two things in her diary before the party began at five o'clock. Collecting a piece of jewelry she had ordered custom-made, and collecting Charles and her niece, Jennifer, from the airport at lunchtime.

Parking her truck in the car park of Sebastion and Sons, fine jewelry makers for royalty, she climbed out of the truck, smoothed down her black jeans, and walked toward the entrance. Although there were a couple of people peering at the front window display, she managed to slip inside before they saw her. Thankfully, there were no customers in the shop.

A woman elegantly dressed with flawless makeup approached her. "Ms. Ranger, lovely to see you again." Her hand was taken in a birdlike grip, then swiftly dropped.

"Nice to see you, too, Miss Sebastion."

The older woman nodded and walked back to the counter, where she opened a locked drawer.

Abby approached the counter, her heart racing in expectation. When she was given the delicate ring, her heart skipped a beat.

"Is it all you expected, Ms. Ranger?"

Abby was lost for words for a few moments as she looked at every facet of the ring. Then nodded.

"Her Highness will love it, I'm sure."

Although the words might sound condescending to some, she knew differently. "I think it's beautiful. Thank you, Miss Sebastion, for all your help. Will the jewel maker have the wedding rings ready on time?"

The woman nodded. "Very short notice." Her left eyebrow rose. "However, for such a prestigious event, Maxwell would work all hours god sends to have them completed for the event."

Abby grinned. When she had talked with Sophia on her return from the US about the engagement party date, she'd been surprised but happy when Sophia said in two weeks' time. Though the biggest bombshell had been that Sophia had wanted to have the wedding within three months. It still had her body shaking at the speed. Even though it was what she wanted deep down.

Miss Sebastion cleared her throat. Abby looked at her and shook her head.

"Sorry, it's exactly what I was thinking. I can't thank you enough for helping me with the design process, and in such a short space of time. You are very gifted."

The woman appeared to blush and gave a small smile.

"I love the business, and to help someone create a special piece adds to my satisfaction." She held out her hand for the ring. Abby reluctantly gave it to her. "I will package it for you, Ms. Ranger. Would you like a beverage while you wait?"

Abby smiled, then glanced at her watch. "Unfortunately, I can't today. I must do a pickup at the airport." Miss. Sebastion nodded and left for another room.

Abby couldn't help smiling. The ring, as far as she was concerned, was perfect. Her mind floated to the first time she entered this establishment in a fluster two weeks ago.

Driving around the town, she had been to at least three jewelers, and no one would commit to her idea of a ring in the time scale. Her last-ditch attempt was in front of her, Sebastion and Sons. The building was old tradition and, from the sign, the company had been here for at least three centuries. God, I probably can't afford it." Her legs shook, but she eventually took in a deep breath and entered.

A man dressed in what looked like an expensive, dark grey suit was serving a small, senior woman who had a very ornate walking stick. Abby looked down at her attire, work jeans and jacket, showing their age. About to turn tail and leave, a quiet, gentle voice spoke.

"How can we help?"

Abby looked into the pale grey eyes of a woman who was hard to age, with perfect makeup. She wore what Abby considered expensive clothes, which immediately put her on the back foot. "I was hoping that…maybe you might…" Abby retrieved the scrunched-up drawing in her pocket.

Delicate hands took it from her. There was silence for what seemed a decade to Abby.

"It's a lovely concept but might need tweaks." Those pale grey orbs caught Abby's. "Will you allow me to improve the design?"

Abby nodded. God, I'm going to be paying for this for the rest of my life.

"Have a seat, Ms. Ranger, tea, coffee, or something else?"

Startled, Abby opened her mouth to talk, but no words followed. Finally, she spoke. "How did you know my name?"

A tinkle of laughter surrounded them. "I do read the news and have seen you on the TV. I was hoping you would honor us and engage our services. Though I know we have a lot of competitors."

"No one else could do it in the timeframe."

"That is?"

"Two weeks," Abby squeaked out." I'll understand if…"

"Maxwell is brilliant and fast if necessary. You will want wedding rings, I assume?"

"Yes," Abby automatically answered.

"Take a seat, Ms. Ranger. We have work to do."

"Ms. Ranger, your package." Abby gave Miss Sebastion a smile and took the perfectly wrapped item.

"I don't know how to thank you and the bill…"

Miss Sebastion's expression changed very slightly as she smiled. "Allowing us to do this work for you has been an honor. We will talk about the bill when the wedding rings are ready. Have a wonderful evening, Ms. Ranger."

Abby's eyes moistened. "You have been so good to me, thank you."

"It has been a privilege." Miss. Sebastion nodded and moved to a customer who looked much as she had on her first visit—scared to death. Package securely held, Abby left the building and was bombarded with questions from the couple window shopping when she arrived.

†

Jenny flexed her fingers as if she were doing gym instruction. Abby had called, and any moment now, she would be arriving with her granddaughter, Jennifer, and the man who was her legal guardian, Charles.

The sound of the SUV screeched to a halt outside.

Nervously, Jenny opened the door and saw the three occupants of the vehicle step onto the drive.

"Welcome to the Ranger family home."

†

Sophia looked at herself in the mirror and smoothed down the dress her mother had worn on her engagement, a beautiful but simple satin creation. Sophia had needed a seamstress to change it here and there; her mom had been very skinny. In an hour, she and Abby would finally have their proclamation to each other, rubber-stamped by their families and friends, made public.

Turning away from the mirror, she looked at the bear, rather dog-eared but mostly intact, sitting on her bed. "I've always loved you, too, Abigail Ranger. I just needed a nudge in the right direction. I just wish it hadn't been Rupert."

She walked toward the door and gave the bear one more glance, wiping tears away as she left.

†

Abby stared at the mirror and wondered who looked back. Her hair was cut perfectly. Her mom had organized a friend to come over that afternoon to make her, as her mom said, "decent." She liked it; her hair was shorter and easy to flick her fingers through, though that was not what the hairdresser would advise.

"Abby, are you ready?"

"Mom, give me a few more minutes."

"Five max. We've been waiting for fifteen minutes. You did say…"

"I know."

Abby looked at her clothes, simple but expensive, at least for her. The darn trousers cost three months' wages. They did look good. A simple white shirt worked.

Nodding satisfaction, she left her room.

†

Sophia stood in the dining room surrounded by her closest family, which could be counted on two hands, and mostly her papa's invites. Claire, as always, was late. There were half a dozen people she didn't know, and two people who were staff. She had talked to them more than she had with anyone else. They had been timid in their conversation, and she understood those nerves. If only they knew she was as nervous, if not more so.

The door to the room opened, and breath held, she sighed as Claire and her friend entered.

"Soph, looking forward to this."

"Yes, me too. Good to see you up and around." She kissed Claire's cheek. "Jean, good to see you again. I hope my friend here isn't giving you too much trouble."

"Princess, no, not any more than I can handle. Thank you for inviting me." Sophia saw the grateful look, but it was probably more for intervention at the hospital than being here.

"You are welcome. Make sure Claire doesn't drink too much, please." Jean nodded, then smiled at Claire.

"Really, please Soph, someone has to be the storyteller for the evening. I have a lot of stories."

Sophia touched her friend's shoulder. "Exactly. Abigail doesn't need to know details, at least not this evening." They hugged hard. "I'm quite nervous."

Claire chuckled. "Love does that to you, my Princess. Now I know you do love her."

"No one else will ever come close."

"I think I know what you mean." Claire took Jean's hand.

The door opened. Sophia watched as the woman she was going to marry entered with her mother and two others, unknown to her.

"Excuse me." She walked toward the new attendees. "Jenny, wonderful to see you." She hugged her future mother-in-law.

"This is a special occasion for both our families."

Sophia released the older woman. "It certainly is, and who do I have the pleasure of meeting?" Her gaze traversed to the tall older man with a brilliant smile and the child who clung onto his hand.

The man gave a short bow. "Charles Leeston. And this is Jennifer Ranger." He pointed to the little girl, who looked mesmerized

"Welcome, Charles. Abigail has told me some things about you. I hope to find out more in the future." She shook his hand.

"Pleasure to meet you." He smiled.

Sophia turned to Abby's niece. She cocked her head to one side, and there was something familiar that she wasn't expecting. *How odd, she looks like…*

"I'm Jennifer Ranger, and you're a princess. I've never met a princess before."

Sophia laughed. "Who told you I was a princess?"

"Aunt Abby." Jennifer pointed to Abby, who was standing behind her family.

Sophia gazed at the woman she planned to spend the rest of her life with. They exchanged smiles. "I do believe your Aunt Abby is correct. Welcome, Jennifer." She held out her hand, and it was taken by a small yet strong grip. "Do you mind if I speak with your aunt alone?"

"Nope, as long as you kiss her soon. She's missed you."

Sophia sucked in her lower lip and tried not to laugh, then she looked at Abby, who had turned beet red.

Jenny shook her head and herded Charles and Jennifer farther into the room.

Sophia was left alone with Abby.

"She's quite the minx, isn't she?" Abby said.

"Indeed, she is." Sophia moved closer to Abby. "Are you ready for this?"

"You sound nervous?" Abby linked their fingers.

"Are you?"

"No."

Sophia looked Abby full in the face. "No?"

"Because I love you, and this is my dream come true. The only thing I'd be nervous about is if you changed your mind."

Sophia grinned. "Never going to happen." She kissed Abby slowly, and the room exploded with shrieks of delight and applause.

EPILOGUE

The room was filled with merriment and conversation. Even the household staff Abby had invited shrugged off their nervousness and appeared to be enjoying themselves. She glanced in her papa's direction. For the first time in many months, he had a happy smile, not the false one he had assumed when Rupert had died. Sophia walked over to the large open doors that led onto the terrace, breathing in the cool air as she stepped toward the wall separating the terrace from the garden below. Her eyes were caught by a figure standing by the fountain where the colored lights were switched on in celebration of this evening's event. For a moment, and it was only a moment, she thought it was the ghost of her brother. However, she knew better. He hated water. He had once said that, when he became Crown Prince, he would have the fountain removed. She had been appalled, but he was the elder. Now the old fountain had a new lease on life under her rule.

Smiling, she walked to the steps that led down to the garden, and a few minutes later, she was close to the person standing by the water. She was placing a gentle hand through the rivulets that reached the edge of the fountain wall.

"I wondered where you were?" Sophia softly spoke.

The figure stopped their action and turned, a sheepish grin on their full lips. "Never too far from you."

Sophia chuckled. "I like the sound of that." She moved closer, and a bear hug was her reward.

"I love you."

"I love you, too, Abigail Ranger. So, you told me a white lie, you are nervous, otherwise, why are you here?" Sophia snuggled into the broad shoulder.

"Not a lie. At least I wasn't nervous about the party."

"Ah, so what makes my gentle giant of a fiancée nervous if not that?" Sophia turned in Abby's arms to stare into her eyes.

Abby bit her lip and then removed her embrace.

"I'm sorry, Abby, if…" Abby gave her a gentle kiss.

She watched as Abby reached into her jacket pocket and withdrew a small box. Then, unclasping the lock, she held it out.

"When I asked you to marry me, we had one thing missing. While I was away, I designed something to rectify that."

Sophia was lost for words as she took the box and gazed at the delicate but perfectly crafted ring. It was a mixture of three diamonds in the center, with an emerald and ruby on either side of the cluster. As she lifted it from the box, she was entranced by the filigree pattern on the shoulders that held the gems in place.

"Do you like it?" Abby quietly asked.

Sophia held out the ring and saw Abby's grave expression, and she shook her head. "Please, will you place it on my finger?"

Abby's expression went from distress to joy in a fraction of a second, as she shakingly did as she asked. "Do you like it, really?"

"Abby, it's beautiful. Did you have this made abroad?" Sophia gazed at the ring, mesmerized.

"Oh no, right here at home. I have a wonderful woman to thank for taking my scrappy design and making it happen."

Sophia looked up into Abby's face. "I haven't a ring for you. I don't know how I could possibly have forgotten..." Abby grinned, then kissed her.

"I have you. Believe me, that's enough. Besides, I don't wear rings. They don't go with my working environment." Abby pulled Sophia into her body.

"I will arrange the wedding rings."

Abby chuckled. "Too late, all arranged."

Sophia dragged Abby into a deep kiss. When they surfaced, she leaned into Abby. "Why here? I confess my first thought when I saw a figure at the fountain was that it was Rupert haunting me."

Abby giggled. "Hmm, I doubt Prince Rupert would haunt you, Sophia. He loved you."

"I know, and the thought was fleeting. But why come here if you were nervous about the ring?" Abby frowned, and Sophia gently placed a finger over the furrow.

Abby placed her forehead against Sophia's and whispered. "It was the first time I realized I loved you, when I was twelve years old."

Sophia gasped. "I was surely...five, perhaps."

"Six, you were in the fountain and struggling to get out. Your brother had pushed you in. I rescued you."

Sophia gazed into Abby's eyes. "It wasn't Rupert?" Abby shook her head. "I always had an inkling that he didn't. He hated water." Sophia gave a weak smile. "You've loved me all that time?"

Abby shrugged, then gave a wry smile. "I had to be reminded. A long story."

Sophia looked directly at Abby. "We are going to have time for long stories. Right now, Abigail Ranger, all I want is for you to kiss me. Then we will return to the party and show off my ring. It's gorgeous. Papa and Claire are going to want to know where you had it made."

Abby laughed. "At your service, my Princess."

They kissed beside the fountain, which burst into a rainbow light show.

The end…of course not! Fairy tales never end. If you want a Christmas update in 2026, to answer your unanswered questions, bombard the publisher with a request for more.affinityebooks1@gmail.com

About the Author

JM Dragon a New Zealand citizen, though originally from the UK. Lives in the beautiful Canterbury countryside on the South Island, with magnificent views of the Southern Alps in the distance. She adores her animals, 3 cats, 1 alpaca, and over 100 bantam chickens. Her other passions are writing (of course) and her business interest—Affinity eBook Press NZ Ltd.

You can contact JM by email at:
jm1dragon@yahoo.com
https://www.facebook.com/julie.dragon

OTHER AFFINITY BOOKS

Without Borders by Stacy Reynolds

When the opportunity to become a war correspondent opens at her news agency, journalist Nicole Sheppard jumps at the chance to go to Ukraine. Her lifelong goal to gather news firsthand in the heat of battle and to test her mettle against the turbulence of war will finally be realized.

What she doesn't anticipate is having her heart and emotions tested as well when she meets the beautiful French doctor, Marie Dubois. As Nicole dodges bullets and Marie extracts them from the wounded, the two women struggle against a growing attraction to one another.

But when Nicole and Marie are kidnapped by a ruthless Russian mercenary, they must work together to find a way to escape.

The only thing they can't escape is falling in love.

The Invisible woman by Annette Mori

In a world where logic meets the extraordinary, Tamara, a brilliant forensic scientist, discovers a mysterious purple plant that blesses her with superhuman abilities, including invisibility. Teaming up with her best friend, Annalise, a passionate FBI agent haunted by scars from her past, the two friends embark on a quest to bring down a brutal serial killer known only as The Hunter. As the danger intensifies, their bond deepens, and secrets are revealed. Will Tamara and Annalise finally admit to their feelings despite being polar opposites? Join these extraordinary women in this gripping tale of love, friendship, and the fight for justice, where heroes are born from pain.

<u>All that Pride by Livia Janes</u>

Lizzie Gardner is ready to ace every class her senior year, ready to perfectly balance school, her friends, and her family.

But school has barely begun when her stepbrother Jake starts a secret relationship with popular jock, Charles Lark. Suddenly, Lizzie has to coexist with Charles' best friend, Darcy, whom Lizzie hates. Then, Lizzie's biological father resurfaces and claims an interest in reconnecting with his children.

As the strain of Jake's secret, family drama, and surprising feelings for Darcy become stronger, Lizzie struggles to tread water. How can she keep her options open when everyone—Jake, her parents, Darcy—wants immediate answers to their questions?

<u>Never Too Late by Glenda Poulter</u>

After the death of her long-time partner, and a scandal at the school where she taught music and art, Janice Halston emerged as a shadow of herself. Feeling shaken, cautious and artistically blocked.

Tam Murphy lost her wife and son within a short time of each other. She tries to fill her emptiness with her daughter Mae, and granddaughter, Ocee.

Janice and Tam are brought together by the precocious Ocee. As their friendship deepens, so do their feelings for each other. Their deepening feelings send both women spiraling…in different directions. One toward what could be, the other away from fear of another loss. Will their spirals lead them back to each other, or further apart?

Nothing But Net by Ali Spooner

Hunter James, a rising star in college basketball, has her career and life sidelined after experiencing a family tragedy.

An opportunity for a fresh start opens the door to return to what she loves most: playing basketball. Hunter rushes through that door to make the most of her second chance.

Back in the basketball arena, doing what she loves, will she open herself and her heart to another chance to forgive herself and fall in love?

The Kitten Trap by Annette Mori

Inspired by the classic movie, *The Parent Trap*, two adorable black kittens, Midnight and Onyx, play matchmakers for their human mothers, Mac and Carmen. Struggling with the complexities of farm life, Mac can barely believe her beautiful girlfriend, Carmen, has agreed to move to the drafty old farmhouse to live with her and her beloved Pops. When Carmen is forced to leave the farm to care for her ailing mother, Midnight and Onyx as well as Mac and Carmen must struggle with the difficult separation. Just when it appears Carmen and Onyx may come back home to the farm, cruel fate raises a further challenge, one that will need the help of two mischievous kittens to overcome.

To Autumn by Katie M Hall

Sixteen-year-old Robyn Gale, along with her younger sister Anne, is sent away for the summer holidays of 1997 to stay with her grandmother at a caravan park in Devon. Robyn's had a tough few months: trying to cope with the fallout of their mother's attempted suicide, messing up her GCSEs, and finding herself attracted to girls. Perhaps getting away from her real life is just what she needs…she can focus on finding a boyfriend, watching *Neighbours,* and swimming. A solid plan, until she meets charismatic Australian lifeguard, Autumn, and her life is turned even more down under.

Fairytail Farm by Ali Spooner

Dr. Hill McCall and her wife Alice dreamed of developing a sanctuary for unwanted cats and dogs to live out their lives as a retirement project. Hill has secretly worked on the project for months when a wealthy benefactor surprises her with a large donation, allowing Hill to be more aggressive with the project's opening. A group home operator approaches Hill about summer volunteer positions for four girls as Fairytail Farm becomes more than just a sanctuary for the animals. It creates an environment of love and kindness for the animals and all that support the project. Several love stories develop from first love to mature couples who have found their forever person. Fairytail Farm is more than a dream come true. It is a home for happily ever afters.

The Love Demand by Annette Mori

In the dazzling realm of reality television, where love and drama entwine in a complicated dance as old as time, a groundbreaking series emerges that transcends the ordinary.

The Love Demand is not your typical reality show. Lacey Fellows isn't sure she wants to subject herself to further humiliation, however, on the off chance her girlfriend may agree to accept a second marriage proposal, Lacey reluctantly consents to participating in the new reality show. What she doesn't count on is meeting a kindred spirit—one she can't seem to shake from her thoughts. Jaimie would do almost anything for her girlfriend, including following her to the ends of the earth and participating in a conniving television show that puts her in front of a camera, which happens to be her least favorite place. Her girlfriend, Sabina, hasn't met a camera she doesn't like. They couldn't be more opposite, but Jaimie still hopes Sabina will want marriage, kids, and the whole shebang. The last thing she expects is to fall in love with someone else. Let the games begin.

Sullivan's Trace by Ali Spooner

Micah "Sully" Sullivan has settled into a solitary life at the family horse ranch after her father's death. When her long-term vet, Doc Barton, plans to retire, his granddaughter, Bryn, arrives to take over his practice. An attack on one of Sully's prized horses throws Sully and Bryn into a whirlwind as they fight to save the young animal. Just as Sully is becoming comfortable with her growing attraction to Bryn, tragedy occurs, and her brother and his wife are killed in an accident. Sully's solitary life drastically changes when a family of three is born.

Love Sins by Annette Mori

Jessica Green's life is predictable and boring. As the chief engineer for Solar Flair, her career is right on track. Her love life, not so much. The last thing she expects is a call from her estranged father's attorney. Too curious to ignore the message, she can't resist meeting with him and discovering more about specific instructions related to his estate, as well as the letter her father left for her. Rattled by what she finds at her father's home, she promptly dials 911.

Special Agent Amanda Forrester is perplexed by a call to join a homicide investigation until she arrives at the scene and learns the victim is not only a serial killer but an elite assassin the authorities have been after for years. To Amanda's increasing irritation, the daughter recognizes a picture of the last target and insinuates herself into the investigation. As the case takes a surprising turn, Amanda finds she has landed smack dab in the middle of a complicated and dangerous situation. The facts lead her to a puzzle weaving together the recent suicide of a wealthy businessman with the activities of several prominent politicians. Amanda must join forces with a mysterious organization and the persistent woman she finds increasingly hard to resist. Her instinct to protect the alluring and vulnerable Jessica Green kicks into high gear, taking the reader on a roller-coaster journey for the last book in *The Next Generation* series.

A Wild Moon Rises by Jen Silver

Successful author, Malory G Holmes, has had a rough year. Wounded by an emotional breakup and writer's block she returns home after eight months travelling to discover the startling results of a DNA test. Apparently, through her mother's side, she is related to a baronet with an estate in Briarbay, Northumberland. She decides to visit the place to find out more about this unknown side of her family.

Selene Wylde is content with life, running a bookshop in the small hamlet of Briarbay. She also looks after her father, Reginald, who is grieving over the recent death of his husband, Sir Alan Guyatt. Reginald is worrying about his claim to stay at Briarbay Hall as the Will of Sir Alan has not yet been found.

With the arrival in her shop of a very attractive, well-known writer, Selene's world begins to tilt alarmingly. Malory and Selene become entangled in a web of secrets and deceptions with the added complication of a rapidly growing attraction.

The Wolf and The Unicorn by Ali Spooner (Erotica)

Ready to explore a steamy, passionate, and tantalizing erotica romance….

Keagan and Celeste have built a solid relationship on trust and independence. A successful surgeon, Keagan understands Celeste's supercharged libido and her desire to experience a variety of sexual encounters. Everything changes when Sky, a new doctor, arrives at the hospital, and Celeste is immediately drawn to the younger woman. Keagan is surprised when she is also attracted to Sky, who shares common interests with Celeste and her. When more than a physical attraction develops, the three women discover a loving relationship beyond the bedroom.

The Blank White Page by Ali Spooner

Tatum Chastain, Corporate Officer of Chastain International, her family's real estate empire, accepts the challenge her father, Charles, has set forth. Charles has tasked Tatum and her brother, Charlie, to survive in the wilderness for six months to prove their skills in taking over the family business once he retires. Charles fails to realize that Tatum would fall in love with the southeastern Alaska cabin he has chosen for her to test her resilience and creativity. Tatum prepares for life in the bush, and shortly after she arrives, Poe, a beautiful raven, becomes her companion and guardian. When River Foster, a designated hunter for her village, crosses Tatum's path, she finds a different kind of love awaits her.

eBooks, Print, Free eBooks

Visit our website for more publications available online.

https://affinityebooks.com/

Published by Affinity Rainbow Publications
A Division of Affinity eBook Press NZ LTD
Canterbury, New Zealand

Registered Company 2517228

www.ingramcontent.com/pod-product-compliance
Lightning Source LLC
LaVergne TN
LVHW020657110826
845149LV00012B/2027
* 9 7 8 1 9 9 1 3 5 7 2 8 1 *